I0675051

Arcanium

HAUNTED

AURELIA T. EVANS

Haunted
ISBN # 978-1-78651-840-8
©Copyright Aurelia T. Evans 2019
Cover Art by Erin Dameron-Hill ©Copyright June 2019
Interior text design by Claire Siemaszkiewicz
Totally Bound Publishing

HAUNTED

Chapter One

Wednesday after the Funhouse found Neve where she'd never expected to be.

"I think this is the weirdest thing I've ever done," Valorie said, setting down her wine glass.

"I feel like we're going to get in trouble," Caroline said, "for doing something so…"

"Normal?" Neve poured herself another glass of red then settled cross-legged on one of the cushions in Kitty's tent, which was the largest tent that wasn't the big top and somewhere the men weren't likely to interrupt during the week. "I wasn't the one who came up with the idea."

"Still, an Arcanium book club. Is this even allowed?" Caroline asked.

"Maybe if we discuss books while tied up in shibari bondage?" Maya offered.

"I'm tied up enough. I don't need that here." The Spider had refused a wine glass, opting instead for the flask she'd brought in. The woman knew what she wanted.

"Me too." With hands rather than rope, which meant Neve didn't have to worry about rope burns, but sometimes her wrists still bruised a little, depending on how hard she struggled when guests passed by.

After the Funhouse event, the golems had provided coffee and breakfast for the road, and once in the vehicles, the cast could sleep a little while longer, but they'd still had to stumble out of the caravan and get themselves done up for the circus opening in an hour. Neve hadn't had a good chance to breathe, away from things touching her, until Monday. With the promise that there wasn't another Funhouse event for another three weeks, she'd take all the no-contact time that she could, even though the hands in the haunted funhouse had aroused her all over again. It was curiously relieving not to act on her desire for a few days, despite the distraction, and to have something like this to do instead.

"It's a good idea." Kitty had brought her knitting, which made the set-up even stranger. "I'm surprised we never came up with it before. It's been thirty-five years since I've been in school. I used to read a new book every two days."

"It hasn't been so long for me," Caroline said. "But it was nice to read something that I hadn't before. And have the *time* to read it, you know?"

"It's been about twenty for me. I don't remember the last library card I had," Valorie said.

Neve shrugged. "Anything to knock some books off my reading list. Thanks, everyone, for agreeing to it. We get so much physical stimulation around here. Yes, that kind, but also all the physical demands like contortion, tumbling, climbing… It's been really nice to engage in some intellectual stimulation for a change."

"Boredom is one of the biggest problems in Arcanium that no one ever talks about," Kitty said. "We're so concerned about the interpersonal interactions, setting boundaries and keeping ourselves and each other safe. But even when everything is as it should be, we can only fuck each other so much. Intellectual stimulation has been nicer than expected. Is it strange I thought of the world in the book as the weird one, where they don't have to think about human-demon peace talks or circus politics? And is it bad that I laughed at some of these characters thinking they're outsiders?"

"I think everyone feels like that," Neve said. "Perfectly normal people feel like that, because everyone has at least one thing that isn't 'normal'. The Internet made finding other people with the same weirdness easier. But people are so quick to call you out if you're even the slightest bit not normal."

"Normal is overrated," Joanne said.

"Normal doesn't exist," Kitty pointed out, literally using the pointy ends of her knitting needles for emphasis. "It's entirely relative, and no one fits all the criteria of *any* normal, which makes the fact that people enforce it even more frustrating. If normal means average, a lot of terrible things are normal. If normal is simply the measuring stick, it's a pretty narrow stick, and no one needs it rapping their knuckles every five minutes."

"Weird is overrated, too." The Spider, like the twins, took up a lot of room, so they got their own chairs. She stared at her flask, which Neve was pretty sure had been emptied. "Normal is Stepford. Weird is Arcanium."

Since no one else asked, Neve did. "What's wrong with Arcanium?" She could think of plenty of answers to the question, but she couldn't know which the Spider would pick.

"Arcanium isn't the worst that weird has to offer," Kitty said quietly. "It could be so much worse, Elizabeth."

"That's why it's hell." The Spider picked up her book and turned it around in her hands. They were pretty much finished talking about it anyway. "It sucks you in, makes you complacent. You're okay with some of the people. You can live with it. There's room for love. But you still can't leave. And it could be worse? That's true of literally anything. Well, I'm sitting in fire ants, but it could be worse, I could be dunked alive in an acid bath. And here's the thing… If it can be worse, who's to say it won't be someday? As much as things around here stay the same, Bell gets bored just like us, doesn't he? And we all serve at the pleasure of Bell Madoc. What happens when Bell's pleasure changes?"

"And on that note…" Neve swallowed down the rest of her wine, grimacing reflexively.

"I'll toast to that," Maya said. She drank the rest of her wine as well. Kitty gave her an odd look.

"Hear, hear," Joanne and Jane said together, raising their glasses.

The Spider, her work there done, labored to her feet. "That's enough from me. Same time next week? Valorie brings the wine, I'll bring the harsh dose of reality?"

"Sounds like a plan," Neve said.

The Spider stopped at the door. "In case you couldn't tell, Neve, your boyfriend's outside, and I think he's here for you. Proximity's a bitch, so I'm going to go get this handled. Goodnight."

"Really?" Neve leaned forward to try to see through the open flap, but he wasn't in her line of sight.

"You mean you couldn't feel that?" Caroline asked. "It's like the temperature went up ten degrees ever since he arrived."

"I always have those temperature fluctuations. If he's not deliberately emanating, this is how it is all the time."

"Oh, sweetheart, I'm so sorry," Caroline said, only half-joking.

Joanne and Jane shifted uncomfortably on their ottoman. There wasn't any other way for them to shift, but despite their jokes in Kitty's tent after Neve's first night with Mikhail, both twins appeared troubled that the subject of humor was right outside the tent.

After a moment, Neve remembered that Lord Mikhail was supposed to have been obsessed with them at one point. Joking meant that he wasn't anymore, but their expressions made Neve wonder whether they'd ever completely move on or whether moving on was just a coping mechanism in a contained environment.

Neve rested her wine glass on the vanity, for lack of anywhere near her to put it. "I'll go take care of it."

"Is that what they're calling it these days?" Valorie said.

"Actually, yes, sometimes?" Maya said.

Neve followed the Spider out of the tent. Elizabeth headed right toward the midway, her walk steady — either she could hold her liquor and a flask wasn't enough to render her tipsy or four legs were better than two when the earth decided to move.

Mikhail stood to the left, leaning against the big top canvas, which was as thick and taut as a wall.

Neve raised her eyebrows in surprise.

Ever since Bell had promised her more comfortable things to wear while ensconced in the circus and out of sight of anyone on the outside, she'd happily schlubbed around in her new collection of sweatpants, leggings, customized sports bras, cotton shirts and oversized jackets. House clothes, things that were intended for comfort rather than sexiness. She was wearing a T-shirt dress, oversized sweatshirt jacket and leggings—hardly the stuff romance was made of—and happy for it.

Lord Mikhail wore the same suit from the Funhouse event but with a tucked white shirt underneath. His hair had been tied back, exposing lines on his face that Neve swore hadn't been there before. And his hair—which had always been black and wild, gleaming as though moussed—was liberally shot through with dark gray and silver that also salted the hair on his face.

"What prompted this?" He was even wearing shoes. She hadn't known the circus strongman had shoes.

"Do you like it?"

"Excuse me?"

"I cannot control every aspect of how I look in this form, but I can alter some of my features and I can dress like a gentleman." He stepped forward, almost shy, and spread his arms to present himself.

"Congratulations?" He looked like he could punch someone's head off and make wise investments at the same time. It was a good look, but it was such a far cry from the leather daddy he usually played, or even the upscale hired gun ensemble he'd sported at the Funhouse event. And the gray hair...

"Isn't this what you want?" he asked.

"What I want? Why would you think I wanted these things? They look wonderful, Mikhail, don't get me wrong. But why did you feel the need to change what didn't need changing?"

"Because you will not allow me to have you except in the direst of circumstances, but you gave yourself in an instant to the wealthy man."

Neve didn't think she was capable of blinking so many times per minute, but she still wasn't sure all this was actually happening and not from something Valorie had slipped in the wine. "And you think the reason I gave him a hand job instead of you is because he was older and wore a suit? I also let Lennon take me in twelve different ways when he was full-on Lovecraft, but I don't see you turning into a wriggling monster with copious mucosal secretions."

Mikhail lowered his arms in frustration. "But if it is not those things, then tell me what I should be for you and I will become that man."

"You don't get it, do you? You don't mean to be this awkward. You *really* don't get it." Her ambivalence about Lord Mikhail suddenly became clear. "You don't understand why I'm not falling into your arms, why you don't get to have me whenever you want, because I'm *capable* of withstanding you, even though it's difficult. You don't understand why thinking that all you need to do is tick off some boxes so I'll want to have sex with you is reductive, insulting and one of the chronic systemic diseases in the dating scene. Which is why I was so glad I was out of it."

Neve scoffed, running her fingers through her hair and shaking her head. She was smiling, but more from a lack of adequate expression for her bewilderment. "You really don't understand these things, and I think I know why."

Mikhail glowered, but he hadn't stormed away. "Enlighten me."

"I've been on the receiving end of your seduction, so I know as well as anyone how flawless it is. But that's all you've ever had to do—turn on the charm and get your way. After that, everyone dies. You know how to seduce a woman, but you've never had to figure out what to do afterward or what to do with a woman who doesn't want to be with you all the time."

"I know what I want, and I know what I need," Mikhail said. "If it's a matter of pleasure, you know I can fulfill you. Why do you hesitate?" Annoyance drew his eyebrows together, the furrow between them comically pronounced. "Why do you laugh?"

She tried to stop giggling, but every time she looked at him in costume as a mature, wealthy patron, it kept getting funnier and funnier.

Absurd. That's what this is.

Still shaking her head, she went around Kitty's tent and into Oddity Row. If he was making the other women uncomfortable, she wanted to lead him away. As she'd hoped, Mikhail followed, likely confused about why she'd laughed, why she'd left or both. In any other place in the world, she might have been wary about turning her back on a man of Mikhail's size and strength when his intentions were so clear. Strange to have Arcanium be safe in that regard when it wasn't in so many others.

"It was not my purpose to amuse you," he said.

"I know. It was your purpose to sweep me up and fuck me for the sole reason that you want it and I want it, and I'm the only one available right now."

"There's nothing wrong with that. I thought you were a practical woman. What could be more practical than yielding?" When she stopped walking away, he cupped her elbows and rested his cheek against her hair. "What is the purpose of fighting what you desire, Neve? There is no *reason*."

She briefly savored the immediate electricity of contact, her nerves seeming to sway her closer to him. Then she continued toward the food court, Mikhail on her heels. "Just because the reason is emotional doesn't mean the reason is invalid, especially when attraction is composed of many elements—one of which can be mutual respect, for instance."

"I respect you. I wouldn't pursue you as I do if I didn't respect you," Mikhail said.

"And the fact that I'm one of two people you can have nonfatal sex with in Arcanium, that's what respect means to you? Not killing me? That's not something you decided. That's something that was done to me that you can take advantage of. Lady Sasha is your equal, Mikhail. I'm just a piece of ass to you. A piece of meat."

"Now it is my turn to laugh at you." He didn't. He didn't even look like he wanted to. "You keep expecting me to be human, but I'm not. You *are* a piece of meat to me. That doesn't mean I do not respect you or desire to please you."

"So you can have sex with your meat," Neve said.

"It's what I am!" It was the first time he'd ever raised his voice, and she put one of the food court tables between them by reflex. He stopped short at her reaction and held his hands up to calm her like she was a spooked horse in his barn. "It's what I am," he said more gently.

"It's not what you are. Do you see Lady Sasha losing her mind?"

"Succubi don't have to work as hard, and in Arcanium, she has much more meat available. She will never be as desperate as I. Her food source is secure. You like science, yes? That's what Bell tells me. Do you need an ecology lesson from an alternative species?"

He gestured to the picnic table, a surrogate student desk.

Neve complied, sitting down and spreading her fingers on the wooden top. "Your class, professor."

"Almost every creature of this planet is created with three primary needs—food, shelter and proliferation. One might argue that food is more important than the other two, which are often sacrificed in pursuit of it. Incubi and succubi, as demons go, are hybrids with much in common with humans. We're born of fire, but we can also be born from a human womb. Some of the demons here in Arcanium are fortunate. Not all demons need food or shelter or need to procreate. But Sasha and I, though immortal, are driven to feed, driven to spread, and driven to protect ourselves, just like human beings. Where we differ is that the sex drive and the drive to consume are one and the same."

Neve opened her mouth, but Mikhail raised a finger to signal that he wasn't finished. He sat down on the edge of the table and met her gaze. "You are part of a comfortable world, little girl—or you were. But even in this comfortable world, you are still driven by these needs, although you have shifted how they are achieved. Your ancestors spent most of their energy and waking hours hunting and foraging. This eventually transitioned into subsistence agriculture, then bulk agriculture. Once a small handful of people became responsible for keeping the rest fed, the others no longer needed to pursue the source of sustenance as stringently and could take on other tasks in return. A system of barter for goods and services was eventually replaced with a currency stand-in that drives commerce today. All the work your people do, at its most fundamental level, is for the purpose of affording food, shelter and sex. It is a single-minded pursuit cluttered with frivolous distractions to pretend you are no longer so primitive. If I seem single-mindedly bent on sex, Neve, it is because I am. I want to feed, little girl. I *need* to feed. Just tell me what *you* want, what *you* need in return, and I will give it to you."

He was right. It was a fully pragmatic way of approaching relationships — biology and transaction. And he wasn't wrong, as far as Neve could tell. He just wasn't all the way right.

"Say 'subsistence' again," Neve said.

It was Mikhail's turn to blink.

"You're a lot more eloquent when you're trying to convince me to have sex with you. This part you're really good at. You should teach more often, sir. 'Pursue the source of sustenance as stringently'? You really are trying to get me into bed."

Mikhail narrowed his eyes in suspicion. "You're laughing at me again."

"I'm not laughing at you. I'm amused at myself." Neve climbed up to sit on the tabletop, putting herself more level with him. "That kind of single-minded pursuit of sustenance, as you call it, makes sense in scarcity, but the reason other things have taken the limelight is because our food sources are no longer so scarce, if you have the money for it. In addition, your food source in Arcanium is managed by Bell, creating false scarcity, and in your case, a false sense of imminent starvation. The fact is, one of the main reasons I haven't been humping everything in sight upon arriving in Arcanium — although getting used to it was hell — is because I know it won't kill me. If you've been doing this as long as you have, how on Earth have you not learned to manage the cravings that you *know* will be satisfied and won't kill you if they're not satisfied *now*?"

"A human's sex drive isn't the same—"

She held up her finger to interrupt him. "How long can you hold your breath?"

He stared at her, although he kept whatever thoughts passed through his mind a mystery. But he understood what she was really asking. "Indefinitely," he muttered.

"If I were to touch you now, would you hold it, or would you use that contact to get what you want?" Neve hovered her hand a few inches above his, close to the bared skin of his wrist. Cufflinks glinted at the buttonholes. She had to credit his attention to detail.

He raised his fingers in response, interlocking them with hers. For a moment, lust she hadn't felt since that all-nighter shot through her, as dangerous as a jolt of electricity. It stole the breath from her lungs and made her wonder, underneath that lust, whether this was it, whether she'd have to cut him off entirely, like an Arcanium restraining order. Then, after sucking all the air from her lungs, he pulled everything—or most of it—back, the way he'd done at the Funhouse. He panted briefly, closing his eyes from the effort. When he opened them again, they were black, glinting red, but touching him was only a little different from touching someone else she was attracted to.

"See?" Neve licked her lips and crept her fingers over the veins and tendons of his wrist.

Mikhail swallowed thickly, his hold wavering but staying strong. "Would you have me hold my breath indefinitely, then?"

"Would you?" She pulled her hand away and felt along the sleeve of the jacket, the texture its own seduction over her palm without his added help. "What if I told you that if you did, I wouldn't mind spending time with you, providing you human company? Everyone who isn't Lady Sasha avoids you. But if you're like human beings, surely you also have a drive for company that isn't just sexual."

"A sexless relationship. Is that what you seek from me?" Mikhail said. "From an incubus?"

Neve shrugged. "Not necessarily, but why the hell not?"

She'd apparently rendered him speechless.

"You talked about sex drives. Well, most of my life, I didn't have one," she said. "My desire for nonsexual interaction with men hasn't diminished just because my desire for sexual interaction has increased. But turning into a voracious nymphomaniac *has* made it harder to have nonsexual interaction with men, because once they know they have a good chance, they pursue, and I have to fight not to give in. And I want *more* than that, damn it!" She hit the table with the flat of her hand, angry out of nowhere — at men in general, at Bell, at Mikhail, at herself. "I want someone — *anyone* — to look at me and not see the sex they want to have. Is that so much to ask?"

A large strongman flinching was an uncommon image. "I don't think you want me to answer that question."

Neve slid down the table a few feet away from him. The distance between them seemed wider than that. "Is that so?"

"There are four levels by which an incubus experiences attraction," he said quietly. "When a human is attracted to us but not us immediately to them, their attraction incites our own, triggering our magic to intensify the attraction. Two, we can create attraction in cases where neither we nor the subjects are immediately attracted to each other — with the exception of those with an incapacity for attraction." He nodded to her. "Then there are the people who we find attractive on our own, but they initially do not. Then there are those attracted to us and we to them at the moment of meeting. That connection explodes with tension, as you well know."

He deliberately stepped around the table closer to her. "Every time I look at you, I want you. I can mask the effects, but I can't make them disappear. And I feel what other men want from you. With very few exceptions, no, no one can look at you without wondering what it is like to sleep with you. Women's responses are either more nuanced or come from a place of envy. But you cannot alter how fundamentally attractive you are—across multiple generations, multiple cultures, multiple centuries of trends. You are timelessly sexy, Neve. If you're looking for nonsexual male companionship, perhaps you should seek out a gay best friend."

What he said gave her too many feelings, one after the other—contradictory and on completely different sides of the multiplanar spectrum of emotions. Flattery, irritation, a primal sexual heat at being so wanted rather than just needed, despair at the confirmation that she was a perpetual sexual object to strange men even outside the objectifying context of Arcanium, fury, pride, depression, grief, pleasure, nausea, gratitude…

She tried to keep all those emotions out of her voice when she said, "You really think I'm beautiful? You don't just want everything that breathes and has breasts—and sometimes even those are optional?"

"If I had my way, Neve, no matter what restrained me, I would break through it just to bring you against me and have you in your bed, in mine, in whatever bed is closest—and only a bed, because we could stay there more comfortably all night and all morning like we did.

Even though you wanted nothing to do with me when you first saw me on Oddity Row, I saw you and wanted you with a power that you couldn't have known before Bell got his hands on your wish."

Still careful, he closed the distance completely. He traced the frame of her face, curling her hair around his finger, then released her with visible effort—still holding back the effect of his magic as well as he could, only a stray wisp brushing her like fragrance passing on the wind. "I called then. You didn't hear me, but when you called for me from miles away, I followed you. I've had many women, and I thought many of them beautiful. You are beautiful, too, Neve, but beautiful in a way that makes it hurt to desire you, to desire a woman who doesn't want to want me. I don't understand why or how you resist so stringently."

She *didn't* want to want him. To give in to him now would undercut everything she'd just said. But even without the full measure of his magic pulling her under like a riptide, he was wearing too much and so was she. Her mind projected the image he'd given her of him taking her back to her trailer, filling up the small hallway, filling her bed, filling her, or kicking in the door of someone else's home and throwing her on some random bed just to wrap himself around her and sink into her all night. Or his bed. She'd never visited his trailer, a whole place that would carry his scent deep in its matter, the way everyone's houses eventually did.

For a moment, she thought she understood what it was like to hunger for sex like a succubus—as physical a craving as for food. She wanted his taste in her mouth.

"Not a sexless relationship." She coughed, because it had come out in a whisper. "But does every encounter between us have to be about sex? Am I really just going to be the resident Arcanium slut and that's it? Is that all you can be for me? Is that all *I* can be for *you*?"

"What do you mean?"

"When I considered men to date, a bare minimum of what I did with them was sexual. I enjoyed contact for intimacy rather than to satisfy some sexual tension. I married my husband—my ex-husband—because I could talk with him, laugh with him, cry with him, cuddle close to him, stay up all night binge-watching TV shows with him, visit museums and national parks with him. And the entire fucking thing dissolved because I didn't like sex with him."

Hate-filled resentment, surprising in its once-again abrupt vehemence, gave her the strength to back away again. "Haven't you ever wanted anything more than sex from the women you had sex with? You called their deaths a waste. That's why you came to Arcanium. Even though you're an incubus with a drive to consume sex, isn't there more to your life? And if there isn't, do you want there to be?"

Mikhail lowered himself to the bench of the picnic table, his legs comically angled because of his height. The age smoothed from his face, the gray from his hair, until he was just himself—or whatever counted for himself in this particular form. "Yes."

Neve inhaled deeply. She'd been unaware that some part of her had been holding her breath. Then she sat next to him. "Bell clearly had the two of us in mind when he made me impervious to whatever makes your feed fatal. But I don't want to fall into bed with you just because you won't kill me, okay? I suggest, just as an experiment, that we suspend sex unless we're both desperate—the point at which Bell would send you out of Arcanium to hunt. You think you're nothing but a mindless animal, that you're just made for sex and strength, but I've actually really enjoyed talking to you. You're charming. You can be considerate. You're not afraid of multiple syllables or evolutionary biology, overly simplistic though it can be. Maybe it sounds radical, but what if we just...dated?"

Mikhail's expression appeared angry, but the blackness and red glow to his eyes faded until his irises alone were black. "Dated."

"Dated. Did things that weren't just sex. You were waiting outside the newly formed Arcanium book club. Kitty knits. Caroline watches shows with her men. Troy draws and tattoos out of his trailer. Besides attacking helpless men and women and practicing choreography with Lady Sasha, what else do you do? I know you don't pump iron to look like that, and I've never seen you jog around the fence line like some people here. Is your entire life truly nothing but the pursuit of your next meal?"

"I, um..." Mikhail appeared completely taken aback by the question. It occurred to her that, like his awkwardness trying to figure out what kind of man she wanted to fuck because he'd never had to put that much energy into making himself desirable, he'd never reached a point with a woman where she'd asked him what he liked to do — standard small talk for a first date, but small talk he rarely had to employ. "I like nature series and documentaries."

"That explains a lot. Stephen Fry or David Attenborough?"

"Attenborough, although both are calming. I... Are you honestly asking whether I want to just sit and watch nature films with you then *not* have sex?"

"Yes. The actual person's version of 'Netflix and chill,' because who wants to get it on while watching *Breaking Bad*? *Hemlock Grove*, maybe."

"I don't know that one."

"Not a fan of horror, big guy?" She slid a little closer to him until her knee touched his. That was all, but he still appeared completely confused by her signals.

"We live horror here. I see no reason to perpetuate it in my escape."

"Fair enough. So, what say you? If you don't want to get to know the woman you're having sex with without killing her, you don't have to. And if you don't want me to know the incubus haunting me, you can keep yourself a mystery. It's your decision. But if dating isn't your scene, then you need to stop creeping on me and doing all kinds of sexual gymnastics to try to get me to sleep with you all the time. We'll chalk our sexual encounters down to legitimate necessity, each of us taking impersonal advantage of the other then moving on. I don't know about you, Mikhail, but that doesn't sound appealing to me. Sounds more like going to the doctor to get vaccinated."

"But no sex."

"Your focus on that suggests it's a sticking point...or a deal-breaker."

"I've so rarely encountered people attracted and attractive to a sex demon who request that they not have sex," Mikhail said. "If no sex is to be had, would what you ask of me be mere friendship instead?"

Neve patted his thigh. Again, he looked down at his leg as though it were covered with alien lifeforms. "There's nothing 'mere' about good friendship. I have—had—male friends. The difference is in chemistry—a desire for closeness, for contact that doesn't automatically lead to sex. It's keeping our clothes on while stripping away the layers to the mind." She shook her head in amusement. "Many men

Aurelia T. Evans

are presented with this journey and choose a different path. They wouldn't think any less of you for refusing."

Mikhail looked out toward the midway, where some glow-in-the-dark features were luminescent from a whole day of recharging. "If I say yes, must I offer you flowers?"

"You may. It's not my preference, though."

He scowled, but though his frustration could snap a metal wire and his anger could melt a stop sign, his expression was less dangerous. "Very well. But may I kiss you tonight? I haven't been able to since that night, and you've done many things since then that made me want to kiss you." He rested his knuckles against her cheek, but though it could have been aggressive, all he managed to portray was tenderness. "Just a kiss, I promise."

When she licked her lips again, they and her mouth seemed bone dry, despite the fact that she'd been salivating ever since she'd stepped out of Kitty's tent. "If you break your promise, you break so much more than that promise. Do you understand?"

Lord Mikhail nodded as he leaned in, holding his breath still.

He brought his hand to her neck, almost as though to choke her, and she flinched automatically, but he just smoothed his huge palm up her neck, caressing the length of her throat with his thumb in a gesture both possessive and unbearably intimate.

He stayed gentle, as chaste as a centuries-old incubus could be, his magic simmering under his skin. It tried to reach for her, but he kept it leashed as well as he could as he kissed her, parting his lips to savor hers. All her focus narrowed to that contact. Her nature made it electric enough, the same as it had been for every other man she'd touched, save for a thin extra layer of arousal

25

that threatened to shift inside her — like his cock in her cunt — if he let his control slip even a little.

But other than that, kissing him was like kissing any other man, and it was still honey-sweet and sultry, early autumn instead of midwinter.

When he pulled back, both of them gasped for breath. Neve knew why she had, but Mikhail still appeared surprised by the whole affair.

"Is that how humans kiss when they date?" Mikhail asked.

"I think you're confusing dating with romance. Sweet romance, anyway. Some like their romance spicy. Some don't want romance at all."

"And you?"

"A little bit of all three. I'm going to stop this now." She retreated back around the table, which was a better barrier than willpower. "Not because we wouldn't both enjoy the outcome if we stayed here, but because we've agreed...or I thought you had. Do you agree, then? There's no pressure to date, Mikhail. It all seems very weird, even to me. This whole evening has."

Mikhail crossed his arms, this time in contemplation. "Must I hold my breath indefinitely?"

She shook her head. "I'm looking for a partner, not just a sex partner. I want dating to eventually lead to sex as a natural consequence, not as an immediate given. With my appetites, is that unrealistic?"

"No," he said quietly. "It's merely...unprecedented."

"Dating with sex is unprecedented for me, so we're both in unfamiliar waters."

"Beware, little girl. Here there be monsters." A tentative grin.

"You don't say."

"I'm willing to try." He stepped around the table, but all he did was offer his hand to shake.

26

Which she did.

As she turned to head back to the caravan, he slapped her ass hard.

When she spun around, shocked, he raised an eyebrow. "A little spicy, no?"

She couldn't restrain a smile. His tentative grin broadened, caution in his black eyes, but also wonder.

Chapter Two

After a few weeks of comfortable cotton clothing, even when the circus was open, pulling out one of the thin silk dresses that were barely dresses from her wardrobe made the sensation of the fabric over her skin all the more sensual. She wondered whether that was why Bell had originally given her nothing but the fancy clothing at first — so it wouldn't be such a shock to the system when she had to switch.

Tonight would be a special Valentine's Day Funhouse, so she'd chosen a dark red dress the color of blood. Neve had gone digging through Kitty's small collection of costume jewelry from which she sometimes used pieces for the corsets, headdresses and fascinators she made for herself and Maya. A fat red heart nestled in the dip of Neve's cleavage, sparkling with glass facets. She'd never liked Valentine's Day as a couple's holiday, but she liked the things that came with it — roses, chocolate, rich reds and hearts. She liked those things all year round, but the holiday gave her the opportunity to indulge.

While the golems were still hustling and bustling around to pack for the Funhouse event, Neve wrapped herself in a jacket, which didn't match anything but at least was warm, then cautiously approached the large Airstream trailer.

The metal exterior had been etched with serpents weaving among carnations and sunflowers, the detail more stunning the closer she came. The artistry of the design wasn't Troy's style at all and the golems' work didn't seem particularly crafty. It could have been Bell's doing, but Neve suspected that Lady Sasha owned every scratch, the way Troy had done some work on his own trailer—albeit with a bit more irony.

She wasn't sure that coming here was a good idea, but she forced herself to knock on the door before she lost her nerve.

"Wait," Sasha called, muffled inside the trailer.

Neve waited. There was nothing to be gained from disobeying a succubus with an army of both venomous and nonvenomous snakes.

Lady Sasha moved back and forth across the trailer, which creaked and rocked with the movement for a few minutes. Then she opened the door. She wore nothing, and while Neve had grown more accustomed to nakedness since arriving at Arcanium and hadn't had much of a problem with human anatomy beforehand, she hadn't expected Sasha to be naked.

To be fair, what Sasha wanted to wear in her own home was her business.

She'd never been this close to the succubus. Like most of the people in Arcanium, she only experienced Lady Sasha from a distance, generally while she was performing, and Sasha made sure to maintain that distance, cognizant of her own culpability if she touched anyone.

It occurred to Neve that Lady Sasha had to be as lonely as Lord Mikhail. His loneliness had been made all the more apparent by the time they'd spent together so far in their careful, sometimes tense experiment.

He acted like she had back when she'd been single. It didn't matter if one was naturally solitary. Sometimes, even the solitary needed a little social interaction, and whenever Neve had been too alone for too long, she'd talk her friends' ears off when they'd finally get together.

Lord Mikhail had introduced her to his favorite nature shows and films—some of which she got to enjoy for a second time from previous viewing outside Arcanium. And she'd already known he had a lot to say if someone got him started. She could listen to him talk forever, because his voice was beautiful, soothing, rich to her ears, the way the odd chef's hot chocolate was rich to her tongue. And he was just as enthusiastic as she was about the old Bill Nye episodes she showed him. A large, tattooed incubus with bulging biceps geeking out over children's shows was one of the more delightful things that the rest of the world would never get to see, and Neve was just fine keeping that rare jewel to herself.

Lady Sasha wasn't smiling. "Can I help you?" Courteous, though with a chill to the question.

"Am I interrupting anything?" Neve asked.

"I'm feeding the snakes and cleaning out some of their enclosures."

"May I watch?"

Lady Sasha hesitated. Neve forced herself to focus on the woman's face and not the rest of her. Sure, she was a woman, but she was still stunning without a stitch of clothing or makeup on—with a dark golden complexion that appeared healthy rather than sallow, skin smooth and poreless, hair as dark as Mikhail's but with strands of gold threaded through that sunlight would eagerly catch. Voluptuous. Not beautiful like a fashion model at all, nothing about her airbrushed to the eye. The quality that would resonate most with someone looking at her was that she was *real*. She carried the same strength in her limbs as Mikhail, but it had been wrapped in a softness that he didn't have—a swimsuit model rather than a gym rat, everything about her defying gravity but still subject to the laws of motion.

Her face hadn't been made up for the Funhouse yet, but she could go without it if she chose, with natural coloring to her cheeks and lips, eyelashes dark and thick to match her hair, black eyes warm without added smoke over the eyelids. Even without the rest of her, Sasha's face also distracted, particularly the darkness to her lips, a color Neve couldn't hope to match without lipstick, not that she could pull off such a tone.

Finally, Lady Sasha nodded and backed up into the Airstream. "I'll need to open the venomous snakes' tanks, but you shouldn't be in any danger. Please sit on the cushion behind the table."

The trailer was more spacious on the inside than the outside, the way Kitty's tent was bigger than it appeared. Neve attributed that to the considerable collection of snakes that Sasha had amassed. She'd anticipated the giant python tank, and she'd already seen the boa constrictors and the king cobras, but the cobras were housed in separate tanks, the boas were in the same tank, and all three giant enclosures took up only half a wall. Above them were shelves of smaller tanks, each one labeled like they were at zoos. The whole room was a little cooler than Neve found comfortable, maybe to compensate for all the heat lamps working so hard.

On the other wall were three shelves of enclosures of various sizes. Three of the tanks on the bottom were filled solely with white mice.

"I used to feed the excess to Bale, but I have to find another method of population control, because my babies don't eat them fast enough." Lady Sasha smiled a little as Neve took in the sight of the white mice crawling over each other like some kind of laboratory nightmare.

"Does David not eat mice?" Neve asked.

"No. He just looks like a serpent. The way Bell changed him, he didn't acquire any new appetites. More's the pity, although I hardly need another overgrown pet. You can look closer at the tanks when I'm through feeding and cleaning. I don't want to risk brushing over your skin."

"Do you have to worry about that with women, too?"

"It's best not to tempt fate. I never touch without permission from Bell." She avoided looking at Neve when she answered, resentment in the set of her shoulders and curve of spine.

The back of the trailer was exclusively for the snakes. There was a bathroom and kitchenette near the door but no bed, just the huge boa constrictor tank between the two walls. A large feather pillow had been tucked into the corner. The two constrictors, one colored for camouflage and the other albino, were big enough to fill the tank, their bodies a cradle that Sasha presumably slept in instead of a bed. Neve stared intently at the tank, wondering if sleeping with two fully grown boa constrictors was comfortable or whether the snakes went out of their way to make it comfortable.

"Have you always been a snake charmer? Was it how you were born or was that something Bell did to you?"

"I was born a snake charmer, as Mikhail was born with preternatural strength. But both of our natural abilities were enhanced in Arcanium. He became stronger. I was given more control. Before Arcanium, I could tame venomous serpents, but if I was bitten by one, either by animalistic pique or accident, its venom would harm me as it would a human being. Now, a slip of my influence will not lead to agony or bring me near to death. It has allowed me to keep serpents I was never able to touch before."

She put her hands in a diamondback rattlesnake's tank and picked it up. It never rattled, of course, because it wasn't threatened. The rattlesnake slithered up her arm to her shoulder, uninclined to climb the way a constrictor would but maintaining its balance around her shoulders. It poked its tongue out in Neve's direction, scenting her, but it remained calm.

"I assume the bite would still hurt, the way a needle hurts," Sasha murmured, stroking a line down the viper's broad head to its spine. "But now they don't even want to harm me when I'm not controlling them. As the spiders and other vermin serve the Spider, so the serpents serve me."

It seemed Lord Mikhail wasn't the only sex demon with a fondness for alliteration.

"If David wanted to, he could command them as well, but he's happy letting me handle them on my own. Snakes make him squeamish."

"Maybe becoming a giant snake wasn't the best move," Neve said.

Sasha smiled. She opened her fist and dropped the white mouse she'd hidden there into the rattlesnake's tank. The rattlesnake swiftly slithered back into the tank to follow his dinner. "You probably know by now that Bell has a fondness for irony."

"I had managed to observe that, yes."

"You seem a pleasant enough guest, Neve, but might I ask why you're here?"

Neve sighed. "I have multiple agendas."

"You'll fit right into Arcanium." Lady Sasha lifted the lid of a tank where a skinny, bright green snake rose from its branch. Neve was pretty sure it was a green mamba, and while she was slightly terrified to bump into something and startle it, she was also as excited as she'd always been in the reptile house of a good zoo. Sasha dropped a baby mouse into the enclosure then closed the tank again.

"The first is to ask whether you have any issue with me," Neve said.

"Because you're in Arcanium, because you're having sex with Mikhail or because you're dating him?" Sasha shook her head, amused for her private reasons. "Cute, although you display remarkable willpower for a clearly attracted woman — in such close proximity with him for weeks and nothing more than kisses. It's driving you and him crazy, and his effort at restraint is driving me crazy. How much longer do you expect to abstain?"

"I'm not holding out hope to wait past tonight," Neve said. "I'm surprised we lasted this long."

"I imagine the reason it has lasted is because Mikhail's tasting something from you he cannot receive from another woman." Sasha still had her body angled away, her back to Neve as she tended the next serpent, but Neve couldn't shake the idea that Sasha was entirely focused on her — kike a serpent herself, able to strike in an instant, although Neve couldn't say whether striking was Sasha's intention.

"Not even you?" Neve asked.

"The interaction between an incubus and a succubus is quite different from that between an incubus and a human woman. He settles for a succubus. He was made for a human woman."

Lady Sasha brought out a plain brown snake that Neve thought might be Australian.

She could kill an army with the contents of this trailer alone. Kids come to this circus. Far be it from her to argue with a snake charmer, but Neve couldn't help but shiver a little.

"You and Mikhail arrived together. He said you were born of the same flame, so you've been with each other all that time."

Sasha rested the brown snake on her shoulders while she cleaned out the tank and arranged the habitat again. "We are familiar with and quite fond of each other, but we weren't made for each other. And our interactions are almost solely sexual. Our magnetism only intensifies in proximity. But being near him… Being near him is like being home, so we stay together."

Neve chewed idly on a nail. It wasn't her habit, but she didn't know quite how to phrase the question. "Not to bring up what might be a sensitive subject, but as long as you have a deadly snake around your neck and I'm in immediate danger of your wrath, wouldn't being born of the same flame as Mikhail make you brother and sister?"

Sasha straightened, brushing her hair behind her ear to look back at Neve again. She and Mikhail had the same skill at hiding their thoughts behind a beautiful mask. "Would you like to hold him?"

"What?"

"The eastern brown. Would you like to hold a venomous snake? I'm well-versed in the excitement in an enthusiast's eyes."

"I don't know. Do I want to hold him?"

Sasha's lips twitched in the direction of a smile. "I'm not going to set him on you. I rarely get to share my snakes with anyone. No one comes to my trailer anymore, not that Bale was interested in any other reptile but himself. Not even Mikhail, since I don't have a bed. They're all quite docile as long as I'm here and nothing is a threat to them. Snakes only bite for two reasons, and you're too big to be food." Sasha brought the brown snake to the table and held it out.

Neve clung to the fact that if Sasha killed her with a serpentine murder weapon, death would be too merciful in comparison to what Bell would do to her. She held out her arm. Sasha carefully placed the brown snake in loose loops around her.

"I can't believe I'm doing this," Neve whispered, unable to speak any louder for the tightness in her chest. "And there's no danger?"

"Oh, they're still dangerous. I don't remove their venom sacs because there *have* been unwelcome visitors to this trailer. Other exotic pet collectors covet my collection. I still haven't figured out how Valorie managed to get my coral snake without my knowing. But as long as they're calm, they don't bite — and I told him not to."

"Out of curiosity, is that the Rotting Man's crime, or is it entirely unrelated? It's just that many places on his body look like advanced necrosis — like, say, what might happen to a man with multiple hemotoxic snake bites." Neve gently hoisted the snake closer to her body. The brown snake was a creeper, not a climber. Its head was less than a foot away from her face. Minute flinches shook her body every time the snake flicked out its tongue.

"You have a good eye," Sasha replied.

"My research lab works with natural toxins, including snake venom, exploring their medicinal uses. We have a pretty good idea what each toxin does to a body in case of a lab accident."

"He was a dealer looking to collect for a wealthy client. He caught me sleeping, thought he'd take more than snakes. Why he believed taking advantage of a woman wrapped in boa constrictors was a good plan, I'll never know, but the smartest men tend to leak intelligence in my presence, and he was not the smartest man."

Lady Sasha crooked her finger to beckon the brown snake back to her. "You asked me a question no one else has been brave enough to ask, though I've seen them consider it. To be born from the same flame is not the same as being born to the same mother. We weren't born from a womb, as some of our kind are. We were born fully grown, with instinct and the capacity for knowledge. To be born from the same flame connects us, and we are like family, but" — Sasha shook her head, whispering lightly to the snake in her hands before putting him back in his tank—"I suspect if our DNA was tested, they'd present with similar backgrounds but no familial match. We're like two babies born in the same hospital at the same time. It happens all over the world, but despite the coincidence, it doesn't mean they are born from the same mother."

Neve could breathe so much better without a brown snake on her shoulders, although she knew she was still far from safe. "As long as I'm asking personal questions, why *are* sex demons born both from fire *and* from a human mother? Curious minds want to know."

Lady Sasha slid into the seat across from Neve, angling her legs away so they wouldn't accidentally overlap. "We're born of fire because we aren't born of a womb fast enough, and we don't proliferate more quickly than we're destroyed—by demon hunters, by each other, by stronger demons. When there are too few of us in the world, we spring from fire. It surprises me you never asked Mikhail, with all the time you spend not fucking."

"We haven't returned to the subject since he first brought it up. We talk about other things."

"You do more than talk. I feel it every time you meet, every time you do more. The atmosphere of the entire circus changes."

"Dating couples do more than just talk, too."

They never watched TV shows or movies while propped up in either of their beds. It was less comfortable to watch in Lord Mikhail's oddity tent, where Bell had provided a loveseat and an ottoman for them to set themselves up with Neve's entertainment tablet. No proper Internet, but at least they had access to what they needed. They sat at either end of the couch—minimal contact, if any—with the tablet propped up on a stand on the ottoman in order to watch together.

At the end of their dates, though, Mikhail closed the distance between them. She didn't bare a lot of skin, but he went shirtless again—no more expensive suits, but also rarely leather during the week. He wore just plain jeans that hung from his hips in a way that made Neve want to trace the edge before pulling them down his legs.

Mikhail kissed her senseless, kissed her until she was melting and half-reclined on the small sofa, leaving marks on her neck like a teenager but with none of the overindulgence that Neve remembered from her teenage years—the kind that hurt when a boy sucked too hard or bit her like a puppy. Mikhail's kisses were tender, deliberate, even the pressure of his teeth pleasurable. He cradled her head and left his bruises and nothing more.

No, not nothing more. He left plenty behind. He'd maintained the control he had promised, withholding his magic like a fist struggling to hold wet sand as it dried. But as they continued to feed their arousal without satisfaction, that control was beginning to fray. She'd broken their make-out sessions in the beginning, but now he had to, which so clearly went against every grain of instinct in his incubus body, a body designed to prey on women, to take from them, to consume them, to fuck anything that would let him.

But when she would stroke over the front of his jeans or slide her palm underneath, somehow he retrieved a mental fortitude equal to his physical strength to take her hand from his full, hot, straining erection and lift it back to his chest—or to hers, where he wordlessly requested her to pleasure her own breasts for him, his hand over hers, as he continued to kiss her.

The contact Neve wanted to permit them was becoming far too brief, their impulses bringing them closer to sex more quickly every time. On some of their dates, she'd asked that they not make contact at all, and Mikhail had seemed to be in complete agreement, despite the desire chiseled into every angle of his body—which meant that something about these innocent date nights was doing something for him, too.

Maybe that was why she kept crawling over to his side of the sofa and sitting on his lap, sometimes before the show or movie had concluded, to take his face in her hands and kiss him. Because he'd shown—through all the things he *wasn't* doing to her—that what he wanted sometimes had nothing to do with his desire for her body. All that did was make him more attractive to her, make her want the taste of his tongue on hers, the salt of his skin, the scent of him on her clothes.

The wait made the arousal just short of unbearable. It was a test to see how far they could go, how long they could last without giving in to purely physical need.

Three weeks was certainly not very long in comparison to her original stretch of abstinence. But in the quiet, rational moments when Mikhail wasn't near her, Neve reminded herself that she was a different kind of woman from who she'd been, different from any of the other women she'd grown up with and had judged without knowing she was doing it. And Mikhail was a different kind of man. She had to adjust her expectations.

Especially since the rest of it was going so well. She hadn't anticipated Mikhail accepting the premise of the experiment or that spending time with him engaging in activities that had nothing to do with sex would be almost as fun as her time with her husband. She hadn't expected to be charmed by the way he enjoyed self-education, how he was open to trying any genre she showed him, how he'd read a book she'd suggested just because she'd suggested it and how he'd said something that she'd then brought up to the book club, which had sparked a whole new discussion. She'd started this experiment to know Mikhail as something other than an incubus, to get to know his mind and learn whether he cared at all for hers. It had only been three weeks, but he hadn't pushed for more, which she knew he could do as eloquently as a master orator. Nor had he ended their dates, which he could do at any time without it getting in the way of his having sex with her in the end.

She supposed that was why she was here. She'd thought it would fail. It was *supposed* to have failed. She'd thought Mikhail wouldn't be able to fill the time the way that Joseph had. He was supposed to get tired of her or try to take something he shouldn't. They were supposed to go their separate ways except when the laws of nature demanded that they meet.

But there was more to him than sex, so much more than anyone else in Arcanium could have known because they couldn't go near him. And he seemed to enjoy the parts of her that had nothing to do with sex, too.

"I hope you weren't here just to ask me the difficult questions about incubi and succubi," Lady Sasha said.

Neve stared down at her hands, tangling her fingers into knots on the acrylic table in front of her, her knuckles white. "I asked the difficult questions because I wasn't sure what Lord Mikhail is to you or how you feel about him with me. When Bell brought me into Arcanium, you were upset—and you haven't taken that out on me, which I appreciate—but I need to know if what I've done since arriving has in any way exacerbated that anger, if I'm intruding where I'm not welcome."

Sasha closed her eyes with weariness, lowering her head into her hand. "If I were to become jealous of every woman who gives in to my firemate's charms, Bell would have killed me years ago. Sex demons can become possessive of their own, but it's foolish to indulge in anything so human as jealousy over sexual favors or affection. My frustrations are with Mikhail for his lack of control and with Bell for rewarding him. I have no quarrel with you, and if you can aid Mikhail with his control, all power to you. I would rather not have another series of messes like what he did to the twins and what he did to Seth. However, since then he's demonstrated more restraint. The Ringmaster's blows must have finally snapped deep enough into his flesh to imprint within his brain as well. I rubbed potion into his wounds for a week, and demon flesh should heal much faster on its own."

Neve filed it under Things I Don't Want to Know, but she had a responsibility to ask. "What exactly did he do to the twins and Seth?"

"He stalked the twins, attracted to their dual energy in one person. You know how persistent he is, how he loses sight of what behavior is appropriate when he desires something he cannot have and when there is nothing to distract him from his hunger. He thinks he hides, but with magic spilling from his pores in a deluge, he might as well shout from wherever he stands."

Lady Sasha shook her head. "Joanne and Jane were vulnerable. They didn't have anyone to claim their attention and discourage Mikhail, and with a long enough abstinence, he would rather accept the consequences of succumbing to his desires than endure them any longer. Bell was there to slap his paws away, but when Seth and Lars arrived and gave the twins their distraction..." She sighed. "After the Ringmaster was through with him, I gave him my own beating. If he was going to be impulsive and desperate, we had no business staying here. He leaves the twins alone now, and Bell trusted him enough to touch Maya, as Bell trusted me to touch John. He's proven himself able to endure. But with so little to feed upon on a regular basis, I still worry that he's going to be the death of us both."

"You think I should give in more often, too." Neve's knotting fingers threatened to tighten into fists but she managed to keep her voice even. "You think I should soothe the savage beast."

Sasha straightened, her weariness yielding to resolve. "What? No. By no means do I suggest you have sex with Mikhail simply to placate his appetite. I would never put that burden on anyone, not even if his love can't kill you."

"Do you think what we're doing is doomed, then? Dating like normal teenagers — normal human teenagers — which neither of us has ever really done?" Neve asked. "Do you think it's a mistake, like trying to domesticate a wild animal? I don't want to make him worse than he already was."

Lady Sasha stood from the table and turned away again to attend to the tanks and terrariums on that side of the trailer. "I think you need to discard the notion that you're responsible for the actions of the men in your life, Neve. I have my own faults, but having been with Mikhail since our beginning, I'm also well aware of his. If he is attempting to challenge those faults because of his obsession with a human woman, rather than indulging in those faults because of his obsession with a human woman, I see no problem with him and that woman engaging in something perfectly human. Incubi and succubi are not so different from you. Like other hybrids, we're often considered beneath the rest of the demon world because we're so similar and suffer the same needs. For all that we require sex to live, we do crave affection. We just have fewer avenues of pursuing it, because it is so often sabotaged by the sex we engage in."

She raised a large viper Neve didn't immediately recognize from its habitat and whispered to it the way

Neve remembered whispering to her cat when she was young. "I have my serpents. They are charmed by me but they have no mating urge for a succubus. I may handle them at will, and they love me as a serpent can. I sleep in the python's and constrictors' embrace, held as though in arms, stroked as though by hands. It is not as good as human contact, but it satisfies the basic need for touch-based affection unlinked to sexuality."

"Have you tried stuffed animals?" Neve asked. "That was one of my methods when guys were too interested in sex for me to keep dating them. I had to rescue a stuffed Cthulhu from the midway after I was so unceremoniously kidnapped."

"I've indulged in a few stuffed animal hugs myself." Sasha's smile appeared less wry as she put the viper back in its tank and lowered a mouse into the enclosure. The viper immediately snapped it up, pumping its venom into the tiny creature and killing it in seconds. Neve got up from the table to watch, fascinated. The label on the tank read 'fer-de-lance'. Above it were more colorful venomous snakes, including the aforementioned coral snake, its elapid head deceptively slender rather than triangular.

"Your collection is amazing. Possibly illegal, but still amazing, and I know they're cared for instead of trafficked," Neve said. "Like, seriously, if I were immune to snake venom, I'd live here. Do you keep antivenin on hand in case of accidents?"

Lady Sasha nodded. "If I carry them with me and someone tries to touch me, they sense my moment of fear and they will strike. One of the king cobras was rescued from one of my very ex-lovers, who'd cruelly had its venom sacs removed. I'll sometimes carry him when in denser crowds like the Funhouse events. But when I bring out the other venomous snakes, yes, accidents happen, though we've only had to use antivenin a handful of times. I mostly go out with my boas or ball pythons, who are used to being handled and less inclined to bite."

She lifted one of the ball pythons from its large habitat and wrapped it around her shoulders, providing her arm for it to climb. "If you came here to ask for my blessing, Neve, you don't need it. What Mikhail does only concerns me when he threatens his own life with his foolishness. I love him as the man who has been with me since birth, but he is my lover of convenience, and we can never be more than firemates. I don't know whether abstaining from sex is sustainable, but from the way Mikhail described it to me, it was never intended to be."

Neve shook her head. "No. I just need more than spectacular sex. That didn't change after Bell transformed me. It was just harder to tell. I'm selfish that way."

"Not selfish at all, darling. Would you like to meet Raphael? He's my cuddlebug. He loves climbing people, and he's the go-to I use for children." At Neve's raised eyebrow, Sasha smiled. "Maya is often there to help, but my touch does absolutely nothing to humans before puberty. And I wear more than this when offering snake-handling and souvenir pictures."

As she watched Neve stroke the snake's strong body, Lady Sasha's expression warmed all the more, though her nipples tightened. "Do visit again if you want to help me with the snakes. Just make sure I'm here when you do."

"I'd like that," Neve murmured, utterly enchanted with the active python wrapping around her wrist. "Now all I have to do is ingratiate myself more with the Spider, and I might actually die of happiness."

* * * *

She and Mikhail stayed separate on the way to their next Funhouse. They'd agreed the night before not to interact at all before the event began, because the tension between them would be good for the atmosphere. Mikhail's emanations were exquisite torture for every single one of the women wherever they went.

When they arrived, Neve blinked as they stepped out onto a neighborhood cul-de-sac rather than in front of an impersonal, anonymous building like the last Funhouse. The golems hadn't brought any of the semis—a house wouldn't be able to sustain even the flimsiest of Arcanium's infrastructure. Arcanium vehicles not holding cast were ushered under an arch with an open gate to a larger parking area in front of a seven-car garage where the neighborhood wouldn't have to see them. Once all the cast were out of the trailers, those vehicles joined the rest.

The long cul-de-sac supported only three houses total, and each house had a good amount of property attached—a breadth of land one wouldn't expect so close to a city where space was at a premium, but the owner of the house could clearly afford that premium. The house was what people liked to call a McMansion, the kind of architectural monstrosity that marked wealth in terms of gables, turrets and stone, modern castles with no sense of balance.

The Mediterranean stucco and clay tiles were aggressive in their pretentious declarations, the lawn manicured in a way that made it abundantly clear that the homeowners had nothing to do with it. But a man and woman came out to meet them through the front door rather than the back, and they seemed like nice enough people. Both the woman and the man wore some kind of collar visible over their bathrobes. They shed their robes as soon as everyone had entered their travertine foyer. Underneath, both of them had donned leather of the sort neither would likely want their neighbors to see.

The rooms of the lower floor were all for Arcanium, the woman told Bell after they'd greeted each other with kisses on both cheeks in European fashion. Most of the non-essential furniture had been removed prior to their arrival. The kitchen was set up as a wine bar, with plenty of hors d'oeuvres for both cast and guests, which meant that the odd chef didn't have much to do.

The cast was ushered out onto the covered porch, which had been set up for outdoor entertaining and what Neve presumed would also be the site for the stage performances. The guesthouse was for them to change or use the facilities, and they were free to swim in the heated saltwater pool during the first half of the event and intermission. The fences on either side of the property and the trees on the far side maintained visual privacy. As long as they kept the noisier activities inside, they could do pretty much anything they wanted, and as far as this couple was concerned, the cast were guests, not merely entertainment.

Obscenely rich or not, Neve hadn't yet met a kink couple she hadn't liked, and this couple, the head of the local chapter, didn't break the trend. They were enthusiastic, friendly people, shaking everyone's hands, asking everyone's names, talking with some of the cast members they recognized from visits to Arcanium or the five other Funhouse events they'd done.

Instead of setting up partitions to make hallways and rooms, the golems hung the black curtains over established walls, draping them partway across arched openings to create more separated rooms. Cast members were assigned about two or three to a room, depending on how much space they took up. Most of them did the same things they'd done in the last Funhouse event, although there wasn't enough room for glass cases, and Melanie was transferred to the pool.

As much as Neve had liked the industrial feel of the previous Funhouse, this one was far more intimate and comfortable, reminding her of the private munches she'd enjoyed while experimenting with her husband.

Neve was assigned to the master bedroom, which still had its king-sized bed, although the sheets had been stripped for whatever else Bell wanted to do with it. Bell led her by the hand to the platform on which the bed had been arranged. She couldn't help but laugh at having to step up to reach the bed then having to climb up another series of stairs just to reach the top.

Silk wrapped itself around the bed under and over her, with more red silk draping over the posts until she was in her own little luxurious circus tent.

Bell climbed into the bed with her, his weight denting the mattress on either side until he was on his hands and knees above her, contemplative. She swallowed, her mouth dry, so keenly attuned to sexual stimulation that just the movements of his body, the subtler flex of his muscles and the dilation of his pupils in the shadows made her imagine him lowering himself over her, taking her without a word or request for permission—just taking her the way she could almost swear she saw in the reflection of his eyes and in the thickening of his cock underneath the thin, ivory, bohemian cotton trousers he'd chosen to wear tonight instead of leather.

He wanted her. She still had the taste of her first desire from his kiss on her lips. And she wanted him—eventually. Once she'd established her place in Arcanium, perhaps. Or when she was no longer afraid he would use her for sex just because he seemed strained by Maya's continued absence. If he took her now, she'd enjoy it but never trust him again. And if he could read her mind, he had to know that.

Bell stroked the frame of her face. "What Lady Sasha and Lord Mikhail do to this circus is beautiful. It thrills me every day. But the quality of your desire is intoxicating—you and the Spider both. I don't know why I torture myself with it." He clenched his teeth and pushed himself back to sit between his heels, demonstrating effortless flexibility. "Would you like the same scenario as before or do you have ideas to change it?"

Neve nodded. "Could you have them be gentler on my dress, though? I know you can repair it, but I like this dress."

"The color suits you." He shook her foot affectionately then rocked back to stand on the mattress, holding the red curtains draped above as he took in the sight of her. "I'm going to bring the Horned God and the Creature in here with you. Neither will be tempted to join you in the bed, and the Creature will have your fear to taste, which should please him. Despite the lack of glass walls to protect you, you are safe. The guests will be instructed to maintain the usual 'look but don't touch' policy unless otherwise invited. These more intimate venues allow for more interactive exhibits, but you shouldn't feel pressured into letting anyone into this bed who you don't want here. Do you trust me?"

She nodded again, already trying to get into the headspace of her character, bracing herself for the hands, for the relentless string of orgasms, for the sex demons' magic to cut through her all the more keenly...and for Mikhail's resolve and her own to eventually snap. She took a shaky breath, craving touch but afraid to ask Bell to touch her, in case her own willpower couldn't convince her not to push it farther.

"I'll see you later this evening, then," Bell said. "I trust you won't be performing tonight?"

"Not tonight. I'll...mingle." She thought of Samuel. She thought of the collared couple. Of perfect strangers. Of Mikhail watching her with these perfect strangers, sending out his magic until her already insatiable need became unbearable. Her thoughts had been purely pornographic ever since she'd left Sasha's trailer and snakes could no longer distract her. Every time she'd brushed one of the other women in Kitty's trailer, the result had been nearly painful. The demon hands wouldn't have to work too hard on her tonight.

"Good girl." He jumped off the bed and turned off the ceiling lights, leaving only a few lamps on in the room. A trio of couches in the center of the sitting room area one level below the bed's platform all angled toward her.

She closed her eyes, and as the golems and other cast members entered, she tried to prepare and rest. She wasn't going to leave the bed for a good few hours, but the demon hands would keep her busy. *No rest for the wicked.*

* * * *

The end of the walk-through portion of the Funhouse culminated with Neve turned over on her knees on the bed, her face pressed into the sheets, the bodice of her gown pulled down over her breasts and her skirt over her hips — wrinkled but not torn, the way she'd asked — and demon fingers deep in her pussy, ass and rubbing over her clit while her arms were bound behind her back. She'd taken the silk sheets between her teeth to muffle her screams, because the demons who had her in their grasp were pulling no punches, and neither was Mikhail.

"Mine. Need."

The absence of eloquence told her that they weren't thoughts so much as feelings, but those feelings were all the stronger for barely being words.

She imagined the feelings she sent out in kind weren't much more coherent. The last orgasm wrenched out of her as though wrung from inside her pussy. She jerked back and forth against the hands holding her down, but she didn't expect them to let up or let her orgasm stop until they'd milked as much of it out of her as she could give.

The people still on the platform around the bed stared at her, eyes wide and glazed, the dominant partners speaking softly to their submissives. Some had been told to put their hands on the bed or kneel so they had to strain to see. Some of them were being pleasured or were pleasuring themselves at their Dominant's orders.

Neve was hit with a strong memory of being at a munch with Joseph where they'd experimented with her as the submissive. What would it be like if Joseph had been a part of this community and could see her now? She squeezed her eyes shut and bore down on the last of her orgasm.

The guests were so much closer than in the last venue. There were faces not two feet away from her cunt, able to see parts of her she could only ever view with a mirror, able to see her dripping with the cumulative effects of seven hard orgasms, three of which had been triggered via G-spot and surprised one of the women who had been in the way. When the liquid had struck the woman, she'd jerked back but laughed hysterically. Sharing fluids without prior approval was a major rule-break, but the woman had been too close and had surely known what might happen. Given that Neve was bound to the bed and not in control of anyone else around her, there hadn't been much she could do, and the woman had just kept laughing, although she'd dropped into the master bathroom to wash up. Neve would have asked if she was okay, but her mouth had been full with demon fingers at the time.

In general, though, most of the visitors were eminently respectful. There had been a man leashed to a woman who had politely asked whether he could insult her because his Mistress asked it of him. She'd nodded, and for a submissive, he'd unleashed such a string of expletives and epithets that would have made Shakespeare blush that she'd almost lost focus on the fingers entering her ass.

After her last orgasm, which garnered her a round of admiring applause, a golem entered the master bedroom. "Everyone is invited to the kitchen for their dinner and to the backyard for an intermission so we can let our Arcanium cast recover before the next part of our evening."

Some of the guests thanked her as they left, but all too soon, the demon hands had receded back into the sodden sheets, and she was left alone while still vulnerable. Neve spat the silk from her mouth, fighting tears from the sudden hormonal and emotional drop.

"Shhh, child. Don't cry. You are not abandoned." The Creature was there to take her hand when she shakily raised herself up.

"You feed on fear, don't you?" Neve sniffed and used a part of the top sheet that hadn't been smeared with something to press against her eyes before the tears fell. "Can you taste the kind of fear, the way wine drinkers taste different notes?"

"I can." He waited patiently, the red of his eyes opaque all the way through, but he didn't *seem* to be leering at her breasts as she pulled the straps over her shoulders again. She wondered how he could see or if he could see at all. He was quite bat-like, so she wondered if he used a form of sonar at a frequency she couldn't hear. She'd ask later. Right now she just wanted his help getting down from the bed while her limbs were still shaking.

The Horned God stood by the door. He'd shed the satyr or half-centaur fur from the last Funhouse and simply wore his horns, the rest of him smooth and bare as matte marble. Unlike the last time she'd seen him, which had been at the beginning of the Funhouse event rather than the end, he was turned on, but even after the sex demons' hours-long onslaught, he'd managed only a partial erection. His face still lacked any expression at all. The Creature was a quiet thing with an expressionless face as well, but there was substance beneath it — intensity, life and intelligence in those swirling red eyes. The Horned God revealed nothing of himself except what biology forced him to show.

The Creature was turned on as well, but he'd replaced his loincloth, which at least covered him — and he was as well-endowed as the other monsters and demons of Arcanium — whereas the Horned God appeared more average. Either way, though they were both men, their emotional restraint kept her from feeling like they would take advantage of her while she was like this — a mass of nerves, eight orgasms not enough while Mikhail's magic was still in play and demanding its own satisfaction. Their tranquility in spite of the magic that Lady Sasha likely sent out as strongly as Mikhail served to soothe the finger-fucked wreck she'd become.

The Horned God opened the door and the Creature held her hand as she stepped down from the bed's platform. He guided her in front of him to enter the hall protected from both sides.

Then the Horned God veered into one of the bedrooms without a word at the sight of the hulking shadow at the end of the hallway. All the bulbs had been covered with a film to light the hallway red. In that light, Lord Mikhail looked like a demon. He'd once again strapped his body in leather, but the bladed gloves and the bladed muzzle for his cock had been removed, and his erection was huge and thick in his hand. He panted like a bull. Neve half expected smoke from his nostrils and parted lips. She could practically feel his fever burn her, despite their distance.

The Creature rested a hand on her shoulder, perhaps tasting trepidation now that she faced Mikhail again, who clearly intended to do much more than a quick blow job where no one could see them. It was a given that he was going to feed on her through more than just her mouth tonight. And she wanted him to. She wanted him to fuck her every way that Lennon's tentacles had had her, every way the hands had taken her tonight.

"Out of my way." He didn't snarl or yell at the Creature, but a hint of a growl roughened his voice, which came from that place inside him that made the walls and floors vibrate.

Neve touched the Creature's hand on her shoulder and nodded, but she didn't take her eyes off the strongman's shadow. If she couldn't reach him with her hands, she could stroke over him with her gaze, her imagination achingly vivid, just short of sensory.

The Creature slipped into the closest room with the Horned God. Neve couldn't say whether that room led anywhere else through a shared bathroom or whether the two cast members were stuck in the room until Mikhail passed it, but their inconvenience dwindled in importance to her.

She'd done the work to make her gown presentable, but now she lowered her shoulder to let a strap slip down, and she slowly pulled her arm out from underneath it. The silk flowed down like water, baring one breast, the nipple hard and dark and tender from the demon hands' bruising abuse.

As Mikhail advanced, Neve backed up, but not to get away. Before she could hit the door, he reached her, grabbing her legs hard enough to leave more bruises and shoving her against the door himself, his body crowding her and stealing her breath.

He lifted her, the muscles of his arms flexing, though she knew it didn't require much effort from him. His strength was needed for restraint, for the patience required to remain still, calm, to bring her up the door, up his body, to not respond to her touching his arms, his chest, his shoulders in a way she had fought against during their dates, because she knew how it would weaken her resolve. She studied the movements of his muscles, the hot pulse under his skin, the thump of his heart as she stroked over his chest. Her silk-covered abdomen drew up against his erection, precum smearing over the fabric, the weight of his cock without anything containing it intimidating all over again.

Neve slid her hands up to his neck, along the rasping line of his jaw, the bristle of his facial hair rough over her palms. He bit her thumb when she brushed his lip, their breath mingling between them. They were still holding back, still holding their line, because arousal rose high and taut and torturous the longer they waited.

Who will blink first – the incubus or the nymphomaniac?

He canted his hips deliberately against hers, his erection slotting between her legs now. Her labia parted underneath her gown from the pressure of his girth. He moved a rough hand up her abdomen to the breast she'd teased him with. Her breath shuddered from her open mouth as he squeezed her in his massive paw. Then he took the nipple and pinched it, rolled it, twisted it – not as hard as the demon hands had in the bed tableau, but her clit twitched like an erection, her cunt clenching tighter and tighter and tighter....

She wrapped her arm around his neck and lowered her mouth to his with a shaky moan, tasting his tongue and chasing it as she rocked against his erection.

Mikhail pulled her away from the door, keeping her against his body by her hold on him and one arm around her back as he drew up the skirt of the gown, just enough to get it out of the way before he shoved her against the door again. Neve thought she heard something crack, but she figured Bell could make any necessary structural repairs that the golems couldn't.

He didn't take her immediately. He kept his cock between her folds, rubbing against her, and she rode him that way, grinding her clit against the underside of his shaft as he sank his fingers into her messy mass of hair and took control of the kiss.

His magic seeped into her as though she were sinking into a hot spring. He was already feeding from her, just from their kiss, just from his cock against her clit. When his kisses couldn't muffle her cries anymore, he bit his way down her neck, took the bared nipple in his mouth and closed his teeth over the nub hard enough to really hurt before leaving bitemarks all the way back up her neck again.

She pressed him closer, her head falling back with a thud against the door. She slid her clit up and down his erection and tried to make that enough, tried to come. But he purred in her ear and licked its edge, softening his touch until she punched his shoulder blade.

The man had the audacity to laugh, but he lifted her up by her ass, his hands steady as a chair, and flexed his cock until it found her cunt. Her entrance, labia and thighs were already plenty slick with her arousal from all the orgasms that the demon hands had given her — foreplay, in comparison.

Her nails left grooves on his back as he entered her, lowering her until she'd taken in half of his erection. She was turned on and already well-stretched, so she could take that much even without magic easing his way. He fucked her like that, controlling completely how much of him she took, no matter how she tried to grind down. He held her steady as he pulled out then pushed back in until resistance kept him from going farther.

And it hurt. It hurt like her lips being stretched too far and the grooves cracking, hurt like lifting too much weight, bending down to touch her toes when she hadn't done yoga for a while. It hurt, but he kissed her like he did during the other nights in Arcanium, slow, excruciating, deliberate, an assaulting sensuous feast rather than the sexual one happening between her legs. She swore he was trying to make her cry, the bastard.

Then he wrapped her in his magic the way a spider wraps its prey in silk. She was pretty sure she was drawing blood with her nails, but he barely flinched. He was inside her, all the way inside, a strangled sound issuing from his throat as he paused their kiss, still open-mouthed, still breathing each other's air.

"Need."

He opened his eyes, black to their edges and glittering with red, like a cross between the Creature and the purer demons whose eyes simply went black. He fucked her and watched, watched her lean in to kiss him. They were only ever almost-kisses, their lips *almost* meeting, his teeth *almost* taking her lower lip, their tongues *almost* touching, but he kept pulling back until she had to give up trying to forge that form of connection. Part of her panged at not kissing him when he was finally inside her, because it meant one of the links she'd grown so attached to had been broken. She leaned her head back against the door again and struggled to keep her eyelids from fluttering shut as his magic sang through her blood, rang in her ears, trembled through her mind like his thoughts.

"Beautiful."

He used his weight to hold her against the door now. He caressed the length of her thigh, massaging more bruises, bringing her knees almost to her shoulders and changing the angle of her cunt around him.

"Oh, please..." She couldn't get enough breath. Each thrust felt like it knocked the air out of her, and his chest was pressed against hers, her nipples still hard from the friction. Her moans were turning into something like sobs. She scrabbled at his shoulders, leaving more claw marks behind.

Just take me. Consume me. Kill me if you have to. I need to die a little. It's the only way to make this pleasure release. Please don't leave me alone in here.

"Mine."

He surged up into her, stopped holding himself back and let the animal free, kissing her until she didn't have what little breath she'd had, screwing her so hard it sounded like he was driving a nail into her. She certainly felt impaled, but she'd accept this death. She'd take any he doled out to her if he would just make her come…

She slammed a hand against the door as the taut tension in her cunt snapped. Her orgasm rolled through her, staying high as he groaned into her mouth. Neve could almost taste his pleasure like that, and the taste of it intensified when he stilled and stiffened inside her, coming in little bursts of heat that accompanied the arrhythmic grasping of her cunt around his erection through her climax. The bursts were mini orgasms of their own. He slid his tongue over hers as though to taste her moans as well, feeding from the pleasure of the kiss and from their collective climax. He pulled her into him, thread by thread, until she was threadbare and vacant, growing limp in his arms.

Lord Mikhail didn't take as much of her as he could have, as he had at the last event. Again, knowing that this wasn't his last — knowing that his resource wasn't scarce, in their parlance — meant he didn't have to be so greedy, hoarding pleasure for leaner times.

She felt the way she had the one time she'd drunk too many margaritas. It didn't help that they'd been delicious, the alcohol in them insidious, and she'd always been a lightweight because she wasn't much of a drinker. Mikhail had left her bleary, lethargic with euphoria, but still awake. In theory she could still talk, but she didn't need to. Mikhail kissed her more gently now, soft on all the places he'd made his mark on her neck — a warm, decadent dessert to the meal he'd made of her as well as the orgasm he'd given.

Once she could move her limbs, she wrapped them around him again, stroking where she'd clawed him.

When he raised his head, he swiped his fingers over the paths of dried tears.

"Hello," he said.

She smiled. "Hi."

"In all my years, I've never had sex with someone with whom I am intimate." He dented her swollen lower lip with his nail before briefly kissing her again. "I have often experienced sadness during a feed, but I don't think I've had an emotion quite as strong before." He attempted to do some justice to her tousled, tangled hair, but only one of Kitty's brushes would do the trick. She guided his hand back down. "Was this solution palatable for you?"

She pulled him in to kiss him again, rocked over his continued erection, which drew out a prolonged groan from both of them at the same time.

"I want you again," he murmured against her lips. "Shall we save it for tonight, or is once all you will permit yourself?"

Neve pushed herself up high enough for his cock to slide out of her and through her folds, smearing his cum and her arousal over her labia and inside the skirt of her dress. But she whispered in his ear, "I want you outside by the pool during the performances. I want you to take me while the monsters are taking them. I want people to see it. I want people to see you fucking me."

Mikhail had become so still, he was almost a statue. He was immortal and didn't need to breathe, which only enhanced the impression. "Does this end our experiment?"

"Do you want it to end?"

"My answer is far more complicated than the question," he replied.

"You want both, don't you?" Neve breathed in the dark scent of his hair, sucking his earlobe between her teeth. His cock twitched between her folds. "If you had your way, you'd have sex whenever you wanted it, but you'd also have what we've been doing."

He nodded, continuing to otherwise hold himself still as she seduced him, subtle reactions giving away his pleasure.

"How often would we have our date nights if you could have sex with me as often as you want?"

After some thought, Mikhail grinned against her neck. "Your logic is unassailable. Perhaps a balance can be struck—a more generous allowance, so that we do not need to wait between Funhouses. They do not continue into the summer, and the autumn season is too preoccupied with Halloween."

"We can renegotiate terms when we're a little less horny and back in Arcanium, okay?" With some reluctance, she wriggled to indicate he should let her back down to the ground. She had to pull the skirt of her gown up over the pole of his erection while he laughed at the sight. "But sex is what everyone's here for. No reason we shouldn't indulge."

He kissed her again, a kiss of affection rather than seduction. Then he spanked her—no small gesture from a strongman but one he'd discovered she quite enjoyed.

"Go in without me," he said. "If I have to watch you leave, you're not going to go very far."

In response, she slapped his ass, which was framed by leather but not covered by it. Without silk muffling it, his flesh made a much more satisfying sound than hers. "I thought I was the only one."

Still laughing, braced against the door—which appeared more or less intact, fortunately, although its interior probably had its share of weak spots now—he determinedly looked away from her as she went through the corridor to the kitchen to find something to eat.

One of the guest rooms was an Introverts' Escape, which Neve thought was the most considerate thing she'd ever heard of, and she wondered why she'd never been at a party with one before. Anyone could go into the room, which looked like it usually functioned as a study, and spend some time alone.

Mindful of what had happened the last time she'd eaten with someone at a Funhouse event, she brought her plate into the Introverts' Escape and took one of the solo ottomans with a nodded greeting to the other two occupants—both guests who earned props by respecting that just because she was cast didn't mean she didn't need all the benefits of an introvert room like them.

As soon as she was finished, she closed her eyes in the peaceful quiet of the room, braced herself then stood up and went back out into the open kitchen and living room. Bell caught her on the way through the French doors to the porch, where night had fallen and lanterns lit the evening. Porch heaters and a fire pit kept everyone not of Arcanium from freezing. Without a word, he took her hand and sent his cleansing magic over her to leave her dress and her good as new.

He kissed her cheek, which she angled for him to reach, and they went their separate ways.

That damn wish gremlin is really growing on me.

Out on the porch, the festivities had heated up nicely, the privacy rooms set up all along the walls of the house and the edge of the pool like kink cabanas. They only moderately blocked the sound, and some of the rooms had their curtains pulled back so that a small crowd could watch whatever scene the Dom and sub had agreed to offer.

Good times, good memories—but not her scene anymore. Arcanium was kinky enough on its own.

Just as Neve stopped browsing, she thought she recognized a man reclining on a beach chair in front of the heated pool. The closer she came, the more she thought he might be the man with the fedora, Locke, although he wasn't wearing his hat. He had his legs crossed, his enigmatic smile and bright eyes unmistakable as he took in the variety of people around him, with the guests almost as interesting as the cast.

It didn't make sense for him to be here, though. Arcanium had its groupies, a handful of people who followed the circus all over the country, and each of the oddities had their fans. But this was the Funhouse, and as far as she could tell, the Funhouse was far more exclusive, each event hosted by different groups, different kinds of people—as long as they were rich, apparently—with no overlap between a private party of socialites in one state and a kink convention in another.

Furthermore, having been in a kink community, she knew there were a lot of rules, both spoken and understood, to protect its members from outsiders looking to mock the culture and from assholes looking to exploit what they saw as easy prey among the single submissive women. Most parties like this had RSVPs, no unexpected plus ones, couples and established groups only and the occasional single woman if vouched for. Single men were verboten until a kink community got to know them in more public munches, like at a bar or a club if they had a leather night.

Locke was alone, and he certainly wasn't from around here.

Curiosity alone would have been enough to draw her toward him, but the prickling of arousal along her labia offered another reason.

While slowly weaving through the crowd, she attracted the attention of more than a few people, though she was one of the least interesting cast members of Arcanium. Lust hooded and darkened their eyes as she passed them, and they seemed hypnotized by the movement of her breasts in what could hardly be called confines and the swell of her hips and ass against the silk. She'd never liked that kind of attention from strangers, but here it was expected — and even better, the voyeurs in question didn't *leer*, didn't think that just because they enjoyed what they saw, she was heading for them or ought to take a detour.

Locke's aimless gaze inevitably found her. A pale woman in redheaded straight for him had to be hard to miss. His slight smile widened, genuine delight in his expression but the shift of his body pure sex as he started to stand.

She was so focused on getting through the crowd that a low, fierce hiss was her only warning before she collided with Lady Sasha, who hadn't been able to back up due to a group of people behind her she'd have to touch. Her protective king cobra reared back then darted forward to snap his teeth over her arm.

Neve didn't have to worry about venom with this particular cobra, although her panic didn't know that in the first few seconds. She'd been bitten by a venomous snake and she'd touched the succubus. Both had her backpedaling as fast as her feet could take her.

Straight toward the pool. Heated or not, Arcanium warmth or not, it was still dead of winter and she wasn't dressed to swim. A number of people reached for her, their fingers glancing over her arms or slipping over the silk.

Before Neve could topple backward into the water, Lady Sasha grabbed her forearms and hauled her back onto the porch, changing the direction of her fall.

But that was somehow worse, because she fell right against Lady Sasha, and all of a sudden, both of them were struggling to breathe, because Lady Sasha was naked and Neve's arms and most of her chest were bare. This wasn't just touch. It was full skin on skin, and Neve blearily realized that at least part of the reason Arcanium sex magic hit her so hard on top of an already high libido was the same reason Carlo was perpetually aroused — because she was just as affected by the succubus as the incubus without even knowing it.

Direct contact and the revelation combined to hit her full force with Lady Sasha's magic, as though she had fallen into the pool then been dragged under, drowning in the warm saltwater, wavering light behind her eyes and each gasping breath killing her.

She wasn't unfamiliar with the effects of a sex demon. She just hadn't prepared herself for it, and neither had Lady Sasha.

"Calm down," Sasha whispered through her labored breathing. "Calm down." It was a moment before Neve understood she was talking to the snake.

The succubus swallowed thickly then raised Neve's arm, where two puncture marks bled jagged lines down her skin.

"You'll be... You'll be fine," Sasha struggled to say with some semblance of composure. She drew her hand down the length of Neve's forearm. Someone put a towel over Lady Sasha's arm, which she quickly wrapped tightly around the wound. The king cobra around her shoulders had since obeyed his mistress, his hood retracted and his head hovering behind her back as he returned to his watch over her.

Sasha licked her lower lip, hunger a glow in her eyes. "I just...didn't want you...didn't want you to fall."

"A little late for that —"

A cheer rang out over the porch as Sasha yanked Neve back against her and kissed her. The succubus' experience kept it from going horribly awry, because Lady Sasha clearly wasn't thinking, wasn't in anything approaching control. Then again, neither was Neve.

Just like she hadn't expected to run into Lady Sasha, expected to back into a pool or expected to have any contact with a succubus' skin, she hadn't expected Sasha to kiss her. Everything was happening too fast for her to keep up, so all she could do was grasp at Sasha's shoulders, slide her hands up to the woman's face to urge her closer and kiss her just as fiercely as her mind struggled to make sense of what was happening. God, even though she was standing, even though Sasha was a firm body against hers, Neve was still falling...

A good portion of the crowd, including cast, groaned when Bell wrapped his hands through Sasha's long hair to pull the succubus' head back and the whole woman away from Neve.

Neve's legs gave way. Two of the guests caught her before she collapsed onto the stone tile. Arousal —

intense, tight and hot—still shuddered inside her, brought so quickly to the cusp of orgasm, yet with a sense that there were still many miles left to climb if Sasha had had her way.

Bell wore leather gloves that looked like they belonged to a falconer but which probably belonged to the Ringmaster, because they were too big on him. However, they allowed him to get close enough to Sasha to hold her back. She gasped for breath and fought against his hold, but the twist of her hair around his hand was as strong as rope.

"If you hadn't lost your temper with me at the beginning," he murmured loudly enough for both Sasha and Neve to hear, and as few of the guests as possible, "I would have told you that her immunity is universal—and so is her desire." Bell gave Neve a brief, almost imperceptible wink.

"You goddamn bastard!" The succubus was a far cry from the quiet, collected woman who had been so careful with Neve in her trailer. She wrenched and shrieked, teeth bared, eyes wild.

Neve hadn't blamed Sasha from the beginning, and she didn't blame her now. In fact, she agreed. But she couldn't be mad. She was too stunned—and too fucking turned on.

Because *of course* she was bisexual. Because *of course* the succubus' magic affected her. She didn't know why it hadn't occurred to her, with all the other things that turned her on that never had before. It wasn't as though the list had been long to start with.

Before Arcanium, she'd only been attracted to men romantically, but once she'd entered Arcanium, the wish had meant all bets off and no holds barred. Her husband had even told her about his fantasy of watching her with another woman. They'd talked about the possibility of a threesome to see if it would spice her up in the bedroom — which had been its own kind of desperate, looking back, because if a woman had spiced her up, then Joseph really wouldn't have been the man for her. She'd ultimately nixed the idea because she'd been having enough trouble satisfying one person and had no interest in adding another. But she should have known that Bell wouldn't have let something that juicy slide.

"I know," he said. "It really isn't fair. But now is not the time for this kind of unrestraint, love. You may explore this little dynamic later when you've had a chance to gain control of yourself. Excuse us."

There were more groans of disappointment, but the crowd parted to let him through. The sight of a man in gloves dragging a struggling woman into the house didn't faze them, especially since it was clear to everyone that if Sasha wanted to hurt him, she could easily do so. They must have figured it was some kind of roleplay.

"You okay, lady?" asked the man holding Neve's right arm.

"Yeah," she said, her voice wavering only a little. "Everything just caught me by surprise."

"Understandable," the man on her left said. "I feel like I've been hit with a bag of bricks myself. It's not unpleasant. You good to stand?"

Neve nodded, testing her balance as the two men let her go. She'd more or less recovered, although her hormones were still working overtime, of course. Not only would she have to contend with being bound to Lady Sasha and vice versa — because, like Mikhail, Sasha couldn't kill her to sever the connection — desire was back as powerful as it had ever been, as though

Mikhail hadn't taken a bit of it away. The men who had been holding her were enough to make her beg.

The sheer magnitude of what coursed through her body terrified her. Not every impulsive affair could be as considerate as Victor or Samuel. If the men who flanked her had started feeling her up instead of making sure she was okay, what *wouldn't* she do was the question. It would be so easy for her to get blindsided by the wrong person in the wrong place at the wrong time…

She managed not to reveal the fear in her voice. "I'm fine, gentlemen. Thank you."

They returned to their partners after double-checking she wouldn't fall again. When she turned back to Locke, she glimpsed Mikhail nearer to the house, wearing his blades as deterrents again. She didn't know what he'd seen, but from the shadows, he observed the present display with the two men as he went down on a piece of fruit—or at least that was how her one-track mind interpreted the sight of it.

"I came out when I heard Sasha screaming. She'll be fine. She's just as overstimulated as you. I wish I could have seen it. We shall have to form a support group for sex demons forced into an obsession with you, little girl."

"Are you going to watch me all night until performances?" She still wasn't sure about the mechanism that allowed her to be heard sometimes and not the rest, but she could only trust it when he answered.

"I wouldn't look anywhere else."

Neve was more careful as she made her way to Locke again, who appeared thoroughly entertained.

"I'm so glad I amuse you," Neve said as she approached him.

"Oh, you do. You really do." He held out both hands for a more personal greeting, clasping them in a gesture somehow intimate, though there was still enough room between them for another person. That didn't last long, though. He barely had to pull her in for her to come closer. "You're charming."

"As charming as a camel," Neve said. "Almost falling into a pool in the middle of winter. Falling onto a naked person's lips instead. Getting bitten by a venomoid king cobra." She lifted the towel. It would have to be thrown away, but the wound had already clotted. "My evening has been a steady stream of charm."

"The night is still young. There are still so many ways to stumble."

"Don't remind me. I promise I'm not usually such a klutz." She wanted to touch his chest, run her hands down his crisp white dress shirt, which was unbuttoned just enough to look casual. The idea of being so demonstrative in front of everyone excited her as much as it made her nervous. She'd engaged in public displays of affection with her husband before, which had been performative in its own way, too. But Locke was as much a stranger as Samuel had been.

"You're fortunate I know better," Locke said. "I've followed you since you arrived at Arcanium."

"A fan of the circus?" she asked.

"You could say that."

He continued to close the brief distance between them, taking possession of both of her hands again. Whatever his game was, she was more than willing to play. His wicked smile and those eyes — even brighter and more unsettling up close — were driving her crazy. It was all she could do not to fall to her knees. She wouldn't need her hands for that.

"I've been interested in the circus for a few years now. Always something — or someone — new to see and experience. The Funhouse events have been a nice touch. And you, Neve, officially have my attention."

"Is that what that is?" Neve canted her hips forward. As close as she was, she could feel him without doing that, but the size and weight of his erection against her abdomen had her cunt clenching, hungry and unbearably empty. She blamed her collision with the succubus, but part of it was just him. His warm hands. His sureness that walked the line of arrogance but hadn't crossed over—and she honestly didn't know whether it would matter if he did.

At the brush of her hips against his erection, he clenched his teeth. He used his hold on her hands to force them behind her back, which had the dual purpose of bringing her flush against him. The tightness in his jaw eased at the moan his body coaxed out of her. He lowered his head, almost meeting her moan at her lips, but he stopped just short, his grip on her hands painful.

"You've driven me to distraction since the last Funhouse, Neve. That isn't easy to do. I flatter myself that I might pass through your mind now and then."

She tried to chase his mouth, but he stayed just short of a kiss. This time when she whimpered, it was because he was squeezing her hands too tightly, but he shifted his grip to her wrists instead, one hand cuffing them both. That freed him to curl a finger around a wavy lock of hair, tilting her head in another feint. He avoided her mouth and brushed his lips over her marked neck instead—too little for what his cock and the mocking patience in his eyes promised her.

"Indulge my vanity," he murmured just above her neck. "Have you thought of me?"

She nodded.

He ran the tip of his forefinger over her lower lip, pouting it just to show he could. "What did you imagine?"

Neve swallowed. Her gaze darted around them. Everyone maintained a respectful distance, but there was no denying that the two of them had garnered attention, not the least from Mikhail, who burned like a winter coal in the shadows, his erection full again…and dangerous.

Locke drew her face back to him. "Eyes on me. Don't worry about them. They don't matter. Tell me what you imagined me doing to you."

During those experimental days with the BDSM community, she and Joseph had played more with sensation than with this kind of dominance, but she'd watched scenes where the Dominant subjected their submissive through mental control, through their command, through mild to extreme humiliation. Neither she nor Joseph had ever developed the knack for doing that without giggling at themselves or each other, but Locke had mastered the voice and the stare that marked someone comfortable as Dominant, mastered the posture, presence and presentation, as though he had been doing this for years. It captivated her in spite of herself, the way Bell sometimes did—but Bell was looser with his approach to dominance, at least from what he'd shared with her. Even when he commanded, he framed it as a request. Locke didn't bother wrapping his commands in something to soften the effect or make her think it was anyone's idea but his.

Her stomach twisted slightly. *If he's such a good Dom, why is he single at a private kink party?* There was always the possibility he was a free agent with enough experience in this community that they trusted him alone or as a Dominant by request, but she couldn't shake the thought that he was as much a stranger here as she was.

"I…" Thinking was like running through cobwebs. The succubus magic must have hit her harder than she'd thought. "I imagined that instead of pairing us with monsters at the Funhouse, Bell selected you to spin the wheel for what *you* would get to have. I saw you with that man as you watched me. I dreamed I crawled from the stage after the scene was finished, as filthy as the monster made me, and crawled over you, rubbed the mess all over you, ruined your clothes as you kissed me as fiercely as you fucked that man's mouth. I dreamed I tore through your clothes and rode you with everyone touching us, stroking themselves over us, sliding over the mess to spread it around until everything was slick, sticky, until we were nothing but a mass of limbs writhing together all night, until everyone else had collapsed, exhausted, but we still hadn't stopped."

Her throat felt thick, her tongue heavy, but the words kept coming, spilling from her while he stared at her lips, at her breasts. His unnatural eyes darkened.

"In the haunted funhouse, I imagined the hands pulling my dress down while you watched, lifting the skirt so they could rub my clit and slide into my pussy, and you would unbutton your pants and stroke yourself as the hands did everything you wanted them to do, and people would come through the funhouse and see what you were doing to me, to yourself. But that one I guess you got to experience, didn't you? Different hands."

There was something about what had happened when she'd first met him. Something that she was supposed to remember, but he shifted his hips against hers, little movements that she hoped distracted him as much as it did her.

She leaned in to mouth over his chin, his jaw, avoiding his lips as he had hers. "I don't know you, but I don't need to know you. If you want it out here for everyone to see, I'll do that, but I'd prefer one of the black rooms. I'll fuck you however you want me to. You've already seen how easy I am to please, and I'm so turned on right now that I'd do anything."

She shouldn't be saying these things. A person wasn't supposed to say how much she wanted something before the seller told her the price. But she hadn't said a word that wasn't true, and his cock seemed to grow bigger against her abdomen. For a man outside Arcanium, the feel of it was impressive. She scratched at her own hands to alleviate some of the pressure under her skin from arousal.

He caught her mouth in one closed but intense kiss.

"Why do you think I chose you?" he whispered.

A chill passed over her lips with his breath.

"Come with me." He swept around her, changing the way he held her. With a hand possessively grasping the back of her neck and the other cuffing her wrists, he walked her to one of the empty privacy rooms. He let go of her neck to yank the cord and close the curtain behind them.

Once in there, he released her wrists as well, but she didn't take them out from behind her back. In the small room, the sound of her breathing was magnified. She could barely hear him as he came back around her and lowered himself onto the settee. As though he was completely unaffected by her, he relaxed back into the seat and draped his arms over the back, drinking in the sight of her.

"Remove the dress. You don't need it anymore."

She undid the side zip then shrugged the straps down. The viscosity of the silk did the rest of the work. It puddled at her feet like blood.

Locke didn't move his arms from the back of the settee, but he crooked his finger to beckon her forward. If his gaze weren't so warm, she wouldn't have liked the way he seemed to just expect her to obey. But the grin was gone from his face. He was almost solemn, utterly serious. He stared at her as though committing her to memory.

"If you still want to rip the clothes from me, now is the time."

Neve didn't have the luxury of thinking twice. She climbed onto the bench over him, straddling his spread thighs and running her hands over his shirt the way she'd wanted to. It was thin material, and he wasn't wearing an undershirt. He was lean, like Bell, and like Bell, his strength was surprisingly compact, his slouch belying the coiled intensity underneath his clothes. The dress shirt was already loose over his trousers. All that was left to do was…

When she jerked his shirt open, his head fell back and he laughed, his teeth bared with a primal ferocity. Three buttons went flying. Another jerk ruined the entire shirt. The sides fell open like wings. She slid her hands on skin instead of fabric, over contours she'd already mapped.

Neve didn't waste time, though. She pulled his head back to her, and this time she wouldn't take no for an answer, so it was a good thing he wasn't interested in playing anymore either. She used her whole body to simulate sex over him, against him, and she kissed him for all her worth. He tasted strange to her, his rhythms different, the darkness of his scent different, everything different from everyone else she'd had so far. It was hard to believe that everyone could be so different, that every action could feel so new and exciting. And there was a whole world out there that she hadn't yet tasted.

Locke dispelled the illusion that he was the disaffected Dominant, his kiss just as hot and fast as hers. He let go of the settee to jerk at the front of his pants, pulling at the zip then pushing the fabric away from his cock. Neve leaned back, struggling to control herself so she could watch him stroke his erection less than an inch from her cunt, his knuckles brushing her folds.

"No time," he said. "Take it in. Get up and fuck yourself on my cock, Neve. I'm not going to take you. I want you to take yourself. Let there be no room for you to pretend you only had a passive role in this. You want this? You'll have to take it. Goddammit…"

Almost without warning, Neve clutched his shoulder, raised herself up then took his cock to set it against her entrance. Before he could finish swearing, she sank down nearly to the thick base. She squeezed her eyes shut as tightly as her cunt squeezed his cock, because he was bigger than he looked, and in spite of taking an incubus cock not thirty minutes before, Locke wasn't a demon, and there was no magic to help her take him in. There was only her body and the way Bell had designed it for pleasure like this. Every stroke stoked her need higher. She was already so close that Locke would be lucky to keep up with her. But he'd told her to use him — *commanded* that she use him — so she did.

She grabbed the back of the settee with one hand, tangled fingers in his thick, dark hair with the other, and fucked herself on his cock, as fast and hard as her kiss.

When she let him breathe his own air between kissing him, he purred, "Yes. Just like that. How you need it. How you need me inside you. I can feel you tightening around me. You're so close. You're so close, but I'm nowhere near through with you."

He took both nipples between his thumbs and forefingers and pinched them hard.

She was afraid she was going to hurt him, she came so harshly. Her cunt felt like a clenching fist, pulsing over and over in a vise hold on his erection as he tortured her nipples.

Locke bit her chin gently, laughing and pulling her down against him. "Good girl. Now it's my turn. Do you give yourself to me? Do I get to have you now? Do I get to use your body for my pleasure?"

"Yes." She still trembled through the aftershocks, gasping for breath. Sweat dampened her hair, dripped down her back. In all the activity, she'd somehow bothered the snake bite. It bled and smeared along her arm and his shirt, over his skin.

He licked and bit along her shoulder to the base of her neck, where he worried the already worried flesh. Mikhail must have broken through in a few places, because Locke's saliva stung over them.

It occurred to her that she was bleeding on a stranger, he was licking open wounds and they were having sex completely bareback. *She* knew that they didn't have to worry about disease or her getting pregnant, but he didn't. He'd seen her literally fucked in every hole by a tentacled monster, by demon hands that presumably belonged to a real person because no animatronics could be that fluid. He had no idea where else her pussy had been or who else had been there. Yet he was still having unprotected sex with her, and her bleeding opened both of them up to bloodborne diseases. The golems waited between privacy rooms for the purpose of providing condoms as well as helping with the clean-up, but he'd bypassed all of them.

As far as he was aware, he was willingly having unsafe sex and putting his partner at risk as well, and a respected Dom of the kink community would know better. By kink standards—and legal—to be this irresponsible was criminal.

He stopped fucking her as she stiffened, but his cock remained hard inside her. His easy smile deepened.

His eyes didn't just seem to glow. They really were glowing, brighter than the lamplight in the corner.

"Thank you, Neve." In one fluid motion, he lifted her, turned, climbed over her on the settee and thrust as hard and as deeply as he could, unblinking as he searched her face through his orgasm. To his knowledge, he was putting her at so much risk like that, yet he was still doing it. He stroked over her ass, along her thigh, to hook under her knee, holding her still closer through the heat that filled her. He was the only thing that warmed her, because everything else was going cold.

"I could have accomplished this without you…eventually. But you were a big part in making this possible so soon. Really, Neve, thank you."

Black curtains swung, swirled, closed around her vision, pulling her under.

Chapter Three

She woke up in another bed that wasn't hers. It didn't belong to the circus or to the master bedroom she'd shared with her husband. By all evidence, she'd never been in this bed or in the place that housed it in her life.

The room reminded her of the first Funhouse — concrete floors, concrete pillars to bear the weight of the ceiling, the far wall all open. Except this place looked out on a skyline Neve couldn't place, and the open wall was glassed in with giant picture-window panes. This stretch of floor was finished, the concrete polished and furniture set up between columns, not just a bed.

"Good. You're awake." Locke uncrossed his legs and stood from the chair that faced the bed, which had been arranged between four columns. There were no partitions, no curtains and none of the windows were covered. He clearly wasn't interested in privacy.

When she tried to talk, her mouth wouldn't move and her throat could only make gulping, choking sounds, although she could breathe and there was nothing on her face or in her mouth to gag her.

Locke approached the bed, stroked her hair over the pillow. "No, don't try to talk. I had to silence everyone. Their questions and insults grew tiresome, but I'll allow some to have their say soon." He had put himself back to rights — his hair tidied, her lipstick cleaned from his face, his shirt buttoned and trousers done up. But he still bore the effects of the night before — a damp stain on his thigh, dry blood on his ruined shirt, wrinkles over the fabric.

When he folded back the covers, it confirmed what she'd already suspected. She wasn't wearing a stitch, and the gown she'd discarded was nowhere to be seen.

"You should be able to move now, but if you try to fight, I will bind you. You won't hurt me, mind. It's just irritating."

Neve carefully sat up, wincing from muscle protests all over her body.

"Good girl. Now, walk with me."

Every single alarm inside her screamed, but she didn't know what else to do but follow until she understood what was going on. She didn't dare defy him as long as she didn't know what he'd do if she did.

The expansive open floorplan didn't take up an entire floor, though it seemed big enough to. He led them to a door, which opened into a curved corridor. She didn't understand the way the corridor was set up until they reached an escalator and the building opened up, revealing four floors of a vast stadium auditorium. Each level had seats facing the center performance ring and windowed rooms that looked like hyper-modern box seats.

Locke took her hand and helped her off the escalator one floor down, as though escorting a princess rather than... Rather than what? A prisoner? A victim? A guest, in an extremely creepy way that crossed so many boundaries that if she could speak, she'd correct him in a heartbeat? She still had no idea what was going on. Her brain moved at the speed of a slug, which wasn't a common malady for her, and she was as frustrated with that as her nakedness and confusion. But she tried to take inventory of what she knew.

Locke had drugged her at some point the previous night or done something else to impair her cognition. From the first time he'd met her, there had been something about him, something enchanting. And until now, she'd believed that quality to be charming, but the enchantment had gone sour.

Because it felt like magic, magic she hadn't even known he was using, except those times she'd suspected — the hands moving over her in the haunted funhouse beyond the realm of teenager-appropriate groping, the way he'd shoved his cock deep down the throat of a man who'd likely never deep-throated another man before, given that most of the guests at the first Funhouse had presented as straight.

And the fact she wasn't in Arcanium but she felt no pain. Despite all the warnings not to step foot outside Arcanium without Bell extending the boundaries beyond the fence-line of the circus or the walls of vehicles, here she was — cold, achy, but mostly painless.

Bell didn't do empty threats. He could be understated or he could be overdramatic, but one thing he hadn't done to her was lie.

She wasn't in Arcanium. That was the fact she kept coming back to. And she wasn't supposed to be out of Arcanium without a wish, certainly not when Bell had barely had the opportunity to play with his new nymphomaniac.

But Bell was nowhere to be seen. Locke held her hand, and though it didn't hurt like it had the previous night, when she tried to pull it away, his grip was iron.

"The last Funhouse a few weeks ago... That was your first Funhouse, wasn't it?" he said. "Bell had to take you through the maze so you could see what you would be a part of. I assume that he did the same thing with you for the haunted funhouse, yes?"

Neve nodded.

"You enjoyed it, didn't you? You like being part of a dark and strange place, even if you aren't dark and strange yourself. There's no need to respond. I know what you think. And yes, I know what you're thinking now. Your attempt to be fierce is absolutely delightful."

He pulled her to him, her abdomen against his hip, and kissed the corner of her mouth. She turned her head away, but that did nothing to fade his smile.

"Allow me to show you *my* funhouse. *My* Arcanium."

This isn't Arcanium. This was a building. A solid building of glass and concrete that smelled of sawdust, popcorn and paint. It was new, slick, modern, the velvet cushions on the chairs far from the cheap acrylic or metal seats at most sports or concert venues. Instead of vinyl awnings or championship banners, red velvet curtains draped over entrances, from the ceiling and around the glass rooms. Men and women throughout the stadium dusted the cushions, polished the glass, swept the concrete. They wore black and moved as though they didn't give a damn, despite the quality of their industriousness.

It took her a few moments to recognize a few of them, enough for her to extrapolate that all the black-clad men and women working on the building were golems. Arcanium golems.

No. This isn't Arcanium.

"No, Neve. This *is* Arcanium." He swept his hand over the scene. Behind the movement of his hands, gold leaf and silver paint in classic circus letters spelled *Arcanium* over one of the concrete foundations between floors.

Magic. That was definitely magic.

"This is what it should have always been — a place of real monsters and demons, of real darkness and strangeness, of real horror. Of which you will now be a part, like all the rest. But how is up to you. Come."

There were twelve glass enclosures on each floor — except, of course, for the fifth floor, which was sealed off to block his apartment from the circus. That meant there were forty-two boxes in total.

He drew her into the shadows behind the seats, under thick ceilings that delineated each tier. The darkness made it easier to see into the first enclosure, which was brightly lit so that there was no question as to what was inside.

The three Torsos of Arcanium hung from suspension hooks — two hooks on their shoulders and two where their thighs would have started — their bodies angled forward. The chains connected to the metal scaffold that framed them. This wasn't unlike what Neve had seen Carlo do in the haunted funhouse, except these suspension hooks weren't attached to some form of latex or harness. After anatomy courses and corpse studies, Neve prided herself on being able to tell the difference between gore prosthetics and the real thing.

This was the real thing.

The Blob swung, none of the medical aids attached to his body, so he had to be in pain. His tattoos gleamed with sweat. Carlo's strong arms had been removed so that he would match the other two. He was muzzled with a leather mask, his eyes red and the stitching on his arms angry with infection. Christina, too, rocked under the creaking chains, the tracks of dried tears and snot on her face. She had a ring gag in her mouth.

The glass room had been tiled in industrial white, the floor tilted in the center toward a drain. Other than what silenced them, Carlo and Christina were naked. There were dried yellow stains underneath them.

Oh my God. What the hell did you do?

"Do you see?" Locke murmured, brushing her hair over her shoulder so he could kiss her neck.

She elbowed him under his ribs.

He laughed, unfazed, not gasping or coughing or groaning in response. She found herself stumbling after him as though a collar had been closed around her neck and he held the leash. Christina and Carlo could only watch her leave, their eyes rolling in their sockets.

The next glass room was empty. The one after that had been arranged with a small koi pond on one side, Melanie's hair strewn within like seaweed. Her human half was submerged in the water, face up, through a porthole built and bolted around her waist tight enough that no water trickled out. Her mermaid tail flopped like a dead fish on the tile. She stretched her arms out toward Neve, screaming bubbles from her gills, but she couldn't swim forward or back, and her screams made no sound. She thrashed her tail, but a metal shackle at the base kept it from striking the glass where it might have shattered it.

It didn't get any better. Locke took her from floor to floor, box to box. Cast members pounded on the floor, on the glass, pleaded with her with their eyes, but she couldn't speak, and when she tried to run to the glass doors, Locke jerked her back with his invisible leash.

The glass rooms were purposely reminiscent of the haunted funhouse and the Funhouse maze. A few of them, like the whipping room, had been repeated beat for beat, with only a few embellishments. Men and women were forced onto their hands and knees in wooden stocks fortified with black iron, their bare asses exposed to a wall of torture objects, from whips, canes and floggers to surgical tools and medieval devices, all polished and prepared.

The Ivy Girl had been strung up in a sea of vines threaded through an iron trellis. When Neve and Locke passed in front of the room, the vines moved through Blondie's mouth and between her legs—nothing to hide where they were coming from and what they were doing to her now. The vines and the glass could only muffle so much. Locke hadn't done anything else to steal her voice. He smiled, keeping Neve from darting past the other corner to make the vines stop until he was good and ready to move on.

The flesh-eaten victims hung along the edges of their room, harnessed wherever there weren't limbs or pieces of them missing. The necrotic disease had spread and mutated, creating sarcomas, neurofibromas, boils and other things that Neve couldn't describe in clinical terms, because there wasn't terminology for the black strings that emerged from mouths and ears and open gashes like Japanese demon hair, moving like tiny parasitic worms. Nor were there terms for the things growing in translucent, boil-like sacs on their bodies. Where the sacs weren't growing, maggots made a feast of the dead tissue, and rats had climbed up the jute ropes to nibble on ears, noses, lips and bits of the parasitic black hair.

But it wasn't just Arcanium humans in the glass rooms.

Though Ciarán and Moss had been put in the same room, the metal contraption holding them kept them on separate dental chairs in black vinyl. Metal threaded over their ankles, thighs, upper arms and necks in contours that matched their proportions to a fraction of an inch so they couldn't struggle too much. Their faces had been muzzled as well, the leather ventilated just enough to show their bared teeth. The parts of their bodies that hadn't been bound down with metal were bare as all the rest, except for the leather harnesses that strapped around their genitals and kept them erect, their cocks dark with blood trapped inside and pointing at the ceiling.

Moss had been blindfolded as well, but Ciarán's eyes had been left exposed, their blacks bovine in bewilderment. Any anger he had felt had since given way, and he could only stare after Neve in confusion, disbelief and what seemed like betrayal. Ciarán tried to reach for Moss' hand, and Moss tried to reach for Ciarán's, but they'd been placed just out of reach by inches.

"They're the same creature, you know," Locke said. "Bell thought they were symbiotic, but they're not. The little one is part of the big one. They are different parts of the same mind, different aspects of personality, different uses. They can't be apart for too long or their mind connection and what makes them function begins to decay. I've never seen a demon of their kind go mad before. I'm quite looking forward to it."

Locke didn't need to explain what was going on anymore. All he had to do was show her, because everything was becoming clear and she didn't want it to. Tears streamed down her face, and she made a choking sound every time she wanted to cry, but he wouldn't let her, wouldn't let any other sound from her throat. He offered her a handkerchief from his pocket to wipe under her nose, which was more than he'd provided for any of his other prisoners. Unlike the Arcanium Neve knew, all the cast here were prisoners.

Joanne and Jane were still conjoined twins, but now they were connected at the skulls so that it looked like they were sharing the same brain, or as though their brains were pressed together. They were dressed in simple pink sundresses folded back over their bare legs, their hair braided and twisted together, their faces rouged like dolls. Their pink mouths had been sewn shut with thick black cord that pulled at infected skin and buttons had been sewn over their eyes. Bloody tears left tracks down their cheeks. They were set up on reclined chairs similar to Ciarán's and Moss', their heads meeting over the top cushion, their feet strapped into leather stirrups that pulled their legs apart.

Seth and Lars were configured much as they had been for the Funhouse event, but their joining was less fluid. They'd been melted in a partial kiss, eyes wide and rolling in their sockets like Christina and Carlo. Skin stretched like thick taffy where their disparate tones merged and they tried to pull themselves apart, though they were held in place by a double shackle around their necks. Their lower bodies were separated from each other similarly to Joanne and Jane's, except Seth and Lars were facing each other, separated by a metal A-frame that pushed their bodies out. Leather harnesses bound their melded arms together, connected them to the frame and wrapped around their cocks, testicles and buttocks. Unlike Moss and Ciarán, who were forced into a state of arousal, Seth and Lars were strapped into male chastity belts, their cocks mashed against their balls in a cage and leather pulling their thighs and buttocks apart.

Oh yes, Neve was getting a clear picture of what Locke had planned for the cast of Arcanium. And it kept getting worse.

John, the fire-eater, had been trapped in his half-dragon state, bound and hooked down onto fireproof bedding, his head encased in glass and metal that had been scorched, his face a mess of third-degree burns.

Valorie had been knotted like a pretzel and strapped into an elaborate hexagonal device with rings on every side that meant she could be twisted into all kinds of configurations that tested her flexibility and made her ring-gagged mouth and spread thighs accessible. Neve was almost certain that at least some of her bones were out of joint, and her spine might have been broken. It was difficult to discern between her contortionist flexibility and what went too far.

Misha hung like a hammock in his room, giant black dildos forced into both ends.

The Horned God was struck at every side by arrows connected to chains that bound him to his own scaffold, his neck collared, his nipples pierced and pulled out with smaller chains that threaded through the rest, his legs spread, rings through his elbows and knees, and his cock harnessed more erect than she'd ever seen him.

The Serpent King had been stripped of his long, strong body. He was just a man with a serpent's face, bound like the rest, mutilated like the rest, his two cocks kept erect and tied together. Rings had been inserted into his jaw and cheeks to pull his mouth open far enough to dislocate the jaw. He looked like a snake stretching his mouth to consume something bigger than its head.

Lennon was still putting up a fight that looked like a mass of electric eels battling a metal machine. Many of his tentacles had been bound in rings and chains, but there were others sprouting from everywhere he could create one. Little bolts of lightning came from each ring that floated above him, trying to quell him so they could attach themselves. And every moment he fought, the rings electrocuted him again and again and again. He was tiring. There was despair in a face where Neve had only ever seen delight.

Troy had rings of his own, some making use of his piercings and many creating new ones from his eyelids, nostrils, over his lips, cheeks, tongue, plus suspension hooks over his shoulders and chest and under his nipples. He was practically suspended from his own face, forced to stand on his toes to keep the rings from pulling his face off. His cock was engorged over the leather harness around the base.

The clowns had been put into a room together, their mouths forced open, their unnaturally long, prehensile tongues wound around the metal pole to which they were bound and impaled to tether them to the pole, like pasta around a fork. Shackles on their ankles raised their legs to the sides at an angle uncomfortable even for practiced tumblers.

In a particularly big glass room, the small cenobite hell carousel from the Funhouse had been reconfigured, with Riley and Colm in their usual places and with Caroline behind them, the bit forced too far back in her mouth and her mascara running down to mingle with the blood trickling over her lips, maybe from broken teeth. Poles ran through their sides. They'd been forced hands and knees on metal platforms, tendons cut from their knees and ankles, horsehair tail plugs deep in each of them.

Victor wasn't in a glass room. He was affixed to a stone fountain on the third-floor landing, where there were couches and settees set up like a hotel lobby, although no hotel lobby Neve had ever seen included privacy rooms. Picture windows all along the outside suggested anyone would be able to see in at night — which meant the windows had to either be reflective on the outside or enchanted not to show what was happening on the inside. Victor shot water from his screaming mouth, his stretching fingertips, and his cock. He'd been frozen in a single moment of torture, his body stretched to the level of a contortionist's when he was not a contortionist, so that the water could erupt from him in all directions.

In the middle of the third-floor landing, however, in a glass room of honor, were Sasha and Mikhail. Sasha lay on a reclined bench, leather straps forcing her legs open wide, a harness squeezing her breasts too tightly, clamps over her nipples, a leather ball gag blocking her mouth. However, rather than leaving her cunt bare like every other woman in the Arcanium auditorium, she was covered in leather there as well, like a muzzle, the leather extending deep into her like an inverted dildo, keeping her open but blocking any of the skin or flesh.

Mikhail was strapped onto his own bench, arms and legs forced underneath him like those of a dead spider, his face muzzled, his erection as large as it could become, but she couldn't see how angry its flesh was, because leather and padlocked metal encased him like the opposite of a medieval chastity belt.

Neve understood. This way, anyone could fuck a sex demon and not have to worry it would kill them. This way, neither Mikhail nor Sasha could feed. They'd grow weak, but they wouldn't die. The magic they emanated would simply grow more intense and magnify the purpose of the enterprise.

Locke's Arcanium wasn't a series of illusions or reality masquerading as illusion. There would be no mere entertainment. There would be no relief. His Arcanium wasn't a freak show. It was a freak brothel, pure and simple. And, unlike Bell, he didn't give a damn about consent. Neve doubted his clientele did either.

What the fuck are you?

There were cast missing from the glass rooms. As far as Neve could tell, Locke had everyone except Bell, Maya, Kitty, the Spider and the Ringmaster. Neve's heart held on to the hope that Bell had managed to protect them or that they'd left the Funhouse before Locke had…

No, that wasn't right either. Arcanium's prisoners didn't come to the Funhouse events, but they were all here. Not all the golems came to the Funhouse events, but based on their sheer numbers, they were all here, too. Locke hadn't just taken the people and props from the Funhouse. He'd infiltrated Arcanium within its gates as well.

Which meant their only hope was that Bell had spirited a few of his people away before Locke could take them. The ones missing seemed the closest to him—even though Maya had kept herself away from Bell ever since Neve had arrived and even though the Ringmaster's closeness did not necessarily imply intimacy.

"You're an intelligent woman. I do like listening to your head work. It's thorough, systematic, skeptical—open-minded, yet unfailingly optimistic." Locke trailed his hand down the length of her spine as they ascended the escalators once more.

What are you? It was clear to her what he'd done. It was clear what he wanted from the cast of Arcanium. But what wasn't clear to her was how he'd taken Arcanium from right under Bell's nose and how he'd gotten all this done in a day. And those questions all ultimately came down not to how he'd done it but what he was.

"All in good time, Neve. Now that you've seen what I can do, I think it's time to tell you what I want from you."

They went all the way up to the fifth floor again and entered a door on the other side of his home, which really did take up half the edge of the stadium. The views would have been glorious if she hadn't known what was going on in the festering heart of this place, if she hadn't known that he had those views because of whatever magic he wielded.

The floorplan curved because of the architecture of the building, but it seemed to her as though it followed the curvature of the Earth, that he sat and surveilled more than just his small piece of it. That impression only intensified when he pushed her down in front of a golden throne, out of place with the rest of the modern and mid-century décor. Between the four pillars in this section of the home, he had blocked out the grandeur of a prince—a golden throne, a red Persian carpet extending from the wooden platform on which the throne was placed, displays of wealth in glass boxes like those in museums—jewels, antiques, ancient books and artifacts, but also items such as books bound in what appeared to be human skin, skeletons of creatures Neve had never seen before, an altar carved with runes she didn't recognize and with brown stains mingled with goose-fat candle wax.

In front of the throne were three large trunks.

"If I release your voice, are you going to scream?"

Neve had to think before she could answer, which amused him. She wanted to scream. Not to call for help. Anyone who came into Locke's Arcanium wouldn't be coming to help, and they likely wouldn't care about screams, despite what all the gags, muzzles and masks on the cast suggested. If Neve had to guess, the various silencers were aesthetic more than functional, but it also kept the cast quieter until they were needed. No wailing or gnashing of teeth for Locke's version of hell, apparently.

She shook her head.

"Then kneel here and don't say a word until I ask you a question." He placed his hand on her head, the pressure of his palm convincing her to lower herself to her knees.

Once he trusted she would stay, he went to the first truck and took a skeleton key from a keyring in his back pocket. He undid the latches, flipped the cover open then unceremoniously tilted the trunk. Maya, trussed in white rope and duct tape, rolled out onto her head then onto her side.

From the next trunk, Locke upended the Spider, each of her limbs bound to its counterpart then those ropes tied together so that she looked like she could be hung from a spit.

Kitty tumbled out of the third trunk.

Locke pulled the gags off each of them. Maya thrashed against the ropes and tried to close her teeth around the fleshy part of his hand but he moved too fast and gave her abdomen a swift kick to steal her rebellion. Kitty glared murder at him. The Spider's expression was mostly blank, but Neve could swear there was recognition.

As soon as Maya had regained her breath, she laid to Locke without restraint, "You son of a bitch. I'm going to fucking kill you then Bell's going to bring you back just so I can kill you again. I don't need another wish. I'm going to cut you up piece by piece, starting with segments of your prick so you can feel their loss longer. I'm going to shove each piece down your throat and follow them with your tongue. I'm—"

"Going to stop talking," Locke said. "Not that I don't enjoy idle threats, but there will be plenty of years ahead for that. I suggest you save your strength for what's to come."

"When Bell gets his hands on you—"

"I was under the impression the two of you weren't on the best of terms. You no longer act as the illusionist's assistant. And do you think we can't read body language when he's playing sadist with you?"

Locke turned his back on the women. Neve had a few brief seconds when she could have done something, but she couldn't reach any of the weapons around them in time before he turned around to sit on the edge of his throne. With his modern clothing and the giant proportions of the throne, the sight was absurd. Neve fought the suicidal impulse to giggle.

"Do you think he would still move heaven and earth to find you when you've walked away from him of your own accord?" Locke asked. "You're untethered from him, barely tethered to Arcanium since you wished yourself out. You were certainly more difficult to gather with the rest, but I couldn't leave you behind."

"Regardless of whether Bell will come for Maya alone, he will come for Arcanium. You've made a grave mistake," Kitty said quietly. She'd managed to struggle to her knees, but her whole body trembled, clearly as much from fear as from anger.

"You have such faith in your master. But if that mangy dog was the god you think he is, I wouldn't have been able to take Arcanium away from him in the first place. He didn't know what hit him, and when he wakes up, he won't be able to find it. What I take is mine, not his. He cannot find what is not his unless I were to show it to him — and Bell is not welcome here." He rested his elbows on his thighs like a concerned therapist. "I'm afraid he's not going to save you. It is my mercy you must plead for. I do like a good begging."

"You won't have that pleasure. Not from me," Maya said.

"I'll make you eat those words and so much more, Maya. Though the repartee is riveting, we do have business, you and I. If you will work your way to your knees and hold your tongue like my obedient, submissive Neve, we can avoid any more delay."

Maya twisted her head around to glare at Neve, her dark hair wild around her face and in front of her eyes. If anyone could wreak havoc on Locke, Neve would have bet on her if she hadn't been tied up and human.

Neve's lips thinned. "I'm neither obedient nor submissive."

"Then what would you call yourself, you who have done everything I commanded? I barely had to force you."

"I'm practical."

Locke's laughter filled the room, hurting her ears. "Yes. Yes, you are. I like that about you. I like that you know you're defeated, and you don't dare fight back because you know I have all the power and you have nothing but your loveliness and your desire to endear yourself to me. So eminently practical, love. Would you still be so practical if you knew you were the reason I was able to take Arcanium? Without you, you'd all be back in your little circus, playing the family-friendly crowd in tedious peace and quiet."

All three women jerked around to look at her now. Kitty, in particular, was fierce in a way Neve hadn't anticipated, but she supposed a grizzly bear could be a sweet mother, too.

"I didn't do anything!" Her protest was to Locke, but Neve silently begged the women to understand that just because she was compliant didn't make her a traitor. She hadn't conspired against Bell.

Locke's laughter finally died, but he still looked like a little boy at Christmas. "While I would love for you to turn on my Neve and spread your suspicions to the rest, leaving her entirely for me, I'm afraid she aided me quite unwittingly. Bell is the fool in this equation. The blame is upon his carelessness, his complacency, his inadequacy. If you'd left Arcanium when I gave you the chance, Lizzie, *you* would have been the woman to deliver Arcanium to me. But no, you had to develop an attachment to that bottom-feeding gargoyle and your fear of Bell got the better of you. Oh, you would have been rid of him all right, right into my arms."

The Spider twitched as though he'd touched her face, although he hadn't moved from the throne.

"Just when I thought you were perfect, darling, Bell pulled Neve into the web of Arcanium, with all his women's more charming traits and much fewer complications. Almost as though he tailor-made her for me. If I hadn't succeeded in taking Arcanium from him after three years of placing my traps, formulating plans and finding a cast member upon whom to pin its downfall, I would have believed he suspected something. But I will give credit where credit is due. She's a marvelous toy."

This time, Neve felt his fingers on her cheek in a ghostly caress. She didn't pull away. If she could keep him in a fine mood with her...

"Good girl. Yes, do keep me in a fine mood. Now, in addition to the significance I attached to your word, love, and Bell's arrogance, I did have a little extra help once I'd established a foothold. Ringmaster, if you would…"

The Ringmaster, a cut and a bruise on his lower lip but otherwise unchanged, stepped out from behind one of the columns.

"Why, you fucking—" Maya struggled to her feet with uncanny balance that had doubtlessly accompanied her high-wire training. "You fucking traitor." Her face flushed, her eyes and nostrils reddened, and she struggled against the ropes anew, whimpering only when the jute started to scrape through her skin.

The Ringmaster was unaffected by the hatred directed at him, but he would be. The most demonic of the demons in Arcanium. Hellborn. The Punisher. The Enforcer. Without a strip of humanity in his shark eyes.

"What have you done?" Kitty whispered. She, too, walked the knife's edge of tears.

"My allegiance was never to Bell, Katharine. He tricked me into a dungeon that he never intended to use as one then latched me to a leash like a faithful Doberman to bring out whenever *he* saw fit for me to torment, and only when slighted by the slightest sins."

"He gave you so much more these last few years. He gave you all the prisoners in addition to punishments. You were still able to torture. He allowed you me. He gave you Maya. I thought his new Arcanium satisfied you. I thought you were…" Kitty's words caught. She turned her head and closed her eyes in pain as terrible as if the Ringmaster had afflicted it. In a way, he had.

"You thought wrong. Bell was too powerful for me to take Arcanium for myself, but Locke is stronger than he. In his Arcanium, I may be a demon once more. I may hear the screams. I may bring the darkness. His Arcanium is what Arcanium should have been from the very beginning. The jinni harbored too much affection for his collection. He throttled his demons, neutered them, elevated his humans above them when dungeons were created to bring them low where they belong, crawling and crying at our feet, the metallic scent of blood and bone thick above them. I have had enough of playing Bell's faithful dog. It's time for Arcanium to be what it's supposed to be, and it's time for the Ringmaster to master the ring the way he is supposed to."

Locke gestured to Kitty. Magic lifted her from her kneeling position to her feet. The ropes unraveled and fell to the carpet. They had chafed her wrists and ankles, but she was otherwise unharmed.

"As promised, Ringmaster of Arcanium, you may have your human, your one weakness, for yourself alone."

"Don't touch me. Don't you *dare* touch me!"

Kitty tried to wrench herself away from the Ringmaster, but he pulled her into his arms, his size making her look small in comparison. His arms were like the metal shackles and vises in the glass rooms. Kitty used everything she had—her elbows, her knees, her feet, her shoulders. She took a page from Maya's book and bit his hand when he tried to clasp her throat. He gave a low grunt, shaking his hand against the blood drawn, but he still had one good arm around her waist.

She struck him across the face, digging her nails into white-edged skin. Blood quickly pooled in the grooves. The Ringmaster grabbed her wrist and forced it under the arm that held her so that she was pinioned.

Kitty spat at him.

"I would also have Maya," the Ringmaster said. "My whip takes pleasure in her back, and I would see my blows rain down upon her and leave their marks, scar over scar, instead of disappearing after every bout."

"Not a chance," Locke replied. "Maya is Bell's woman, lovers' spat or not, and everyone who walked into that damn circus knew it. They want Valorie and they want Maya. There's a five-year waiting list for her, and I wouldn't waste her on your whip alone. You may take her during the day when she's free and use her all you want, but I won't make her your exclusive pet. Your reward is Kitty alone, for as long as you want. She still has a following of her own I can exploit when you're finished with her. Take one of the east wing rooms on the fifth floor. All other floors are for guests only."

The Ringmaster straightened with Kitty against his red jacket, his black gaze boring a hole into Maya, who was trying just as hard to do the same to him.

Then he gave a stiff bow to Locke and turned, dragging Kitty with him. She protested, her bare feet sliding on the floor, but his arm didn't budge, and no matter how many times she said no—something that would have forced the Ringmaster to freeze in his tracks in Bell's Arcanium—he didn't stop. He flung open the door, threw Kitty out into the hall and slammed the door behind him.

"He's old hellborn, though young in this world, and damn, does that boy have vision. He was wasted on the old Arcanium. All of you were."

"Bell is coming. He's going to find you, and when he does, you're going to wish you were a cockroach smeared under my shoe," Maya said.

"No, Maya. Bell is not coming here. He will not save you. There's just me, my Arcanium and all the demons and monsters who have wanted Bell's Arcanium and will now pay through the nose to get it."

"That's why you did all this?" the Spider asked, finally speaking up, although she'd barely moved or tried to struggle out from under the rope. "For *money*?"

"Money buys pretty things that are less obtrusive when bought rather than stolen. Money buys off other demons, other monsters, with greater desire for wealth than I. More importantly, the clientele that cannot afford the cost will pay me in favors. And that, darling, is far more valuable than money in my world. Let dragons hoard their gold. I want promises. I want their word, because the word is law. What you've experienced under Bell should have taught you that much, my lovelies. What great power alone cannot give me, favors will gain me the rest. So it has always been, so it always shall be."

Locke crooked his finger. Maya's feet trailed the floor as she floated over to him. He deposited her back to her knees at his feet and grabbed her chin to lift her head, inspecting her up close. "What I told the Ringmaster was only half true. There *is* a waiting list for you, Maya, enough to fill your nights for the next five years and beyond. But now that Arcanium is mine, I own you, and I have first rights. I'm curious as to what it is that drew Bell to you. Beautiful, no doubt, but what makes a jinni so careless that he gives his heart to something so fragile and inconstant? Especially something that turns him away."

Maya clenched her teeth. "A demon like you couldn't possibly understand."

"Quite possible," he replied, unfazed. "We were created from very different fires. But it merits further investigation. There are answers to be mined from you, Maya, and the mystery warrants a choice none of the others received. I can spare you. I can keep you hidden away from my clientele and harvest the ripest fruits for my own. You wouldn't be on display or for sale. You would serve me exclusively. You would have every comfort when not in my bed. My only requirement is enthusiastic submission."

He grabbed the rope binding her arms and yanked her up. "I'll even give you points for just trying, at least in the beginning. By all accounts, the tortures I will have for you in here are quite in line with the tortures you enjoy. Out there, I won't protect you. I'll have to heal any life-threatening damage, of course, because you're no use to me dead. And to keep you in demand, I will have to do some surface healing."

Locke squeezed her chin until a deafening crack made Maya buckle and scream. A hissing noise preceded the smoothing of the dent Locke had made in the bone.

"But it's amazing what a human body is capable of surviving after suffering significant internal damage. Am I making myself abundantly clear?"

"If you're such a big demon, asshole, why do you need to tie up little girls?" Maya's anger had diminished, curtailed by the brief but intense pain, but she rolled back to her knees, trying to pretend he hadn't scared her at all.

Locke smiled. A perfectly normal, beautiful smile. A human smile. He wore his camouflage like Bell—because it worked. It was difficult not to underestimate him when he was just a handsome, unassuming, almost shy-looking gentleman, if one ignored the blood on his shirt.

"When you're not able to fight back, I don't have to strike you to keep you down. It just makes these conversations so much easier. But if you would prefer to expend your precious energy fighting me when you can't win, by all means…"

He waved his hand. As they had with Kitty, the ropes fell to the carpet, leaving her little worse for the wear. Maya immediately launched herself at him, her fist poised to strike his jaw.

Locke caught her fist in his palm then closed his own fist around hers. This time, the crunching sound was multiplied a hundred times. Maya screamed again, a wrenching cry that had Neve scrambling to her feet and running for her, whether to help her or put herself between Maya and Locke, she didn't know until Locke opened his fist again. Maya pulled the misshapen mass that had been her hand near her stomach, still screaming.

"You see, keeping you bound is for your protection, not mine," Locke said, mildly pleased that Neve was pulling Maya away from him. "It's better for you to never believe you can win."

He waved his hand again. Maya's hand popped back into its normal configuration, not so much as a bruise to show it had ever been damaged.

Maya wrenched from Neve's hold under her arms. She was crying, but anger came back in full bloom. "If you think I'm going to get in bed with you to save my skin, you're crazy, you fucking bastard."

"Maya, no. Please, think about what you're saying," Neve said, trying to stop Maya from going after Locke again while also trying not to touch her.

"Get off me! Look at you, kneeling like an obedient little bitch to the next master just because you're afraid he's going to hit you. As far as I'm concerned, you're as bad as the Ringmaster. You're a traitor, too — giving in, *letting* him do this."

"You haven't seen it. You don't know what he's done to Arcanium. There's no concern about pain, about well-being, about rehabilitation. Think about everything the haunted funhouse and the Funhouse events have ever created the illusion of. For him, *there's no illusion*, and there's no respite. They're all out there now." Neve pointed toward the auditorium, as though showing Maya where it was would do anything to convey the hopelessness, the pain, the terrible despair...and Locke hadn't even opened the new Arcanium yet. "They're in boxes to display them to whoever pays to torture them. The Spider wondered what would happen if Arcanium were ever in the wrong hands. These are the wrong fucking hands! And he's having fun, Maya! Don't you understand? You fighting is a *joke* to him. He's *laughing* at you."

Maya stared at her as though she couldn't recognize her. What Neve was saying wasn't getting through, and the more she sensed Maya's resistance, the lower her stomach sank and the colder her hands became.

"You go out there and it's going to be a million times worse. You're going to be sold to who knows what. Every night, it's going to be a new torture, and every day, it's not going to stop hurting. It's not going to get better. He's just one hell, Maya. It's a thousand hells out there. Not staying to save your skin is like flaying yourself alive on principle. The principle of what? Loyalty? For the Arcanium ideal? Because Bell would want you under a thousand evil demons if he can't have you for himself?"

Maya struck her across the face. "Don't you dare say his name." Her voice was dangerously soft. "You don't deserve to say his name."

Neve covered her stinging cheek in shock.

"What principle? How about not making deals with devils, Neve? What about that?" Maya shoved Neve away and stood up again. "I may walk the line, sticking with demons and jinn, but they made a choice not to be as demonic as they could be, and Bell's no demon. Locke is a demon, through and through. His only goal is corruption, and that's what he'll give you in exchange for an easier hell in here. No way. You put me in that hell out there, you asshole. It's no less than what I deserve. I won't sell my soul for a softer bed."

"As you say, so shall it be," Locke said. At his snap, Maya disappeared.

"No!" Neve lunged at the place where Maya had been standing, but there was nothing to pull back, nothing to save. She slammed her hands on the rug. "Damn it!"

"I could have told Maya that her rousing speech was wasted on a pragmatist and an agnostic." Locke rose from his throne. "Her righteousness will accompany the thousands of bodies that will keep her warm in the nights to come. I'm sure it's small comfort to know that she's one of the few who *will* lie across a softer bed. At the price I set, my clientele receives the best guest suite in the house to enjoy her."

Neve kept swallowing back her protestations, each one more useless than the last. She could tell him he was evil, sadistic, cruel, criminal, and all of it would be true, but none of it would insult him, and any insult that challenged his power would bounce right off him, clearly false.

"What did you do to her?" she finally said.

"Mmm, I was under the impression you didn't want to see any more. But curiosity always gets the better of your shameless species."

An image spread over the wall above the throne like something from an old-time projector. Maya had been put into her own glass box near the windows in the lounge, across from the incubus' and succubus' box. She'd been stripped of her red dress and given a black leather underbust corset to wear, nothing else. She was spread on a St. Andrew's cross, nails embedded in her wrists and ankles. A sacred heart had been carved on her chest and steadily bled down under the leather. A crown of barbed wire had been affixed to her head and a crucifix had been converted into a dildo.

Behind Neve, the Spider retched and turned away.

Neve covered her mouth. She couldn't keep watching, but long after the juddering projector picture had gone, she couldn't shake the image.

"She'll lose the wounds when she's taken down, clean and ready for whatever her customer plans for her. I put her in the place of honor, above even the sex demons who never earned what little demon blood still flows through their veins. If they're lucky, I'll feed them every quarter century. But see the leather, love? Anyone will be able to get their satisfaction from them. Anyone and everyone at all, to start their evening hard and ready and to bring all the prisoners to their own terrible pleasure in spite of what I've done to them. Bell cheapened his dungeon, a moving house of tricks and illusions to entertain those who should have been brought to their knees by it. I've elevated Arcanium to its proper glory."

He slithered his fingers through Neve's hair. She fell to the ground to get away from the sensation, even though her traitorous skin tingled with pleasure at the contact. The incubus and the succubus were already doing their work, and so was the wish Bell had granted. She was still as subject to it here as in Bell's Arcanium. Locke hadn't seen fit to change that. Why would he? That was the pièce de résistance. He could take her, and she would want him no matter what he did or what he had done. If Bell had been there at that moment, she might have killed him herself.

Locke brushed past her to undo the gag that was still loose around the Spider's neck, then set her free of the bindings. She shivered at the brush of his fingers over her wrists. Locke tightened his jaw as her eight limbs unbent from her body, but Neve doubted it was from anger, the way he looked at her.

"Sometimes, it's the flaws in a gem that make it all the more desirable. I'll keep you, too, love, if you're smarter than Bell's woman. I say that—*his woman*—but Bell has many women, doesn't he? Not just the ones he discarded. You have the eyes of someone who has shared his bed since last we met." He lifted her face up to him, forcing her head back and making her long neck perpendicular to the ground.

The Spider turned her head to look away from him, but she didn't attack like Maya. "Is he out there?" She avoided both Locke's and Neve's gazes, but the tone of voice suggested she was asking Neve.

"Your fear-sucking beast? That monstrosity of man's making?" Locke said. "Would you like to see him?"

"No."

"The irony cannot be lost on you. You finally need him, really need him, and I won't let you have him. If you choose principle like Maya, I'll never let you anywhere near him, Liz. You'll never be spared your fear any more than you would be spared pain."

"Reading my mind isn't charming when Bell does it. It's less charming when you do." She knocked his hand away and climbed to her feet on her own.

The Spider was as tall as Locke. She could stare right into his eyes without being beneath him. Locke didn't appear to mind the contest. He gave as good as he got, and unlike the Spider, he didn't need to blink.

"She's like you," Locke said softly, his whisper almost a caress in itself. "You're like her. You'll know pleasure none of the other victims of Arcanium will be allowed to know. I know you can take orders. I know you can come with me inside you without my help. I know you can come just sucking me off if I tell you to. I may give you more than you can handle, but you'll always have what you need. Or you can go down into the belly of the circus with the rest. Maya's waiting list comes from her years with Bell, the intrigue of her importance to him, the rumors of what she desires, what she spreads her legs for. But you came into Arcanium with a reputation of your own, and your waiting list is just as long as hers from that reputation, brief though your time in Arcanium has been. If you deny me, that's what you can anticipate—so much worse than what the Arcanium scum did to you, so much worse than what your lover did. I can be kinder. All your life, Liz... Are you really so intent on your future mirroring your past?"

The Spider's second set of hands kept clenching and releasing, her elegant limbs poised, but Neve couldn't tell for what.

"You want the Spider of Arcanium's web, do you?" Elizabeth slid her palm over his cheek and parted her lips to kiss him—hesitant at first, but at the enveloping of his arms around her, she gave a distressed moan and yielded her mouth for him to deepen the kiss. He curled his fingers around her second set of thighs to press her hips against his, claimed her in his grip, in his kiss.

Neve couldn't help it. They were beautiful people to her, and watching them embrace, desire raw and undeniably powerful, turned her on. She shook her head as though to chide herself, to command herself otherwise, but it had never worked before, and she had no expectation it would work now.

Locke opened his eyes just enough to look over at her. While thoroughly laying claim to the Spider with the arrogance of someone taking what had always been his, he somehow showed Neve that he knew arousal moved in her, as surely as he would, all too soon. The fact that she had memory to draw upon made watching them so much worse, that memory just a hair's-breadth from being the same as the actual sensation he could provide.

God help her, her body was jealous. She'd never experienced the intensity of shame that burned through her cheeks and down her neck to flush over her chest. To envy a woman for resigning to a fate some might call worse than death—even though it couldn't compare to what was going on in the rest of the building—felt like the lowest she was capable of going. But Locke didn't have to tell her there was still lower to burrow, like a worm wriggling in the earth. She didn't have to have Maya's principles to consider herself despicable for her own reasons. And as he fed upon the Spider's shame, so he fed upon hers.

Then Locke shouted, releasing the Spider's legs to bring his strong hands to her face. She had his lower lip between her teeth. Blood welled up to stain her mouth and his, but the place where her sharp teeth had sunk into his skin was visible from where Neve sat on the rug. Mingling with the blood was a clear liquid with a yellowish tint that Neve would have assumed was lymph if there wasn't so much of it coming from where the Spider's longer fangs had plunged into his flesh.

His shout rolled with an animalistic growl, sharp and metallic. He yanked her away from his mouth and threw her to the floor. She had enough limbs and control over them that she braced herself against the fall and looked over her shoulder at him as she spat his lower lip onto the carpet, spraying blood on the expensive weave. Locke no longer looked like a gentleman. He looked like an extra in a zombie movie, a new zombie too fresh to be a shambler — he would be the kind that was the most dangerous because it was fiercer and faster.

"You want the Spider?" Elizabeth scurried around, her bent limbs eerily reminiscent of her name. She spat blood again. Droplets of venom gathered at the tips of her fangs. "Careful what you wish for, motherfucker."

Blood continued to spill onto Locke's shirt. His bright eyes had narrowed under his dark eyebrows. The thunderheads threatening above them and even outside the windows darkened the room, but his posture remained deceptively calm. He ran his hand over the back of his mouth, seemingly heedless of the fact there was a piece missing.

"Is that a no?" he said.

The Spider hissed, shoving herself to her feet. "I know why you aren't dying, but why the fuck aren't you even in pain? Goddammit, why aren't you screaming?"

He ran his knuckles over his mouth again then lifted his hand with casual interest at the amount of blood it had gathered. "Your venom's hot through my veins, but did you really think you could hurt me? I *am* pain, Elizabeth. I was *born* in pain. But I'll take out every last one of your teeth with pliers if you even think of doing that again."

The Spider's snarl was more vampire than human. "Why? Couldn't you see it coming?"

"I don't need to see the future. Bell can barely see it himself."

"Would have spared you a bite," the Spider said.

"I was startled, not damaged. It certainly didn't kill me, and I assure you, Lizzie, my bite is far worse."

When he smiled this time, his smile was too big for a human face. Neve was reminded of the clowns, except his lips didn't extend from ear to ear. His teeth, though, were just as razor sharp, crammed in neat lines, the ivory bright against the blood still spilling from where his lower lip had been.

The Spider stepped back, but she didn't run. There was nowhere to run.

As his mouth shifted back into something more human, the place where the Spider had bitten through grew back. He was still bloodstained, but otherwise there wasn't a mark left from what she'd done.

"So," he said more emphatically, "are you saying no to my generous offer? Will you join the rest of the poor souls as meat for the beasts?"

"Please," Neve whispered.

She managed to get to her feet, although she swore she'd lost all feeling below her hips, and held out her hand. She didn't know whether the Spider would be as adamant against her touch as Maya had been or whether she'd been just as insulted by Neve's capitulation—as though they really had a choice.

It wasn't a question of whether they'd kneel. It was simply a question of before whom.

"Please don't leave me alone." Something a little girl would say, but her inner child wasn't the one begging.

She couldn't be the only one here. She couldn't have her life filled with Locke and nothing more. She couldn't bear knowing what was happening in the circus then suffering Locke's customized torture all alone. Neve knew better than to think that just because he might sometimes be gentle, just because he might give them pleasure, he wouldn't also deal them pain as sadistically poetic as he had written for the rest of Arcanium. But at least they wouldn't be alone.

"It's just submitting to a new master, Liz. It's nothing new, really." Locke tasted the blood from his hand as though it were strawberry syrup, sucking on his fingers between arguments. "First it was your sainted father. Then it was Dez. Then it was Bell. I'm just another master to you. And I think I can make you a star again, my dear. I really do. The crowds can either flock to have you or flock to *see* you from the distance afforded things that are *mine*. Which will it be?"

Neve didn't say anything else, and she let her hand fall to her side, but she still begged Elizabeth, willed her to stay with what feeble power she could muster in her mind.

Elizabeth's bloodied mouth was a thin line, and she'd lost all color to her face. But she nodded.

"I need you to say it. I need your word."

He kept mentioning their 'word'. Bell had power in wishing, but it required them to use the word 'wish' in particular — which was mercy in itself, because if all he needed was for someone to say they wanted something, any expression of desire, heaven knew what he could have filled Arcanium with. Locke clearly wasn't bound by wishes. Everyone in Arcanium knew better than to use the W-word unless they meant it, so Locke wouldn't have heard it from her. But he did need them to say *something*.

The Spider had caught on to the repeated usage as well. She hesitated before answering, closing her eyes. "I'm yours."

"Yes, you are."

With a whirl of vertigo, Locke swept them from the throne back to his bed, where Neve fell onto the sheets.

"I'll deal with you later, my lovely little Arachne." He pointed to one of the columns. The Spider slammed against it. The stone knocked the wind from her, but when she slumped, a small glass room was there to catch her. The opening that had let her in disappeared. There were only air holes at the top, where the Spider wouldn't be able to reach. "But you must be punished for your insolence."

The Spider groaned when she could finally catch her breath. She pushed herself upright again. Then her eyes went wide.

As though from nowhere, a swarm of spiders ran over her from her back to the front—all the spiders Neve recognized from the creepy-crawly tent over which the Spider usually presided.

"If you think I've afforded you the same protections from your namesakes that Bell gave, you're mistaken. Most of them aren't venomous, as you know, but some of them are. And tarantula hair is awfully irritating when your skin isn't impervious to it. Your venom might do next to nothing to me, but I can't guarantee that of your old friends." Locke unbuttoned his cuffs and shook them out over his hands. "If I were you, I'd stay...perfectly...still until I'm ready to let you out again."

When the Spider tensed, pulling her lips from her teeth in another snarl, the subtle change in her body put several of the large huntsman spiders on edge. The Spider stopped moving again, hardly daring to breathe.

Then Locke turned his back on the Spider, facing Neve. "Now it's just you and me. At last."

Chapter Four

Neve crawled backward over the bed. That was her only avenue of escape as he advanced upon her, even though she knew he was guiding her exactly where he wanted her.

"You aren't going to ask me what I choose, are you?" Neve said.

"We both know what you'd decide, practical woman that you are. If you'd like to dance that dance, though, I'd be glad to ask. You know better than Bell's women what you'd be signing up for if you choose to join the rest of Arcanium."

Locke pulled his shirt down his arms. Then he unbuttoned his pants. In a matter of seconds, he was naked. Most people looked more vulnerable, human beings not very equipped with the protections of other animals and slightly ridiculous because of it. Locke, like most of the demons of Arcanium, didn't look more vulnerable without his clothes. If anything, the lean, firm strength of his body made smooth, pale skin and even the silliness of a cock seem a warning rather than a natural joke.

Like Mikhail, he moved like a predator, a mountain lion pursuing easy prey.

"You know, it's curious… How could Bell make you then not take advantage of his masterpiece? Why hasn't he put his indelible mark upon you like he has the others? What man, demon or jinn would be so foolish?" He pulled the covers back until there was nothing to cover her, nowhere to hide. He crowded her against the pillows, weaving his fingers through her hair and pinning her down. "You going to be nice, Neve?" He slowly lowered himself over her body and brought his mouth to hers. Once bitten… But she didn't have the Spider's meager defenses.

And his flesh sliding against her, all over her, swept through her hard. When she gasped, he took her mouth. He sucked her tongue and rocked his heavy, dense body against hers until she parted her legs of her own accord.

"How on earth could he resist?" he murmured against her lips. "Especially after he tasted you. How could he taste then not take the whole damn thing— throw you down and bury himself as deeply in you as that goddamn water demon could reach?"

Locke raised himself onto his knees between her thighs then slid a hand between them to thumb and tweak her clit, pulling the hood back, teasing her.

"I don't have to ask what you'd choose. You'd choose me every time. You gave yourself to me before you ever gave yourself to him, and I'm sure that knowledge smarts just as much as everything else I took from him."

He crooked his thumb to catch his nail against her clit. She thrashed with a cry, grabbing fistfuls of the fitted sheet.

"No, I'm not going to ask you to choose. I want you to *beg* me to fuck you. I want you to beg me to put my mark upon you, to belong to me, to be my living slave, my faithful acolyte, to devote yourself to my service. I want you to beg to worship me. I know you can beg, Neve. And I don't have to see the future to know you will."

With a hand still in her hair, he closed it into a fist and pulled her upright. His kiss was a brand, his body hotter than Mikhail's had ever been. It stung for his skin to touch hers, but he still rubbed and cut at her clit, his pupils dilating more with every twitch and every whimper he coaxed from her until the blackness expanded beyond the irises and poured like ink to fill in the whites of his eyes.

"I want your word, Neve. I want the power of your word. Beg me to own you, Neve. Do it well enough and you may even come before the circus opens."

If Mikhail had asked her to beg—hell, if Bell had asked her to beg—she might not have hesitated the way she did now. Because when she begged them, it didn't have deeper meaning. Begging them wasn't worship. It just meant she wanted them. It wasn't signing herself away, heart and soul, to a demon who wanted to use her, who didn't love her or even like her. Her religious beliefs might have been more muddied than they used to be, but that crossed one of the more defined lines. In that respect, Maya was right. Consenting to be a slave in exchange for protection hadn't crossed it, but giving him the power of her word that bound her more thoroughly than chains, that burned through her skin hotter than his flesh...

She couldn't do it, not even for the desire that had risen up to meet him as though his skin were that of an incubus. Her flesh remembered him, hungered for him still. She could beg him to fuck her and mean it, to her own self-disgust, but that was as far as she was able to go. And it wouldn't be far enough for him.

'My only requirement is enthusiastic submission,' he'd said. *'I'll even give you points for just trying, at least in the beginning.'*

"Please." Neve swallowed thickly against her stomach's attempt to interrupt her. She ran her hands up his arms and convinced herself to slide closer, even though he repulsed and compelled her in dizzying turns. She moved her hips to meet the arrhythmic touch over her clit. "I choose you. I chose you back in the tent, gave you my word there, as powerful without my knowledge as with it. That's why Arcanium is yours, isn't it? Because I already gave myself to you?"

Locke slowed his insistent fingers over her clit. He parted his lips slightly. She had his attention, even if what she'd said had been stilted, halting, emotionless in her fear. In his stillness, her body protested, demanded more. She shifted closer, her legs spread around his knees, took his shoulder and pulled herself up until her abdomen was flush with his cock. She bit her lip against her gasp, not that it helped to keep Locke from noticing. He moved his tongue behind his lips, as though tasting her desire in the air.

"I told you to take me. I told you to do whatever you wanted with me. That's how Bell made me, and that's why you want me, because I'll do whatever you want — *anything* you want with me — and I'll love it." She slowly tightened her arms around his shoulders, bringing her breasts to his chest, her mouth almost to his. "You can read my mind. You know I'm not lying. So go ahead...just take it. Take your pet nymphomaniac however you want."

He closed his eyes and leaned in, his parted lips brushing hers, not quite a kiss. His cock pulsed fast with his heartbeat, and his body tensed as he made to do exactly that—fall forward and take her however a demon like him desired.

Then he opened his eyes and grinned.

Neve pulled back, brow furrowing.

"It was a nice try. But you don't get to demand, love, not yet. You get to beg, and that means desperation you haven't realized I can create in you. It means subjugation. No, you're not afraid enough of me. You think you know how far I'll go because you've seen it, but seeing isn't knowing, Neve. And I haven't even begun. Let's start small."

He tossed her back onto the bed. Ropes reached for her from the posts, wrapped around her wrists and ankles, spread her wide to him.

Without warning, he slid three fingers into her cunt. She tried to hide her face against her shoulder when he didn't have any trouble doing so. He took her chin like he had Maya's. Neve feared he'd crush her jaw, too.

But he apparently just wanted her to face him with her shame, because he looked down at her like an artist with a blank canvas.

"You are *mine*. Don't just recite the lesson to me, darling. In order to have me, you must *understand* it. And when you have me, it will be because I deign to, not because you have persuaded me. It will be because I favored you, not because you desire. Your desire is *mine*. Your pain is *mine*. Everything your body does, from the greatest pleasure to the meanest functions, is *mine*. Your love is mine. Your fear is mine. Too many others still have these things. You still guard them jealously. But I'll have them, and I'll have the ones who keep the pieces of you that you yielded."

There was a snap like a whip crack. The glass room that held the incubus and succubus appeared next to the bed. The leather over Mikhail's cock constricted in rhythmic waves, and Sasha moved as though the leather inside her was doing the same. But no matter how they struggled now that they saw Locke and Neve, they couldn't break free.

"You gave your desire to them, but they are mine now. They will bring you to your peak, but you will not come, because your climax will be mine alone if you please me. Trust me, darling…" He encircled her ankles with terrible intimacy, as though his hands were greater bindings than the ropes. "You'll know how I want you to beg by the time I return."

Neve jerked violently, but the ropes didn't give her much room to maneuver. The mattress creaked in her attempts to get away from the stinging pain making its slow way through the base of her right nipple. A thin line of blood dripped down the side of her breast as gleaming silver emerged and swirled to curl around the bud like tiny tentacles. The silver that had pierced a thick line through the nipple tightened around it, but though it was metal and felt cold, it moved like it was alive. It swirled and stroked and twisted and squeezed, acting like a nipple clamp, a flexible tongue and a pair of evil fingers all at once, keeping her nipple stimulated, stinging, burning, hard.

As soon as the right one was complete — silver artfully displayed over her entire nipple, the whole enchanted thing wriggling and pulling like a mouth over the areola — stinging started all over again on her left nipple.

Neve struggled to control her breathing. Hyperventilating herself into unconsciousness would be merciful, but she doubted he would allow her that mercy, and panic would only increase the pain. However, practicality could only get her so far. Her body paid no attention to her rational mind, which diminished by the second.

Then she screamed, because that cold knitting needle sensation impaled her clitoris, digging and slithering underneath the nub on the exterior and making its home in the subdermal portion before emerging on the other side. Then it wrapped its smooth ribbon tendrils around the external part of the organ. Her clit swelled above the silver, throbbing, bright pink, larger than usual because of the blood flowing in and not out — a clit ring. But among the pleasure, there was no doubt of the pain from the metal deeper than skin, deep in a piece of anatomy dense with nerve endings.

Locke lowered his head between her legs and swiped his pointed tongue over her engorged clit.

She cried out again, bucking up, wrenching to the side. The ropes creaked from her trying to get away. Both the pleasure and the pain were so intense, side by side, that she couldn't distinguish one from the other — didn't know which poured the tears from her eyes, which spilled whimpers from her throat, which prickled over her skin in gooseflesh, which she'd beg for if she could think well enough to speak.

Locke kissed her belly, between her breasts, the hollow of her throat, her forehead.

"So beautiful," he murmured there, the vibration of his voice intense between her eyes.

He kissed her forehead again then vaulted out of bed and passed the Spider. He rapped the glass to make the spiders scurry in agitation.

"I'll return in a few hours. We'll see what your talented tongue can offer me then. Oh, and don't bother trying to speak to your sex demons. They can't hear you through the glass or in your head. I wouldn't permit that kind of solace. All of you suffer alone."

* * * *

"Neve, can you hear me?"

The voice was soft, just above a whisper. Neve barely turned her head. Mikhail and Sasha on her right, the Spider on her left... There was nothing she could do to help any of them. She didn't think she could stand to see their despair, because it would only make her own more real.

But Locke had said Mikhail and Sasha wouldn't be able to talk to her, so Neve looked to the Spider.

"They've settled. I used to be still like this for hours when I started in Arcanium. The venomous ones are in the corners, except for the banana spider, but it's a few inches away from my hand. Are you with me?"

Neve was glad the Spider hadn't asked if she was okay.

"I'm here." She winced. Talking made it worse, but she turned her head a little more.

The Spider was more or less where Locke had put her, colorless and eerily still for a human being. The giant tarantula was on her chest, a few huntsmen on her legs, but most of the spiders had scurried away from her. The black widow had started its web in the corner, and it looked like a few of the tarantulas had died from one of the venomous ones, because they were belly up or listing to the side, their legs curled in. Spiders weren't Neve's forte.

"Are you hurt?" Neve asked.

"No bites. The tarantulas got irritated with me, though, so my face itches and my eyes burn. Never had that happen before. Now I know why B...why he protected me from it. My nose tickles and I can't move. But my skin's not rotting off. That's something." She was almost inaudible through the glass. She couldn't speak too loudly, lest the sound startle her companions. "I can't feel my leg or my hand. I'm going to try to move. I didn't want to move alone."

Neve blinked, the closest she could convince herself to nod her head.

The Spider slowly shifted the hands bracing her on the ground so that they inched away from the banana spider. It was small in comparison to the gigantic tarantula on the woman's chest and the huntsman spiders that had run in every direction of the glass room, including halfway up one of the walls. The banana spider stirred, but it didn't raise its legs or attack. Some of the smaller tarantulas showed their displeasure, but the Spider checked behind her and slowly pushed herself back, creating more distance between herself and where the spiders had gone.

She stopped when the huntsman spiders on her legs grew restless and started finding new places on her legs to climb, barely breathed as the giant tarantula climbed farther up her chest, its head halfway up her neck now.

"I feel like I've never been so scared, but I know that's a lie." The hand that had fallen asleep twitched. "It always feels worse in the moment. You never remember it as bad as it was."

"I've got fucking needles in me, and they keep moving," Neve said.

"I know."

"It's like someone's sucking and biting pieces off at the same time." Every time she thought they were going to make her come anyway, they tightened, held the blood in the erect tissue and the silver twisted to sting through the pleasure, bringing her back down again. Then they would undulate and squeeze again. "I can't… I can't stop it…"

And Sasha and Mikhail were right there. As soon as Locke had left, she could sense them even when she wasn't looking. Although Mikhail had been hard and Sasha likely turned on by biological stimulation alone, they certainly weren't emanating on purpose— otherwise she'd be bowled over by their pleasure, not distracted so much by the extreme piercings. But that didn't mean nothing came from them.

She'd faced them once after Locke had gone, just once, as her skin prickled and tingled with restlessness and her cunt continued leaking onto the sheets beneath her. Regret had knotted Mikhail's brow as desire had come off him like fragrance on a breeze. The leather over his cock was working him, the silver working her. He'd felt her pleasure. She'd felt his. It was an endless loop that intensified the work that the silver was doing to her. The sex demons were as much a torture device for her as the silver.

He tried to hold back, but he couldn't. She tried to fight him, but she couldn't. And if she couldn't fight

Mikhail, she was no match for Locke. So she couldn't look at Mikhail. She could barely allow herself to think of him, even though his desire settled over her like a fog.

"Don't."

At first, Neve wasn't sure whether she'd heard the Spider correctly.

"Don't fight it."

"What?"

The Spider lowered her eyes. "Don't fight him. He was right. I've been with men like him most of my life. Don't fight him. You won't win, and it only confuses you."

"But…" Her protest was cut off by a moan, followed by a hiss.

"I know that's not what Maya said. Maya doesn't understand men like him. If you fight him, he's going to win, and you're going to do what he wants and like it. But you'll hate yourself and get confused about what *you* chose to do, what you're responsible for. But if you give in to him, he's your master and it's all his responsibility. Let him break your body. It's already broken. But for God's sake, Neve, don't let him destroy *you*. Stay you underneath where he can't find it, where he can't touch it. Otherwise, don't resist him. Don't listen to Maya. Listen to *me*. I've survived this before."

"What if I don't want to survive?" Neve said.

"Please don't leave me."

At the sound of her own words being repeated back to her, Neve's eyes fluttered shut and she turned away to groan again.

* * * *

Time had no meaning. There was nothing but the silver embedded in her sensitive flesh. Each second felt like a minute. Each minute felt like fifteen. Each hour felt like a day. The windows of the apartment faced west, but she was facing away from them, so she couldn't watch the sun's exact progression. If she hadn't had the sun, though, she would have believed she had been there for days. The sun had only just started to lose its brightness, which meant she'd been there for a mere afternoon.

She couldn't hear them, but the incubus and succubus writhed in their glass room, and Neve was about to crawl out of her skin then yank the silver rings from herself, because she was close—always close, never there. The silver kept her from coming, but it kept her high, too, walking on what felt like the edge of a blade caressing her folds. If she didn't reach her orgasm soon, she would... There wasn't an end to what she wanted to do to him. All she knew was that when Locke appeared again at the foot of the bed, she would offer him her firstborn child if he fucked her and let her have his orgasm as well.

"Well, look at us. The Spider is still alive, the sex demons are hot and you are the most beautiful thing I've seen since the old centuries. Do you have something to say to me, love?"

He snapped his fingers. The ropes fell away from her wrists and ankles. Neve drew them in, though the muscles protested the sudden change. A few of them cramped. She turned over onto her side in fetal position, whimpering, twitching, sobbing her moans as she waited for those pangs to pass.

"*Please.*" She brought her freed hands to her clit, rubbing over the hood and the folds around it herself, but every movement disturbed the clit piercing, and she shrieked into the pillow. "Please, I can't... I can't even think. Please, just—"

"No 'just' here, love. Everything I do to you has significance. Everything I do for you is a favor. Don't diminish that. *Just* tell me what you need, Neve. Beg your god for your heart's desire."

She rubbed her face against the pillowcase to smear the worst of the mess off. Then, with all the effort she could muster, she took her hands away from her clit.

Neve didn't know what she was doing or what he wanted from her, but she had to try. He'd made that clear. She had to try. And she had to mean it.

She rolled onto her back again, and without the ropes to hold her, she spread herself again.

Locke closed his hand around the post at the foot of the bed.

"I won't touch myself. My pleasure and my pain are not my own." Neve closed her eyes. Somehow, the words spilled from her tongue as though they had weight, heavier than before. His magic was inside her. His magic made what she said real, true. And she was all too aware how dangerous that was. But she had little choice.

She turned her head toward the sex demons' glass room, but she couldn't convince herself to open her eyes. She couldn't bear to see betrayal or conflict or pain above the muzzle. Because her words had power, and if she were a demon like Locke, she'd make sure Mikhail didn't miss a word.

"Everything here is for you to do with as you please. I am here for you. It is my pleasure to serve you. I'll be whatever you want me to be. I'll do whatever you want me to do. And I will take pleasure in your pleasure, not my own. I'll come for you alone. I'll suffer for you alone. Please, Locke, *your* desire is my command. Do as you will. *Please…*"

"Silence." He stroked down the length of the post, breathing slowly but deeply, the blue in his eyes disappearing beneath the black once more. "You had me at your pleasure and pain not being your own."

She shivered as he leaped onto the footboard in a crouch. His toes gripped the wood. They were longer than normal and more dexterous than human toes should have been.

"You do not know yet what you've given yourself to. It's time for you to see. It's time to make my mark, love."

His clothing pulled away from his body, leaving him naked and just as invulnerable as the last time. His cock was half-erect and growing. But while he'd been large for a man when she'd still thought he was human, it was growing so much more now, the base expanding, thickening and the flush over the shaft and head deepening.

As he lowered himself to the bed and crawled toward her again, his legs lengthened and his feet extended, making it look like his legs had twisted around. His pale skin reddened to a deep vermillion. He pulled the covers up in fistfuls with long fingers, nails thickening and darkening into black claws.

The closer he came to her, the more he shed his handsome human disguise.

His red skin lost its opacity. Through the translucence, Neve could see the flexure and extension of each muscle, the movement of blood through his nearly black veins — as though he'd been flayed and was still in the process of growing a protective layer of skin. But she knew better than to believe his skin would pierce as easily as her own.

His angles intensified, his muscles grew and so did he. He was almost as tall as Ciarán, but his long limbs either made him seem longer or would have had him towering over Ciarán at their full extension. The thick, dark, wavy hair had receded into his scalp. His head was wide enough now for his mouthful of teeth, for the prehensile tongue that traced the sharpness as he crawled over her once more, grabbing the headboard with hands that could have closed around her entire head.

There was no structural trace of the Locke that she knew, nothing left but the demon. If she hadn't watched the transformation, the only way she would have known it was him was his expression, the lust that he made no effort to curtail or conceal from her. Desire was his weapon, not his vulnerability.

Locke was at least four times her size, his cock longer than Ciarán's and thicker than her forearm, and his body was a massive, heated shadow over her, his knees creaking the springs of the mattress with his weight and pushing them down.

Neve fought not to curl back up again. It would be no use. He would call the ropes or force her arms and legs apart by hand. He watched her struggle against cowering, watched her take in the sight of him with fear and awe, purring as he continued to stroke his tongue over the tips of his teeth.

"Are you afraid?" It sounded like him, but darker, deeper, from a vaster cavity.

She tore her gaze from his writhing abdomen, from his still-growing erection, to stare into the black eyes above her. She could see her reflection. She could see what he saw.

"Yes."

"You should be." His fingers were so much like the long legs of the giant tarantula and his joints clicked as he moved—tiny popping knuckles, like the clowns' mouths. She flinched from them, but he only wanted to caress her face. The quality of his skin was somewhere between latex and human skin. It burned, as though the fire that had flayed him had only just gone out. "Ever since I saw that water demon take you, I knew I needed you. We'll have some good times in the years and years to come. I promise you."

When he lowered himself to kiss her, his sharp teeth gleaming behind his lips, Neve forced herself to rise up and meet him. That sent a groan through him and into her.

Kissing a demon, with his mouth bigger and wider, quickly overwhelmed her. She had no hope to control the kiss. All she could do was cling to the pillows and try to convince her taut, trembling body to relax, because he wasn't hurting her. Even the silver piercings had settled into a smoother, sedate slide over the skin, no longer stinging or digging or strangling the flesh. Although they hadn't quite set her free, they were no longer the focus of her fears or her attention.

That was the giant body sinking over her, his knees spreading her legs, his cock heavy on her belly, the sheer weight and heat of him just a little too heavy, a little too hot. Her bones didn't break and her skin didn't blister, but it felt close.

Even so, as he moved his mouth from hers to the delicate vulnerability of her throat, that metallic purr rippled through her and her heat rose to meet his. The shaft of his erection slid against her silver-wrapped clit, keeping the sting alive but also stimulating the hypersensitized flesh. Her hips rose to meet him in spite of the pain, and any whimper was followed by a moan. Before she realized she was doing it, her arms had shifted from the pillows to wrap around his back. She slid her palms up over the exaggerated jut of his shoulder blades. And though her clit still felt like someone was twisting a knitting needle inside it, she wrapped her legs around his thighs and rubbed it against him, desperate as a bitch in heat.

He laughed into her sternum, licked a path from her heart to her mouth then kissed her again as he shifted his hips lower, bringing his cock farther down her body and flattening himself more over her, crushing her into the mattress. But her breathing was already shallow and oxygen highly overrated. It wasn't until the head of his cock parted her folds and probed bluntly against her entrance that her eyes flew open again and she remembered who she was with, *what* she was with.

"Oh, yes, love, this will hurt—but not in the way that you think." Locke looked over his shoulder, the curve of his long neck oddly elegant. He grinned his shark's grin at the sex demons. "I'm going to take your woman, boy. After this, she'll be mine like she was never yours, branded beyond the surface as the slave of a master that Bell didn't have the imagination to be…and that you never had the balls to become."

Neve cupped her hand over his cheek and guided him back to look at her. "He's already disgraced, humiliated. You don't have to mock him like this."

"But it gives me such joy."

Locke's grip on the headboard made the wood groan, and the silver piercings squirmed like serpents over her nipples and clit as a counterpoint to the tremendous pressure of his cock entering her.

He was right. There were no words for what it felt like for him to push into her, for her body to magically accommodate him the way it had for other demons who had fucked her, but for it to still stretch her not to her limits but beyond. She arched, shaking as though in seizure, shout rising into a scream.

It wasn't the physicality of his cock that hurt the way it did. The pain wasn't because he stretched the lips and the walls of her cunt, wasn't because he slid past her cervix and into her womb, wasn't because if the laws of biology and physics were constant, he'd have perforated her uterus and done major internal damage by now…and he was still pushing in, pushing deeper.

Fire spread from around his cock, unfurling and unwinding its tendrils like parasites that bored through her. Hissing came from deep inside, a pit of vipers in her abdomen, sizzling skin. She smelled sulfur, smoke.

He didn't stop until his hips were flush against her thighs. He stretched his neck back, his groan nothing human. In the midst of everything, the curve of his throat captivated her—as though her mind had officially snapped and she couldn't help but distract herself with small things. Like how beautiful that alien neck was above her, the ripple of the throat when he swallowed, the subtle vibration when he groaned, how seemingly vulnerable, how delicate the minutiae of its movements, yet how powerful.

"You have never belonged to anything, not even yourself, more than you belong to me right now." He pulled back. Her body protested the retreat and clung to him like a fist, rendering any movement as painful as entering her. "Scream for me, Neve. Scream so all Arcanium can hear you and know their own despair."

He pulled himself back until just the head of his cock was inside her then surged back in. Neve wailed, the sound raking through her as though he were fucking her all the way up there. Even to herself, it sounded like she was in terrible pain, but the truth was, while there was pain, it wasn't physical. She could barely define it, except that it was everywhere inside her now. And it wasn't just pain. The same as the silver through her flesh, it wasn't just pain. It was agonizing, excruciating, gut-wrenching pleasure that couldn't be contained in a human woman.

Locke buried his face in her hair, his panting deafening, breath like new steam, his purring groans from some primeval beast rather than anything that had ever looked, talked or walked like a man. "They'll never know. They'll never know you begged for me. They'll never know how you wanted this. They'll never know what I have given you. But I will, and every demon who lays eyes on you will know that you've been marked for another. I will make sure every demon who sees you knows they cannot touch you because you have sworn yourself to *me*, sacrificed yourself to *me* and me alone."

She couldn't come, not with the silver strangling her clit. Neve shook, tightened and released, her body quaking. She wrapped herself around him like a vine, her abdomen meeting his as he punched himself into her, but she couldn't come. She bared her teeth, shaking her head, swallowing back her cries when she could. Then he would roll his hips and sheathe himself all the way, and the screams would start again.

"I told you, Neve, like nothing you've ever felt."

In the midst of the chaos wreaking havoc inside her, it took her more than a moment to realize that part of the reason the pleasure was so high, so intense, wasn't just because of Locke.

She opened her eyes. Mikhail's eyes were almost shut from the angle at which he watched the claiming, but the gleam under his eyelids meant he could see her. And Sasha had strained to look over the side of the bench. Desire emanated from them in dense waves, powerful as ocean breakers, and Locke had to know. He had to feel it himself, had to feel what it was doing to her. But despite the fact he wasn't the sole demon responsible for her pleasure, he hadn't stopped them.

Of course he hadn't stopped them. He'd brought them all the way up here, and he wouldn't do that just to make Mikhail a witness. That didn't make them an interruption or intruders to what he was doing to her. It made them tools, nothing more. He was using Mikhail for himself and for her—a kind of twisted marital aid.

The comparison called her attention to the ring on her right third finger, the only thing that she had been left with, cold carbon and platinum, a ring that symbolized the binding of her soul to the man who had broken their vow, who could no longer be her husband. Moved to a neutral finger to shine without significance as a stranger demon claimed her, used her body as no human man ever had.

Now that demon was shunted aside and mocked as another demon, hellborn as the Ringmaster, took her for himself. Of all the things she'd done, it was this devastating ecstasy that seemed like it could crack the diamond deep in its setting. Her whole body burned, but her fingers felt frostbite. Tears streaming down her temples, she worked the ring off with her thumb, threw it to the concrete floor next to the glass room. As he'd said, Locke's mark would go deeper, and she'd promised herself to him with words more powerful than the 'I do' she'd given in a church sanctuary.

Neve closed her eyes again as Locke licked a line up her cheek to taste the streaks of tears. "Good girl," he murmured. "All mine. For that…"

The silver around her nipples and clit loosened. Blood that had been caught to keep the flesh hard and sensitive rushed out and new blood rushed in, sending her into a new tailspin of pain but also giving her the ability to reach her climax.

Locke gripped the headboard with one hand, splintering the wood under his grip, and clawed down the sheets and through the mattress on her other side as he buried himself as deep as he could go and came with volcanic heat through her orgasm.

It wasn't like coming with an incubus. He didn't feed from her, didn't steal life or energy or spirit, didn't render her nearly braindead. No, he didn't take anything from her, but he left something behind. Call it third-degree burns on some metaphysical plane where his cock reached. Call it a brand, a mark on her soul.

She clung to him, unable to breathe, holding his head as he groaned the last wrenches of his pleasure into her hair, held him as tightly as she could, yet she could gain no comfort from him, no love, no affection, no safety, nothing to cling to as she plummeted while lying still.

He released the headboard, his skin without wound as he slowly crawled backward down her body, pulling his cock from her. It seemed to go on forever. She whined into the pillow next to her as the head stretched her entrance like a fist. Then he was free and she was hollow and aching. The liquid dripping from her felt like her own blood, not his seed.

Locke licked her pierced nipples, finding the places where the silver emerged to reawaken the wounds, then down her belly to her clit then to her cunt, where he licked inside her, his tongue like a tentacle.

When he'd completely withdrawn from her, he caught the flesh of her thigh between his teeth before softening it into a kiss. "Welcome to the new Arcanium, Neve. You're mine now. Forever, you're mine."

He left her on the bed. She didn't move. The silver piercings gradually tightened around her nipples and clit again—a reminder that any pleasure was in his hands alone and the rest could only be pain.

"Neve…" The Spider's whisper barely reached her.

"I'm here. I'm with you." She didn't want to be, but her mind wouldn't show her mercy. It kept her there and didn't erase a single memory, didn't allow her the courtesy of fuzziness. She remembered everything, every detail, and the memories kept replaying.

"You did everything right. You won't believe me now, but it will get easier. If your brain doesn't break, it will adapt. You can get used to anything. It will get easier."

Neve turned her head toward the Spider's glass room, wincing. "What happened to you?"

"Not a demon, but everything else." the Spider replied. "I'm here."

An apology seemed insufficient. But the Spider didn't need her to say anything. And Neve didn't need her to say anything more.

* * * *

When Locke returned, he wore his human guise, but now that she knew what he hid within it, she couldn't help but see it in him with every move, every gesture, every expression he made. He was back in his suit, second button undone, fedora angled on his artfully tousled hair like some modernized throwback to the Rat Pack. The only difference from the way he'd looked all the other times was the red poppy pinned to the ribbon of his fedora. Black, translucent fabric draped over his arm.

He held his hand out to her, and she took it. It would have been so much easier to not move, to make him pull her across the bed, make him make her do everything, but giving up would break her vow. The condition of her being with him was clear. She had to try. She had to keep going. She could not yet muster enthusiasm, false or true, but she had to move, so she did. She dragged her body closer to him, rolled onto her front to climb to her hands and knees. Her breasts weighed on her nipples, and the change in orientation placed additional pressure on her clit as well, but she couldn't stop. He continued to hold her hand like the gentleman he pretended to be as she slid shaking legs over the side of the bed. Bad as the sharp ache in her nipples was, it was the silver through and around her clit that had her nearly collapsing.

Locke grabbed her around the waist, lifted her up again until she could brace both hands on the mattress. Then he opened the fabric he held over his arm — a robe, though it would do little to cover her up. It provided a modicum of warmth, however, over her cooled body that seemed freezing in comparison to what Locke had done to her. Any of the protection from the elements Bell had provided to accommodate an outdoor circus had apparently been removed, because this was the old chill she remembered from before Arcanium, when she'd been much more sensitive to the cold.

Standing up sent more of his semen down her thigh. She grabbed the edge of the top sheet and put it between her legs. Locke was patient, an enigmatic smile gracing his expression once again as he quietly took in the sight of her.

When she thought she'd soaked up most of it, she pulled the sheet out from between her legs. The semen-stained fabric had the slightest red tinge. She didn't ask whether it was from him or her. It didn't matter either way.

She pulled the robe on, and he pressed up behind her with his arms around her waist to tie the robe closed. It had been designed to reveal more than conceal her, but it made her feel a little better to have it on—a slight barrier was better than no barrier at all.

Neve took ginger steps around the bed with him, but her legs still couldn't quite support her, as though the piercing in her clit had cut off nerve endings in her legs as well—which she knew wasn't true, but she also knew that the nervous trauma he'd caused could have a broader effect. Adrenaline, too, wasn't the strengthening hormone that people thought it was.

"We will need to be out there when the doors open to greet our guests for the first night of the new Arcanium. You will stand at my side. I would love to introduce the Spider as well, but her punishment has not yet satisfied me." He tapped the glass to set the spiders in motion once more from where they had settled.

The giant tarantula climbed up to the Spider's face. Her hands trembled in her lap, but she had managed to move so she could lean against one of the walls, and her second set of legs acted as an extra bit of support. That would give her a little more time in perfect stillness, but a human being wasn't capable of being still indefinitely. Neve could see weariness worn in hollows under her eyes and cheekbones.

The huntsmen raced like spiders many times smaller than they were, and the tarantulas showed their fangs at the sound. The smaller venomous spiders at the corners didn't appear disturbed. The banana spider, however, bolted toward the Spider and climbed over her feet. Any movement now would result in a bite. It wouldn't be fatal—she wouldn't be so lucky—but it promised intense, practically inevitable pain.

"If you're good, pet, I'll let you out in the morning. Then you can prove to me you'll be as good as Neve," Locke said. "As for the two of you"—he turned to Mikhail and Sasha—"you're due back in the lounge. I'll take care of her alone from now on. After tonight, you won't have to be so close for your need to reach her."

The incubus and succubus' glass room disappeared.

Neve struggled to stay upright instead of doubled over as he led her back to the escalator, but she could either walk hunched over against the knife-like pain in her clitoris or she could stand upright and have her legs buckle. Finally, with a laugh, Locke swept her into his arms.

"You'll get used to it, love. Soon it'll be as though you've always suffered the pain." He kissed her ear as they descended to the fourth floor. Muttering that he needed to have the golems build a service elevator, he brought them to the bottom row of stadium seating on that floor. Then he stepped out over the edge and floated them down to the main entrance on the ground floor.

The doors to the auditorium closed behind him, and he set her down, holding her close so that she could lean against him as she walked. Golems waited at giant glass doors etched in the pattern of the Arcanium gates, which led into the massive, windowed atrium.

On the other side of the doors, a clustered line of people led well into the parking lot, the golden sunset nearly blinding behind them.

Except Neve didn't think they were people.

She tightened her grip on Locke's arm.

"Oh, yes," he said, "demand for a proper dungeon like Arcanium is quite high. Earth-dwelling demons, jinn, fair folk... The greater beings of wicked desire who seek subjugation of the weak will never tire of us. And I might eventually open the circus to a more human clientele of particular tastes, if only for my own entertainment."

He nodded to the golems. They unlocked and pulled open the doors.

Men and women who looked human poured into the atrium, spreading through the empty space like water. In comparison to human beings, they were more subdued, a few of them speaking to each other but otherwise stalking away from the others around them—a crowd of loners. It didn't surprise her that most demons didn't play well with others.

But the creatures who entered in the company of others didn't surprise her much either. If they had company, it was in groups of two and three, the way they'd separated themselves in Arcanium as well— rarely anything more than that. There were a few smaller beings the size of tall children or short adults who came in a larger group of maybe two dozen, but they were an oddity among the rest.

As the atrium filled, some reached for her, stretching out their long-fingered hands, brushing her skin with claws she couldn't see, gleams like hard light on flint in their dead eyes and sharp teeth emerging in their mouths. But when Locke turned to them, they withdrew, lowering their eyes and backing away as though challenged by a king. As terrible as Neve already knew he was, she started to wonder what kind of reputation preceded him, that other demons genuflected and retreated.

He combed through her hair, deceptively relaxed and casual, surveying his guests as they spread out before him. The crowd outside the stadium thinned, trickled in, filled the atrium to the brim. When the golems closed the doors again, there was little room left. However Locke had sold his tickets, he'd determined the exact amount he could spare. Bell charged his guests twenty dollars per entrance. Given the quality of the fabrics around her and the absolutely hideous jewelry that could be nothing but real, Locke charged significantly more. And who knew what that translated to in favors?

"Bell undervalued Arcanium on purpose," Locke said, answering the question when she didn't dare open her mouth, unsure if a slave was permitted to speak in his world. He didn't suggest otherwise. "Made it a poor man's holiday to impress the unimpressive. That was his choice. I choose otherwise. I know the worth of my possessions, and I refuse to sell them short."

He raised his free hand. The low murmur of conversation died.

"Good evening, ladies and gentlemen. Tonight marks the beginning of a new era. For too long, we endured

Bell Madoc's insult of a freakshow circus traveling our world. For too long, his dungeon mocked every intention it had been built for—a moveable feast for demons, a pocket of hell for us to endlessly destroy and never extinguish. Bell turned it into a cheap, pathetic sideshow. All these years, he used the dungeon's laws to keep us from crossing his borders, protecting his precious little dream."

Locke lowered his hand. The crowd was completely silent, their hunger restrained, but Neve didn't think it would be for long. They looked between Locke and her, and every time they looked at her, she saw herself bloody, skin torn to ribbons, shoved down to the floor and her pieces violated in a matter of moments if they had their way. Her knees buckled again, this time from her quiet, silent, shallow breaths, but Locke wouldn't let her fall, wouldn't let her faint. He gathered her in her arms as though he were the lead in a romantic move and she the damsel, but his tenderness was as much a mockery of romance as Bell's circus had been a mockery of a dungeon.

"We've tried since the beginning to penetrate the spells he erected to keep us out and his people in. Other demons have tried. Some have fallen. Some joined him of their own accord when they couldn't win. They willingly put their throats under Bell's boot to perform for him like organ grinder monkeys."

Locke paused, his disgust mirrored in every face before him.

"No more."

The crowd erupted into cheers, raising their fists into the air, human-like shouts interspersed with animalistic howls, roars and a deafening whistling cry. Their expressions turned ugly, human faces melting away to show who they really were. Bodies grew taller, wider, sharper, changed color or texture, added horns or wings, until Neve was surrounded by unfamiliar creatures, not lust emanating from them but dread, cold as icicles through her veins.

"I have humiliated the jinni who denies the darkness of his creation," Locke called over the din, amplifying his voice to be heard. "I stole Arcanium right from under him, taking his power and his people with me. I restored the circus to what it should have always been — an exhibition of degradation, a freakshow not for their pleasure but for ours, a playground of domination and delight, a circus of the enslaved primed for your poison of choice. I have so much more to show you in time, but your impatience shall nevertheless be rewarded. You get first taste of those Bell failed to protect, first taste of their despair while it is still fresh, while misplaced optimism still runs through the flavor. On this, our opening night, we tear the old circus down to the sawdust. We shall bring this dungeon to its glory."

He kissed Neve's forehead, his smile fierce. "Ladies and gentlemen, welcome to Arcanium!"

The monsters and demons around him cheered again. The concrete at her feet trembled, and she swore that the metal between the windows rang with the vibrations. Locke waited until the demonic joy had subsided, although not into the complete silence of before. He turned her in front of him and curled his arm around her chest in an unmistakable possessive gesture, displaying her as well as his mastery, his ownership. If these demons knew Arcanium, then they knew her. She was his demonstration, his proof.

And she could barely stand, much less stand against them.

Once they had quieted down again, Locke rested his chin on her shoulder, peering out over his crowd as he idly stroked the hard curve of silver around one nipple. "In the future, I hope to provide ever more elaborate performances for you, but when I open these doors, everyone is free to visit the exhibits of Arcanium and provide their own performances for the pleasures of your peers. No matter what you do, they won't die on you, so while I urge you not to needlessly dismember my children, you'll do no lasting mortal harm. Golems will provide you with anything else that you need. As for the exhibits unavailable for sampling, they will be made available to you at the midnight auction. This one is not for sale," he added, abruptly tightening the silver to make her yelp and sink back against him, "but you'll find the contortionist and the high-wire mistress on the block."

The doors behind him opened of their own accord, and Locke gestured to them with a flourish. "Ladies and gentlemen, hell is empty, and all the devils are here. Enter and enjoy!"

The demons darted forward like wolves on a scent, shouting and whooping their excitement. Locke laughed against her neck as the crowd spread out through the giant auditorium and left them alone with the golems in the atrium.

He lifted Neve in his arms again and followed his guests into the auditorium, bringing her to the center of the performance ring. He forced her hands behind her back then turned with her so that she could take in the new Arcanium from all three hundred and sixty degrees. She tried to close her eyes and turn her head, but he grabbed her hair and forced her eyes open again. The screams rose all around her—knives to her chest, every one, each tear salt in an open wound.

"This could have been you," he whispered, pulling her robe down her arms and pressing himself close against her. "One day, when I've grown bored and decide to move on, it will be."

Chapter Five

As terrible as the screams and cries were during the nights, what broke Neve completely and what Locke kept her awake for was what followed after dawn, when the demons left and the golems returned the cast to their glass rooms from wherever they'd been taken.

It had Locke's desired effect. When he finally brought her into his bed, she clung to him more tightly, kissed him more fiercely, sank him more deeply inside her of her own accord. In the pain, there was pleasure. In the pleasure, there was comfort—cold though it was in the midst of his fire.

She took it because it was there, but in his intermittent tenderness, she knew she mostly amused him. It was only when he was inside her that she sensed something more powerful from him. Not love. She didn't think he was capable of it, although she'd learned that demons could love in their own ways.

He prized her like a swallowed diamond, yielded something of himself when he fucked her, poured it into her when he came — as though to possess her he had to sacrifice a piece of himself in return. She couldn't define it, but whatever it was crept through her like infection.

When the rest of the cast saw her among them, accusation and hatred contorted their faces. They agreed with Maya, whether she'd shared her view with them or not. They thought she'd been spared. Physically, she had been. A few piercings to keep her weak and the demon's brand inside her, bruises and rope burns, scratches down her back and thighs... It couldn't compare. With all the things done to them, they couldn't understand that she hadn't been spared, and she couldn't blame them for it.

Only the Spider understood. Sometimes they slept together, all three of them, his demonic arms pinning them to the bed on either side of him after he had exhausted himself with their bodies and afternoon sunlight streamed into the loft against their eyelids like the end of the world.

He kept them apart, though, refused them human contact. Only he could touch them. But the Spider's presence alone shifted the drafts of the room, and her breath moved through the same air. Neve could see her, hear her, sense her — and that was enough. She could do without more contact.

After the fifteenth day and night, she stopped counting. Any lingering hope that Bell might find them had faded. As powerful as Bell was, if he hadn't been able to find them in a few days, he wasn't going to find them at all. Locke had proved himself to be more powerful, and that was that.

When she could stand to be in the moment, she still searched for escape, for some way to get out of the building, to break away from Locke. But when she wasn't held against him, he led her on a silver leash and collar that matched the piercings, and when she wasn't with him, he had her locked in his loft with golems patrolling the corridor. She'd inspected the window glass. A bullet couldn't penetrate it, much less anything she could do.

The Spider thought it was cute that she continued looking. So did Locke. He didn't mind, because he must have known she wouldn't find anything, and that only added to the despair. She had more space over which to spread her legs than the other cast members, but she was still trapped.

The performances would begin tonight. Some of the Arcanium cast members were brought from their glass rooms down to the performance ring and promised a few minutes of relief during the course of a show. They could be alone, untouched, their bodies strong and unfettered — as long as they performed well and according to the reputation of the circus.

In addition to the relief during the performance, they were permitted to practice for Locke so that he would know what they needed for the set. Golems worked from the scaffold that hung in the middle of the auditorium like an industrial chandelier. They'd arranged trapezes for Seth and Lars, the ring that Valorie could use for her act and a high wire for Maya. The cast members Locke had chosen weren't given a choice to say no, but they were guaranteed excruciation if they defied him before an audience. If the crowd couldn't enjoy acrobatics, they certainly wouldn't say no to the Ringmaster's punishment in its place. After all, the first set piece was the modified carousel for the Ringmaster's to command, punctuated with his whip.

No one fell, but the routines were hesitant as the performers reacquainted themselves with pain-free bodies doing things they hadn't done in weeks. Locke smiled like a wolf as he surveyed each practice performance. He rested his feet on the back of the seat in front of him, playing with the end of Neve's leash. The collar fitted too exactly around her neck, pressing into the flesh when her throat expanded every time she swallowed. But she knelt at his feet, her hands behind her back, and watched, as he had commanded her.

The Spider had been sent from his side to join the performers in the ring, each wrist and ankle shackled in the same silver that pierced and collared Neve. The shackles had been threaded with the thin white rope that she'd used shibari-style when she'd hosted the creepy-crawly tent. A leather harness that connected her to more white rope from the scaffold was the only other thing she wore. Locke had already determined how he wanted the chains to move her, his marionette of a spider dancing to a sweet music box lullaby. He'd conducted the dance himself, moving his puppeteer fingers, his eyes shining with glee at the broken-limbed lolling of the Spider's body.

It was better this way, he'd told her when she hadn't performed for him voluntarily. She'd given him four middle fingers, but she'd submitted to his control the second and third time he'd run her through the song. She looked like a fairy tale with an unhappy ending.

He had nothing for Neve to do for the performance, but that wasn't a surprise. Bell had only made her look pretty and fuck well anyway, and she was doing that for him just fine.

Of the demons, the only ones he had released for the performances were the clowns, though they weren't given their usual face paint. Locke had instructed them to use their own faces. No need to hide in this Arcanium.

After they'd performed their usual bawdy burlesque as though nothing had changed, Locke threw a bucket of fresh meat to them—which Neve didn't dare identify—. Murphy, the one with the rainbow suspenders and two tufts of curly hair on either side of his head, snarled at Locke, but he was the first to the meat. Tragedy and Comedy followed, gaunt and pale, their lantern eyes glowing in hunger. Tragedy looked over her shoulder at the carousel, but if she regretted what had happened to Caroline, she didn't dare try to go to her.

"If everyone is very good for the next few nights, I might bring back the Funhouse wheel of fate." Locke's voice boomed through the auditorium for everyone to hear. "No limitations, no restrictions, no choices—just chance."

He wound the leash chain around his hand until his link-wrapped fist pressed under Neve's chin and lifted her head. "The role you were created for, love. But I doubt they will be as kind to you as before."

"I thought you wanted me all to yourself," she said, struggling not to cough from the press of the collar.

"This *would* be for me."

"You promised. Sure, you're a demon, but you gave your word."

He grinned, laughing from deep in his chest as he leaned down and caught her lower lip between sharper teeth. "I did, didn't I? I would protect you enough. No worse than you receive in my bed." He tilted his head and possessed her with his kiss, taking her until he'd wrought a genuine moan. As though he knew the irony, he never wanted her to fake her response. She pleased him only when he knew she couldn't stop her own pleasure. "Does that satisfy your objections?"

"Nothing satisfies."

"Except me."

"Except you."

The Spider had been forced to go sober, and it seemed that for each day Elizabeth struggled with not having something to drink, Neve got drunk on bitterness without downing a drop.

"Into your cages, my pretty things. The show starts in an hour, and the audience will be here in thirty."

The cages, like those used to transport zoo animals, were too narrow for the performers to move in, although they could stretch their arms out through the hatch bars. The golems passed a small meal through the bars of each cage, the minimum of nourishment on a dessert plate.

From what Neve could tell, the odd chef had been put to work in the kitchens and commanded a small faction of golems to satisfy their guests' more esoteric gastronomic whims. Neve hadn't seen so much raw meat outside a chum bucket. But he himself had been put on a strict starvation diet and wasn't permitted to prepare his own meals.

Locke led her up to the third floor, where he had roped off a whole luxuriant section of the stadium for himself—in easy range of the lounge, close to the incubus and succubus. And the third floor was where they kept the wine.

This time, he had her straddle him in the lounge seat, the dark pink, translucent silk robe he'd chosen for her barely staying on as he pushed it down her shoulders.

The silver piercings awakened with renewed activity, and he subtly moved her hips over him.

"Not until the evening is done and we retire to our bed… Only then will I let you come."

"And in the meantime, what would you have me do?" She clutched at the arms of the chair as the silver tightened. She'd grown more accustomed to the sensations when the silver wasn't this active, but when it held her pleasure hostage, there was no getting used to it. That wasn't what he'd put it there for.

"Kiss me."

The corners of his eyes crinkled when she hesitated, something she rarely did anymore in his loft.

At times like this, she would prefer it if he shed the human disguise and looked like the demon he was, because even knowing what he was, the disguise disarmed her every time.

In fact, most demons kept their human disguises most of the time. The glass rooms had low ceilings, and the beds in the guest wing were built to human dimensions, but demons also just seemed to prefer doing the most obscene, offensive acts in their human disguise — perhaps to make a point that a human doing it wasn't out of the realm of possibility. Or perhaps she gave most of the demons too much credit when it came to subjects like philosophy and ethics.

Locke cradled her cheek then curled his fingers around her leash. "You asked me what I wanted. Why aren't you doing it, Neve? Could it be because I usually spare you their voyeuristic hatred? Could it be you don't want them to know how much you desire me? Afraid they might think that because you desire, because you succumb, you've chosen a side? And here I thought they'd already found you wanting."

For those who could see out of their rooms and from three floors down in the cages, Neve likely sensed more attention than she had, but that didn't mean no one was watching. That was the point, and she couldn't deny him.

He released the leash to grab her neck as she lowered her mouth to his. In yielding to her, he moaned, a grin curving his lips, because those who witnessed would know she kissed him rather than the other way around—her agency made plain, even though she was the one with the collar and he wasn't.

Arcanium was no stranger to Master and servant. It didn't necessarily make one less than the other. All they would see was that Neve kissed him, slid her tongue over his, shifted over his body like a woman who needed him. His erection pressed against her clit and her folds, and she trailed her fingers down his shirt then pulled it from the waist of his trousers. Locke hummed his pleasure when she reached beneath to take the head of his cock in her grip. He was human-like for now, less intimidating in size and less hot to the touch, though he still ran feverish in comparison to her.

He worked the button open and jerked down the zipper, allowing her to reach in farther and bring him out to stroke in full. Her undulating hips brushed the shaft with her metal-wrapped clit and the dark pink silk that Locke had gathered up to open her to him.

"Up," he said urgently, though any sense he was out of control was usually a ruse. He was only out of control when he chose to be, the one exception the moment he would come inside her. But his urgency spurred her own, and she lifted herself up, held his cock steady and brought herself down over him.

Despite the steady stream of sex from someone who considered her a valuable possession and nothing more, the way his cock felt so good entering her surprised her every time. She kept expecting it to get old. She kept expecting her feelings for the demon to get in the way of her ability to relish his body. She kept expecting him to tire of her. But as she encased him inside her, they both groaned, closing the distance together—Locke lifted his hips, and Neve let gravity bring her to the base and grind down, even though she knew nothing she did would satisfy her the way she satisfied him.

She guided his mouth back to hers, tasting him again without him having to ask or command, and she rode him without him having to tell her what he wanted. It was times like this, when she took initiative against her interests, that he rewarded her with his own enthusiasm.

In that sense, the Spider was wrong. Her desire and what she did with Locke to feed it still confused her, wrapped the gray matter of her brain in so many knots that she could barely think for the guilt and accusation. But she didn't fight it and neither did the Spider, although Neve didn't know what kind of struggle the other woman fought in her own head that made her avoid Neve's gaze after Locke finished with her.

Neve gave in to the lust for which he had chosen her, for which Bell had created her—and which the Lord in His wisdom had seen fit not to give her on His own until the fire-made creations of His plan had taken the matter into their own hands. She gave in, but that submission had always taken place in private before. The concrete and open space of the auditorium did nothing to muffle what they were doing. Their moans echoed back to them seconds after they were set loose, reverberating in her ears with their own stimulating effect.

Locke palmed her aching breast and gathered the flesh of her ass in his fingers, urging her faster. Her pleasure climbed, spiraled dizzyingly high, as though all she would have to do was reach the top and she'd be able to fall. He kept her that high, met her kiss with his own now. With such a short time before Arcanium opened, he had no reason to restrain his pleasure and no time to spare making the encounter last. Her sexual agony that followed would last long enough for the both of them. He could feed off that long after he'd achieved his own satisfaction.

For him, sex wasn't what it could be for people or for an incubus or succubus. Sex didn't seem a necessity. It was just another playground, and she was a delightful piece of equipment he could climb whenever he wanted. Like the best kind of leisure, he never tired. If he could, he'd go on forever and deny her all the while.

But the doors would open in twenty minutes, and he'd want to be ready before then. Locke grabbed her throat over the collar and held her close, held her still, stole her breath until her head spun as he came. A growl came from his chest, the sound so low she was sure no one else could hear it. She whined, the walls of her pussy clenching around him, but she couldn't push herself into her own orgasm. All she could push herself into was the needle-like lightning bolt pain that shot from the piercing in her clit to the flesh around him. And all he appeared to feel was pleasure.

He stood while he was still inside her, rolled her hips a few more times to milk the last of his orgasm from himself, then lifted her up and off to stand in front of him. The milky liquid that gleamed on his erection, a combination of his semen and her arousal, disappeared, leaving him clean so he could do up his trousers again. But though he usually cleaned her at the same time — or at least let her clean herself — he clicked his tongue and shook his head.

"When it comes out, don't stop it. You smell like sex, love. It's an intoxicating aphrodisiac when it meets your skin, my pleasure and yours together. I want them all to breathe it in."

"I hate you." The words held no rancor. Her hatred was simply a fact, the way the concrete compound beneath her feet was a fact.

He spanked her, a deafening crack that repeated through the room. Cheeks burning, she closed her eyes.

"I know," he whispered. He kissed her neck then took her leash again. "It's time."

With every prisoner they passed, Neve prickled with judgment and unfading, inexhaustive lust, and she shivered as Locke's semen dripped down her leg.

As demons and monsters entered the stadium to take their seats, Locke brought her out into the ring with him and indicated that she should kneel market the center mark at his feet. She did so, bowing her head slightly, but she kept her eyes open. If their relationship were more equal, he might have wanted her to close her eyes as well. But he knew how well she remembered things she saw, and he pored through her memories and feelings when it suited him. The more she could see, the more he could experience her fear, her anger, her curiosity, her disgust.

"Ladies and gentlemen, thank you for your patience as I work to establish this circus as more than a freakshow gallery and auction, delightful though they are. It is my pleasure to begin bringing the rest of Arcanium's glory to you. Allow my pretty things to please you and show their worth for your perusal. If you're fortunate, one of them may be yours by the end of the night."

The Ringmaster stood stone-faced and cageless at the edge of the ring, stroking the handle of his whip as though it were his cock.

Neve hadn't seen Kitty since Locke had delivered her into the Ringmaster's hands. For all Neve knew, he'd disposed of her, but she suspected he hadn't. Something like him wouldn't have grown attached to a woman like Kitty just to discard her after a month to do as he wished without restraint. If he loved her, he probably kept her where he lived, far from anyone's reach and far from being able to see what everyone else suffered. If the Ringmaster didn't love her, he could have done anything, but Neve didn't think Locke would have let him kill her. After all, he could still make money off her, and Neve had heard plenty of demons express an interest. In Locke's words, she was always 'unavailable'.

Something about the way he looked standing there next to Maya... But Maya glaring knives at Neve kept distracting her attention. In the cage twelve feet away, the Spider kept a wary eye on Maya, who'd soured toward her as well. Just as Neve understood why the rest of Arcanium hated her, though, she more or less understood why Maya hated her most.

"Without further ado, I present to you the master of our ceremonies, the legendary demon set free from Bell's shackles to become what he was always meant to be—the Ringmaster of Arcanium."

The spotlight found the Ringmaster, who unhooked his whip and sent the leather whirling with a quick-shot series of cracks as the music rose and the modified carousel descended from the scaffold to raucous, ecstatic applause.

The carousel's mounts were harnessed in rare style. Reins tethered them to the floor of the ride, the short length forcing them into a bow, but they strained their necks up to avoid the stiletto knives aimed at their throats to ensure perfect posture. The leather and their bodies had been oiled until they glistened.

The Ringmaster leaped onto the foundation then took his place on the grand pedestal at the center. He raised his whip to a new wave of cheers.

The carousel began to turn to the music. The reins loosened as the plugs and dildos pushed into the mounts and the poles holding the stilettos rose to make the mounts rise and fall in rhythm. The Ringmaster took his time turning in the opposite direction, surveying his options and allowing the audience to pick the one they most wanted beaten. Then he raised his whip again and brought it down in blinding, blurred succession, sending the lash in every direction.

When he was finished, though, the audience gave only a smattering of applause. The rest squinted in confusion. After at least two dozen cracks and blows of his whip, none of the mounts bled — not so much as a welt.

It took the mounts just as long as the audience to understand that he hadn't broken through skin, muscle or bone.

He'd broken through the reins.

Caroline was the first to stand, scrambling off what had impaled her and darting for the man in front of her to help him ease himself up as well.

"What—?" At the edge of the ring, Locke started forward, inadvertently jerking Neve onto her hands. But he was just as bewildered as the audience and the ones the Ringmaster had freed.

The music wavered then cut out, leaving only the murmur of the crowd and the people on the carousel.

"Did you really think you could hide Arcanium from me forever?"

Chapter Six

The lights switched on in the auditorium and Bell stepped out into an aisle. Not in any apparent rush or fear for his safety, he took his time coming down the stairs to the edge of the ring then vaulted over.

He looked tired but more or less like himself.

"You... You shouldn't be here." Locke's fist trembled around the leash, his knuckles white and nails digging furrows into his palm.

"Yes. You did make it difficult to find what no longer belonged to me, and leaving me weak and wasted behind you kept me from pursuing Arcanium as briskly as I would have otherwise. But eventually I gained enough power to find creatures who *did* know where Arcanium was." He reached into his pocket and pulled out a ticket. "Not in my name."

Locke looked up at the carousel's pedestal where the Ringmaster still stood, arms crossed over his chest and whip at the ready. "I gave you Kitty. I gave you anyone to torture at a moment's notice. Your immortal soul burns as pure black as mine. How could you choose him?"

"You gave what I wanted. Bell gives what I need," the Ringmaster said.

Locke pointed at Bell. "Hellfire and damnation, people, do I have to do all the work around here? He's right there and weakened. Do as you will."

Just as the audience realized the fight wasn't a spectator sport, Bell blocked the ring from anyone's entry. They struck empty air as though it was a concrete wall.

And with a flourish of Bell's hands, every single glass box shattered outward. Glass that could withstand bullets sprayed over the creatures on every floor. Only those in the boxes and under the dome of protection around the ring were spared.

Chaos erupted.

The weaker demons tried to flee, but the more furious ones leaped, flew, ran or teleported to the first floor to attack. Some tried to steal the prisoners from the shattered rooms for themselves, but every single door in the auditorium slammed shut except the doors to the lounge—until Lady Sasha and Lord Mikhail slammed it behind them. They were still harnessed and muzzled, but from three floors down, even Neve could tell they'd wreak their own havoc now that they had a chance.

"Oh no you don't." Locke yanked at the air.

All the cast members and golems in the auditorium swung toward the center as though Locke had retracted invisible chains attached to invisible hooks. Neve knew they were hooks, because all the bodies floating in the center of the room sprayed the forcefield and the audience with fine droplets of blood.

They hovered like slaughtered meat in an oval around the ring, clawing at their mouths.

Inside and outside the ring, muzzles and masks fell away to display skin stretching over lips like interlocking fingers. Even the twins, whose mouths had already been sewn shut and whose lips had been infected from the procedure but not permitted to deteriorate beyond a certain point, had the cord crisscrossing their mouths covered by skin.

Neve clutched at her own mouth, dug her nails in where the skin was still trying to meld together, but it pushed under her fingers and rose to the surface. She could barely part her teeth, couldn't push her tongue far enough through to shove against the layer of skin. It was smooth and thick under her fingers, like keloidal scar tissue.

Locke's chuckle broadened into a laugh that filled the auditorium. The demons around them joined him, even though they were still picking glass shrapnel from their flesh.

"You lost Arcanium fair and square." Locke strode around the carousel, dragging Neve behind him as she struggled to stand from her hands and knees. "Look at you. You're already tiring. You don't have nearly enough power to face me. If you aren't prepared to leave Arcanium to the victor with some dignity, then you'll be a part of her again—at my behest. That's what you did with the other demons who tried to take the circus for themselves, wasn't it?" He kicked out at the ribs of Colm, who had half-collapsed on the carousel.

Caroline crawled to him as he doubled over, still impaled, bleeding.

"Welcome to Arcanium, Bell." Locke snapped his fingers.

Bell stumbled backward as though kicked by a horse. He clutched at his chest, which had been divested of his shirt and replaced with a complicated leather harness that showed off the heavy gold rings inserted in his nipples. They were connected by a thin but sturdy chain to rings in his nose.

Locke had stripped his leather trousers away as well, caging his cock in a golden chastity belt and prepping his ankles, wrists and neck with gold shackles. The demons who had committed themselves to the fight cheered and howled with laughter to see the once venerable Bell humiliated.

"No one else gets you first, Bell. You're all mine tonight." Locke hauled Neve to her feet, confident enough to be casual. "Maybe I'll strap something onto her so she can fuck you, too. Another on Lizzie, and we'll finally have a party."

Bell shrugged in discomfort, but he didn't appear nearly as humiliated as Neve would have been in the same ensemble. "You know, you look familiar. You're one of our regulars, aren't you? You followed Arcanium across the country. You attended Funhouse events. You favored the Spider, but you were the one to choose Neve at her first Funhouse. I couldn't even *remember* you until now. Is that how you were able to sabotage Arcanium? By camouflaging yourself? By using the gaps in my sight to hide right in front of me?" He clicked his tongue, shaking his head. "Clever, clever. But your soul is unmistakable now. You'll never be able to hide from me again, Locke."

"I don't need to hide anymore. Do you think that because I took my time, because I took Arcanium by trickery rather than brute force, that I must be weak? You tangled Arcanium so tightly around itself, a demon can only take it by snatching it away when you're not looking. I'm not weaker than all the other demons. I'm smarter and I'm stronger. How many can hide themselves from your sight without tripping a single alarm, without triggering the protections you set around Arcanium — far more solid than the flickering shield you just forged?"

And it *was* flickering. Neve couldn't see it, but blood kept dripping through like intermittent rain.

"You came here too weak, Bell. You came because the pain of your people called you here too soon, and now you won't be able to save them. You'll only join them, the crown jewel of my collection. You've lost everything, and all because you loved them too much."

The skin around Bell's mouth crept together like the rest of the cast, but he brushed it away with a swipe of his hand. "For a demon with such power in his words, you talk too much."

"For a demon in need of a wish for his power, you're without another mouth to make it." Laughing, Locke lifted Neve's chin and kissed her where her lips would be. "You used your own wishes long ago, tied them into this circus like a fool."

He stopped laughing when the Ringmaster's whip cracked against his cheek, striking a line under the bone. The Ringmaster's eyes had filled to the brim, darker than the darkest black that science had discovered. From beneath the Ringmaster's boots, black smoke billowed and curled, sweeping down from his pedestal to the carousel mounts, most of whom had had their mouths closed around the bits or around the rings that had been pierced through their cheeks. The Ringmaster didn't need his mouth. He rarely spoke outside the ring, and his power—whatever it was—didn't need words.

"Would you steal them, these animals you betray me to save, into your hell just to get at me??" Locke tossed Neve's leash to the side and nudged her away with his leg, dismissing her to deal with more pressing matters, which didn't include flaunting her.

The Ringmaster nodded in reply.

"You would put them through your most terrible pain to include me among their number? If you think that ash cloud is enough to ensnare me, you're sorely mistaken."

He tore the whip away with his magic and wrapped it around the Ringmaster's neck instead, lifting him from the pedestal to bring him into the air with the others. He, too, was stripped and clothed instead in humiliation—a lacy pink tutu and a tiara accompanied the slave rings and chastity belt.

Demons' claws pierced through the shield, giving way to arms reaching in to spread the openings wider.

"Bell!" The same as with Lord Mikhail, Neve couldn't tell if she'd reached him until he responded.

"He has too much of Arcanium wrapped around him. And I don't have enough of my own power to draw upon. I need a wish. He's taken most of them away from me."

"I wish you had the power to take Arcanium back, then!"

He grinned humorlessly, his brow furrowed as he concentrated intently on the faltering shield. *"Believe me, many of mine are wishing through their minds. It doesn't work. Like Locke, I need words, not thoughts. I need a wish."*

"What now, Bell? Cheap illusionist tricks? Are you going to pull a dove out of my pocket to take back your circus?" With the Ringmaster taken care of, Locke strode straight to Bell, striking him with more power than a fist should hold. Bell flew backward and crashed into his shield, which sent a new torrent of blood rain onto the concrete. It smeared over him as he struggled to stand. But the chastity belt and the chains between his nipples and nose disappeared. He still wore the harness and rings, but he conjured his trousers back, regaining at least some of his dignity. Also, the chains would be highly impractical in a fight.

Bell ran at Locke. Their powers clashed like two blades of flint, sending sparks everywhere. But this time, both of them were thrown back. Blood soaked Locke's white shirt and splattered over Bell. If Bell could land a blow, it meant the scales hadn't automatically tipped in Locke's favor. The fury in Locke's expression at Bell's small victory galvanized Neve.

Bell needed words. Just like Locke needed her to say her promises aloud, Bell needed people to say 'wish'. What that meant for mute people wasn't important right now, although her brain nonsensically dwelled on the question as a kind of ward against her deepening despair.

Bell needed words, but Locke had taken their mouths.

Neve darted her gaze around. Her first thought was of the Spider, but some of the demons who had made headway through the shield were pulling her hair and arms. Even if the Spider had thought of the same thing, she was indisposed, clawing at whatever demon flesh she could. Maya, Valorie, Seth and Lars — nothing, not so much as a wicked heel, since the rest of the cast was kept barefoot like her. The clowns were just as harassed as the Spider, and Neve wasn't sure how intelligent they were.

The smoke still spilled from the Ringmaster like an indoor storm cloud, though its growth had stagnated as the Ringmaster struggled to breathe. The leather was slicing through his neck. If it kept tightening like that, it was going to burst arteries and cut through to the bone, perhaps even severing his spine. In myths, beheading was usually one of the few effective ways to kill something immortal. Whether decapitation would kill him or just incapacitate him, the end was functionally the same — removing the Ringmaster from the equation and leaving only a weakened Bell to resist.

Misha no longer swallowed swords, and the implement room for the whipped men and women was on the outside the forcefield. Besides, there were too many demons between her and weapons for the idea to be of any use.

That left...the carousel.

The smoke that still clung to it had obscured the most germane weapons in the ring — the stiletto knives that had kept the mounts' heads up in their subservient position. She ran for the carousel then leaped onto it. The extension of her legs pulled the piercing in her clitoris and possibly tore something, but she'd distract herself soon enough. Above her skin muzzle, Caroline looked confused, angry and hurt, but as Neve knelt in front of the knife that Caroline had left behind, her eyes widened in understanding.

The knife's point pressed against the keloid. It was her own skin, with nerve endings like any other part of her. She could work a scalpel in a pinch, but a stiletto wasn't quite the same, and she'd be using it on herself.

If she thought about it too long, she wasn't going to do it at all. Pressing a hand between her thighs to use the clit piercing to her advantage, she waited for the first sharp pang of metal disturbing organ before pushing her mouth against the blade. The tip of the blade hit one of her teeth, possibly cracking it, and scraped up into her gum, but it went through.

She screamed as she sawed her own mouth over the blade. Halfway through, the force of her scream helped thin the muzzle, and the blade cut through to the other corner of her mouth. Blood spilled down her chin and dripped onto the carousel floor, but the skin muzzle didn't grow back.

Neve spat out a mouthful of her blood and turned back to where Bell and Locke fought, mingling magic with physical blows, a mixture of all the martial arts and artless violence they'd accumulated in their immortal lives. If Locke saw her like this, he wouldn't let her get another chance.

"Bell!"

With Bell distracted from Neve's shout in his head, Locke struck him across the face with his knuckles, the crack painful to hear, as loud as the Ringmaster's whip. But as Bell stumbled, he twisted toward her.

"I wish Bell had the power to take Arcanium back!" She screamed as loudly as she could, screamed to fill the stadium, though blood gurgled through the last word. Even if she'd lost it, Bell could work with the rest of the wording. It didn't need to be complicated. She was wishing for something Bell already wanted.

Locke whirled around, human face contorting with the emerging demon. Neve cowered. His fury was darker than the Ringmaster's cloud, more terrible than every single time he'd entered her without magic combined, so frightening that she forgot all her pain, because he was worse.

He howled like a hurricane around her, shrieks entering her ears like needles, as though the slowly tightening silver in her body was also trying to pierce into her brain. "You think that wins him Arcanium? Your goddamned whore's wish? I still have your word, Neve! But you won't have another one."

Locke was halfway through tearing her tongue out when he suddenly whipped around, all human guise eliminated, larger than life at his full height.

The Ringmaster fell from his terrible height. All the Arcanium cast and crew did.

They didn't hit the ground.

Bell lowered them gently, saving them from broken bones.

Her tongue stitched back together, and her mouth stopped hurting quite as much. The torn skin muzzle fell away from her face, only the parts of her own mouth she'd cut through bleeding now — though he hadn't removed the skin muzzles from anyone else in the auditorium. Perhaps the amount of blood pouring from her mouth had concerned him. She was cold and dizzy, but that didn't matter much now.

If Bell couldn't win even with a wish, she could stand to get colder.

But demons all around the shield who had made it part of the way through suddenly screamed louder than her, because the pieces of their bodies that had crossed the barrier flopped onto the floor, suddenly severed.

Locke swiped his long demon claws at Bell. They cut through his abdomen like scalpels, tearing through organs. Bell clutched at his intestines and fell to his knees.

The forcefield fell. What was left of the blood poured down on them like a horror movie.

"No!" In spite of the chill shaking through her, the pain in her mouth and the silver that continued to tighten around her nipples and clit, Neve pulled herself in a half-crawl, half-drag to the Ringmaster, who was unconscious but still breathing. She unwound the whip from his neck.

"I have all the protections you wove into Arcanium's web, plus my own," Locke snarled. "You have her wish, but I have her word, and I am still the more powerful of the two of us, because I know what I am and you deny."

"I deny?" Bell's voice was soft, yet it carried. The demons clambering over the side of the ring froze. "I deny what I am? I was born of fire well before hell spat you into existence, millennia before you stepped foot on Earth. I watched humans crawl from caves to build their edifices. I watched their imaginations grow like an ancient oak, branching out into a tree as wide as the world, despite every effort of so many jinn to tear the branches down. If it weren't for their imaginations, we wouldn't dream as broadly as we do. Without their fears, we wouldn't know how to bring them low. Without their weakness, we wouldn't revel in our power. I learned what I was before you first laid a hand on a cowering being to feel it tremble."

Bell staggered to his feet. And as he stood, he, too, began to grow. The slashes through his abdomen filled in, built new skin that showed no trace of the wounds. The new skin started gray, but as the gray spread over the rest of his torso, it richened into a powdery blue. Like Locke, he shed his clothing. The harness snapped and fell away. The piercings dropped to the floor like coins. He'd been fit before, in a lean way, but while Locke was slender, even insectile in his demon form, Bell transformed into something more akin to Mikhail as the strongman, barrel-chested and wrapped in muscle that almost broke bones just to look at it. His short, curly auburn hair went so black that it shone blue and gathered behind his head in a tail.

He was as tall as Locke now — and bigger — but Locke had a longer reach and claws and teeth where Bell appeared more human. But despite the human-like features, Neve couldn't look at him and see human. He was more *there* than she was. If most of the universe was empty space between atoms, looking at him was like looking at less empty space than any other being she'd ever seen. Her mind rebelled at the sight, made him make sense as well as it could, but she thought she might see him most accurately in her peripheral vision.

"I am jinn, with fire and water flowing through my veins, and you are nothing but a worm. To live among them, I chose my limitations. But only a fool believes me to be the sum of those limitations, which I can shed whenever I please."

Bell swept all the cast from the carousel. They rolled onto the concrete like tumbleweeds. Then he grabbed the carousel by its edge and hurled it at Locke. The metal and wooden contraption had to weigh at least a ton, but he handled it as though it were a metal discus. With the shield firmly in place again, the carousel was too big for Locke to evade. It struck him with the force of a semi, sending him across the ring. The carousel screeched and gouged the concrete, the wooden parts and the additions to the foundation cracking off to scatter in every direction. The Spider shouted through her skin muzzle as the carousel pushed Locke into her cage, bending the metal.

Neve had no time to check if she was all right, if anyone was. She spat out more blood, and tested her tongue, which still felt like someone had tried to pull it like taffy. Her cold limbs trembled, but survival instinct kept her moving. If she managed to survive, she would pay for it.

She went for the broken pieces of metal scattered on the ring floor that still held stilettos, grabbing one in each hand. Each metal piece was a different size, and one had been bent at an almost ninety-degree angle, but they worked as makeshift spears. She scrambled to the edge of the ring, out of the way of the god and monster flinging large things at each other.

Locke shoved the carousel away from him. It hurtled back toward Bell, who proceeded to rip the rest of it into fragments while it still hovered above them. Locke gave a howling shriek then ran at Bell with speed his body shouldn't have been capable of.

They clashed in the middle, power meeting power, muscle meeting muscle, tooth and claw meeting foot and fist. The force of their blows nearly deafened her. When they missed and struck concrete, it cracked as though jackhammered for hours. They sent pieces of the carousel at each other until they each looked like victims of an airplane crash, carousel shrapnel sticking out of their bodies. But minimal blood spilled, skin stitching around the wounds and pushing the metal out.

When two apparently invincible immortals fought, how could one achieve a victory?

Neve learned how when their energy began to flag and the cut of claws and teeth didn't heal as fast as the wounds made by metal — something about being struck by another jinni rather than something manmade, perhaps. Bell landed his blows, but Locke could reach him more easily, and his thinner physique allowed him to avoid more of Bell's attempts. However, he moved as though Bell's blows were beginning to take an internal toll — not a permanent one, perhaps, but impermanent internal bleeding and broken bones appeared to have slowed him down.

Even so, Locke finally managed to knock Bell flat on his back. Kneeling over him, he slashed at Bell's chest, sank his teeth deep into Bell's shoulder. They'd forgotten all about the rest of the Arcanium cast — small, puny creatures in comparison, unworthy of sparing a thought.

The carousel mounts were huddled at the side of the ring next to Valorie's cage. If any of them was saying anything to Bell in his mind, she couldn't hear it. She was the only one with a weapon, and she was the only one with a voice. And she only had one wish left. Despair threatened to sink her to the ground — because if a wish wasn't enough for Bell to gain Arcanium back, what use would another wish be?

The sound that Bell made when Locke bit through his skull was that of a dying elephant. Neve couldn't stand paralyzed with indecision forever, and Bell wasn't going to make it much longer — if the battle wasn't already lost.

She took a running leap at Locke, using her weight to add extra force and hoping it was enough to pierce his tough hide. The two stiletto knives plunged into him, one in his back and the other in his side. The blows weren't deep. The blades were barely four inches long, but they were wide, and they had penetrated his body when she hadn't expected them to.

Locke whipped around, his claws extended as he slashed down at her. Neve stumbled back, clutching at her eye, where new pain exploded through her nervous system like a hand grenade. The gash went from her forehead to the corner of her mouth. Vitreous humor spilled between her fingers with the blood. To add insult to injury, the small part of her brain not occupied with the fire lancing through her face noted that Locke hadn't been affected at all by the pinpricks of the stiletto blades in his body.

With his gaze on hers through her one good eye, he took Bell's crushed head and twisted. Snapping a demigod's neck sounded like snapping anyone's — loud and small at the same time.

He stalked her on the ring floor, muscles rippling. The makeshift spears stuck out of him like spines, as seemingly insignificant to him as splinters.

"When I am through with you, you'll think you've been in my hell your whole life. You'll scream your vocal cords out of your throat. You'll beg me to fuck you then beg to die. I'll never let you sleep. You'll have to live this day as your nightmare for the rest of your pathetic span. Did you think this would stop me, Neve? Did you think it would even harm me? Have you not yet learned that I *am* pain?" He yanked the stilettos from his back, flung them to the side then raked his own claws across his chest. "Nothing you do can stop me, stupid human slut. The pain you feel? The pain you give? It is all pleasure to me. And I'll ensure all pleasure for you is pain."

She couldn't hope to get away from him. He was too fast, even at his slow stalking speed, and there was nowhere to go. Pragmatism won out over instinct.

At the moment she stopped trying to escape, he spread his glittering, serrated grin and crawled over her. "Thank you again, my dear. Without you, I would never have proven to everyone how much Arcanium is truly mine. For that reason alone will I allow you any pleasure at all."

He ran his tongue up the gash in her face, gathering blood and eye with it. She could feel him burning in the socket.

"Neve…"

The voice was faint, but the fact that there was a voice at all was a miracle. She glimpsed him under Locke's arm, chest rising and falling. The sunken portion of his head pushed out. He was healing, but slowly. One blue eye fixed on her.

"I wish I could hurt you as badly as you hurt me," she whispered, "make you feel pain the way it's supposed to be felt."

Locke's smile fell. He narrowed his eyes, but he curled his lips from his teeth and reared back to strike her belly.

"Good girl. Use your words. They've always had the power."

"Get away from me, you filthy, disgusting, degrading piece of shit." Obscenity had never come naturally to her, but if ever there was a being it was made for, it was Locke.

And to her surprise—although she didn't know why she was surprised—he reeled back, falling away from her and wrenching away from nothing, as though she'd come at him with hands full of claws. There weren't marks, but he gasped, twisted, the pure confusion on his face almost sad as he searched for what made him feel what he was feeling, which he'd clearly never felt before.

Pain, the way it was meant to be felt.

"You sorry sack of vomit. You violating, raping hell trash." Once she got started, the words came faster. Every last thing she'd kept tidy and tucked away in her brain when she would have gained nothing by saying it aloud now spilled over her blood-slicked tongue. With every word, he shrieked, a beast with bear traps closing down on him from all sides. Instead of a predator, he sounded like a rabbit caught in a coyote's mouth.

"If you think I'm pathetic, you're nothing but a scum-sucking jackal, mangy with disease and pustules bursting all over your body from the parasites. You think you're a demigod? You think you're a big, strong demon, taking over Arcanium and pounding Bell to a pulp? You think you're something special now that all the other demons envy you for what you stole? As though there's any honor in a fox taking the eggs from the henhouse while everyone's asleep…"

The skin around her mouth tried to creep back together, her lips sticking like cling wrap. But she bent down to pick up one of the knives he'd pulled out of himself and cut through the skin again, screaming but determined.

And when Neve screamed, Locke screamed.

She kept the knife but started throwing small bits of carousel shrapnel at him as he scrambled back like a giant crab on the concrete.

"Look at you, the big man, mastering all these humans and a handful of demons and monsters. You thought you were like Bell, but better. You thought you were making Arcanium something purer. But Bell was a collector. Flawed, with evil and good and chaos in his intentions, he took your dungeon and turned it into something different. He made a freak show of your torture chamber to elevate the strange, thriving when freak shows all over the world are struggling and dying. And what do you do?"

Locke rolled on the ground, batting at his body, scratching through his skin. He no longer tried to block the metal she threw at him. She yelled between his shrieks.

"You take his precious, painstakingly curated collection and make Arcanium just another dungeon, just another hell, as though the world or the underworld needed another. You can dress it up in a circus costume, and you can put metal and leather and lace on it, but you're no great man, no devoted collector, no matter how you try to be. You're just another pimp, and your Arcanium's no better than a trafficking brothel." She crouched down to make sure he could see her as she spat in his face. "You're not some grand Master. You're just like any human who needs to subjugate anything weaker to make himself feel powerful—and that isn't power at all. For all your size, your strength, your invincibility, your immortality, you're just another small, evil man."

Locke flailed, catching her across the head, but before she could fall, Bell caught her. Though his giant form had been pristine when he'd begun the battle with Locke, he appeared much worse for the wear—but not as bad as he had been.

"And now he has your word," Bell murmured, cradling her head for a moment. "Thank you, Neve. I can take him from here."

"Ridden bitch!" Locke tried to lunge for her from the floor.

She lunged right back out of Bell's arms, screaming to send him screaming away again. She kept going until her throat went raw and crackling, though he was so much louder than her that she barely knew it. She kept screaming until he'd diminished into the human man at her feet, his beauty unmarred but his natural appearance of strength gone as he writhed.

Then her voice went out and she fell to her knees, the silence between them abrupt and broken only by their gasps for breath.

"You'll regret this," he rasped. "You will yearn for me for the rest of your life. I will haunt you with every touch."

Neve grabbed one of the pieces of metal next to them and gave one last, soundless cry as she stabbed it into Locke's mouth, entering his skull through the soft palate with a wet crunch like a smashed melon.

He twitched then went still.

But he wasn't dead. She knew better.

Bell lifted her back onto her feet and turned her away from Locke as though that would eliminate the image, as though it wasn't branded into her like the rest.

He raised his eyes to the demons around the ring. Then he took down the shield.

The demons ran.

The human cast of Arcanium was still weak, struggling to stand while not being attacked, trampled or stolen by one of the fleeing demons, but the Arcanium demons had recovered enough. Without electric shocks to stop him, Lennon had become the Cthulhuian nightmare. Ciarán lumbered like a mammalian dinosaur. And Lady Sasha and Lord Mikhail were bringing people to their knees with desire, the emanations from them the final surreal assault. Neve closed her eyes, pain burning like a heat lamp behind her eyes, the trembling in her limbs becoming impossible to endure.

"Did any of you really believe that I would allow you to escape?" Bell asked, amplifying his voice as Locke had.

Neve twitched reflexively, afraid for a moment that the deep voice was Locke's rather than Bell's.

Every single light in the stadium went out. In the darkness, Neve felt like she was falling, though the ground stayed solid under her feet—as though the entire stadium was on some kind of elevator taking the Arcanium dungeon straight to the hell Locke had wanted to make it.

The lights came back on. Streetlights. They were standing in a giant parking lot, empty except for the cast lying on the ground and the golems, who stood and looked around aimlessly, which was as close as they could get to confusion.

The cast groaned as they eased themselves up from the far rougher concrete, bleeding from the places they'd been hung or pierced or impaled or amputated. Underfed, exhausted, beaten, broken, destroyed, climbing up on their own was beyond some of their abilities. When another could help, they did, but sometimes helping was too much as well. The ones that Locke had strengthened in order to let them perform were the first to their feet.

Neve blinked, taking in her surroundings in snapshots — the golems, the parking lot, the darkness beyond the cones of hazy light. She wasn't a hundred percent sure she wasn't hallucinating. But when she stepped away from Bell, she fell and hit her knees on the concrete, scraping the skin. The blood from the gash through her eye dripped onto her hands.

There was a sidewalk path at the end of the large parking lot. It led to another parking lot. This one had a full collection of cars and other vehicles, most of them luxurious jewels in the distance. The pathway had once led from the stadium to the parking lot. But now the Arcanium circus stadium was gone. Just…gone.

"What? What? What?"

From underneath Ciarán's great bulk, a small man with rubbery green skin clambered out, wide-eyed and spinning as he tried to orient himself. He bled a darker green from a cut on his head. Neve didn't recognize him as cast or crew, which meant he must have been either another prisoner or one of the demonic guests. Small though he was, Neve knew better than to assume he wasn't dangerous or evil.

"Stop fluttering." Bell was a totem in the darkness, a limned shadow with arms crossed as he stared down at the frantic demon.

"Where did everything go? What did you do? Fekking bastard…"

"I told you to stop."

The demon paused midstride, not just paralyzed but frozen in the moment. He should have fallen, but he didn't. The demon's eyes were the only thing not frozen, wide and white as they rolled in their sockets.

"Every last one of you who came to the false Arcanium for your own condemned appetites are complicit in Locke's crime. Your friends, your sadistic compatriots, are here." Bell gestured to his feet, where an antiqued trunk appeared. The latch flipped open and the lid rose to reveal a collection of crystals, geodes and semi-precious stones. "Imprisoned forever, or until I deem it time for them to be destroyed. Everyone needs to know that Arcanium is not for the taking and that anyone who tries shall fail. Arcanium is mine, and the people in this circus are protected."

"Why spare me?" The demon had to work to speak, but Bell permitted him a voice.

Bell slowly stepped around the trunk then crouched in front of the demon to bring himself to his level. "Someone needs to spread the word. May knives pierce your feet until every demon plagued with envy and conquest knows to never touch Arcanium again. *Go*."

When Bell released him from his paralysis, the demon stumbled, shrieking every time his feet hit the ground.

Bell took him by the back of the neck and flung him toward the pathway. "Run!" he bellowed.

The prospect of facing an angry, possessive jinni overwhelmed whatever pain lanced through the demon's soles. He staggered for the full parking lot.

Bell's shoulders slumped. He lowered his head, closed his eyes. The jinni receded, becoming human, easier for Neve to look at in terms of reality, but harder as well.

The winter night was quiet, too cold for birds or insects. The late traffic from the city around them sounded like water rather than civilization.

The Spider came up behind Neve. She had a perforation in her abdomen from the bent cage bars, but she was walking and had enough strength to help Neve back to her feet, so it couldn't have been life-threatening. The Spider winced, hissing through her teeth, when she saw the mess of Neve's face up close. Neve trembled and nearly fell again. Mentally, she was numb. Shock had been setting in for a while, and it was no surprise it assaulted her now, weaving her in and out of consciousness with her eyes still open.

"Please, come help her," the Spider called, not to Bell but to the Creature, whose wings had been torn into uselessness, his face bleeding from the metal muzzle that had been latched onto him. He was thinner, paler, like a vampire rather than a gargoyle, and his red eyes glowed. He stumbled to the Spider then wrapped his arms around her like he would crush her in his embrace. The Spider held his head as he buried his mouth against her neck.

Neve didn't know how the Spider could stand to be held, to be touched, but she let her head fall back, peace settling over her drawn face like a caul. It didn't last once the Creature had withdrawn, but the furrows that had become permanent fixtures over the Spider's brows had smoothed away at least, even when pain returned.

"Help her," the Spider whispered, guiding his head toward Neve.

"I can't heal her. Bell…"

"That's not the pain I know you can spare her from. Please, give her a moment."

"I'll have more than enough to feed upon now, with the muzzle gone." The Creature lowered himself to his knees in front of Neve. When he brought his hand to her cheek, a tender gesture, she flinched.

It was as though she knew she finally could. All this time, she'd succumbed to every touch that Locke had set upon her. Played her part. Became his slave. But now she could show the fear that had been there all along, the utterly rational fear that had made her choose him in the first place.

A growl rolled over her from behind. Neve jerked around, collapsing to the concrete at the sight of Lord Mikhail in a crouch—an animal protecting its own from her response to the Creature. But Neve crawled away from both. Lord Mikhail was still emanating, the waves raw enough that she didn't think he realized he still was doing it. He would be as starved as the Creature, as desperate. But if he followed her now, she thought she might lose what meager sanity she'd managed to preserve.

"Neve..." Mikhail lowered himself, concealing his teeth again, his posture softening from the predatory.

"I'm not going to hurt her. She's terrified, as well she should be," the Creature said. "I can take her fear. I can drink the poison from her blood. The wound will not bleed so much if her heartbeat slows."

"Bell should heal her first," Mikhail said. "She's cold."

"Bell has his hands full."

Neve looked past the concentrated chaos that seemed to have amassed itself around her. Bell was going from person to person to tend to whatever atrocities and grotesqueries Locke had inflicted. More than one flinched from him the way Neve had from the Creature.

Carlo's arms appeared from the infected amputations he'd been given. As soon as he could walk his usual way, Carlo went to Misha, who was bleeding from his mouth and nose, coughing up thick blood. Bell touched Misha's forehead like a faith healer. Misha fell back against Carlo in visible relief, and when he breathed out again, blood didn't accompany the air.

Seth and Lars had already been separated from each other for the night's performance. They'd immediately darted for Joanne and Jane, who were catatonic on the ground. Bell restored their conjoined status to the base of their spine rather than a shared brain and removed the buttons from their eyes and the thread from their mouths, but they didn't stop staring in their opposite directions, the backs of their heads still pressed against each other. Distress wrote itself across Bell's features, but he had to keep going.

Kitty, who looked as untouched as at the beginning when Locke had given her to the Ringmaster, knelt at the Ringmaster's side. The deep gouge around his neck was already healing. He was well enough to rip from his body the clothes that Locke had given to humiliate him — well enough to care.

The men and women from the carousel were next. Bell went to Colm first. Colm tried to push him away, but Bell gripped him by the wrists until Colm gave a sigh and closed his eyes, slumping to the side. Caroline willingly held her hand up for Bell to take, beckoned for Bell to tend to Riley next and the others after.

Neve didn't doubt that, under other circumstances, Bell would be able to reverse Locke's changes in a matter of thoughts, but he was weary, too — so weary that he was tending to the worst of the damage and not the entirety. There were still holes where rings and hooks had been, cuts where muzzles and shackles had been attached to skin. Anything superficial was left behind.

The fire-eater, John, still shook as though in seizure long after Bell had spared him the worst of having burned off most of his own face, including his lips, eyes and tongue. Bell restored him to the scarred man he'd been, and when John exhaled, spewing fire without any control, it didn't burn him again.

Neve fell back, striking the concrete. It wasn't that she was dying. She didn't think she was dying. She just couldn't convince herself to get up. She stared at the sky, a black mass whose stars the streetlights obscured.

"Neve?" Mikhail came closer, not reaching for her, not touching her, but arousal shuddered through her anyway. She could only cry from the one eye, although what was left of the other one tried — like trying to pass glass through a tear duct.

"Stay away. Stay away from me," she whispered, the only sound she could manage.

"Mikhail, I don't think it's a good idea to be near her right now," the Spider said.

"I don't blame her for what happened. I'm not angry with her. I would *never* hurt her."

"You *are* hurting her. It's your magic. If I can feel it, she can feel it twice as much."

"I'm sorry, Neve. I didn't come to demand anything of you. I'm starving, but I'll try." He inhaled slowly. The power of the sex magic hitting her receded, but it didn't disappear.

"Mikhail, we shouldn't." Lady Sasha came up behind him, placing her hand on his shoulder. "We shouldn't be this close to any of them."

"I can't leave her."

"You can't hold your magic back as much as she needs while we're like this. We need to get away from them."

Mikhail shook his head, his hair sticking in the places the muzzle had been inserted into his face, just like the Creature. "She's dying."

"Bell won't let her," Lady Sasha said, meeting Neve's eyes. "We're making things worse. Come with me, away from them, until we renew our strength. That is how we may best help her."

"No," he rasped. He hovered his hand over her gashed face, but when he realized he couldn't even touch her without causing her more distress and pain, he finally allowed Lady Sasha to pull him back.

Neve wouldn't let herself watch him leave.

"Should I get Bell?" the Creature asked, torn between wanting to feed on her fear and keeping his distance.

"No." Icicles trembled through the Spider's response. "Let him finish. He's avoiding her for a reason, just like he's avoiding Maya."

"Is that true, Bell?" Maya, like Valorie and Seth and Lars, had already been healed enough to perform, so Bell hadn't needed to go to her first, although it must have killed him not to go straight to her immediately, regardless of the tension between them. With so many distractions, Neve hadn't noticed her, but she'd fixed her attention on Neve. She clutched her knees as tightly to her chest as she could, her expression fury set in cold stone.

Bell, who had been holding Christina as he healed her, passed her to Troy to keep her from the rough concrete. Neve hadn't known he was capable of regret, but he moved with weight that his previous size and density hadn't imposed upon him.

When Maya let go of her legs and stood, the Spider broke away from the Creature and put herself between Maya and Neve, curling her fingers to prepare her claws.

Maya scoffed. "She made her choice, and I made mine. We both had to live with our decisions. I've been angry as hell, but as far as I'm concerned, she did what she needed to tonight. Practical to the end, I guess. She fought when she had a chance. That's better than a coward to me."

"You can't begin to understand—" the Spider began.

"I think you'd be surprised," Maya said.

"You're only okay with her now because she fought back. You don't understand that there was never a choice. Locke wanted both of us because he could use sex as a double-edged sword, use our willing submission as his weapon. He wanted us because whether under him alone or whether tossed out into a gangbang free-for-all, no matter how it hurt or how we hated it, we'd still come—and why shouldn't he keep that all to himself?"

Bell silently passed Maya, avoiding her gaze. He stared at Neve as though to fix the image of her there on the ground to his memory, although she'd never known him to have trouble with memory before.

Maya grabbed his shoulder at the same time the Spider held both of her left arms out to keep him from getting closer to Neve.

"But the thing is, Maya," the Spider continued, "I was like this before I came into Arcanium. That's why I had to stay with him, because I knew I could endure it. But Bell brought Neve in and made her like me, gave her this goddamn curse, too. It took me a while, though, to realize why he modeled her after me in particular when he could have modeled her after you, after Caroline or could have made her something new. He made her like me—and in many ways worse—*because* I'm the one Locke came for first. So tell us the truth, Bell. You made her just as helpless of a nymphomaniac then put her out there new and raw and never told her you brought her in as bait."

Neve sat up. Bell remained steady. He didn't turn away, didn't blink, didn't fidget, but he also didn't deny.

Maya let go of Bell as though he burned her. "You knew this was going to happen. I kept telling myself that the reason it did was because this was one of the things you couldn't know. But you *knew* he was going to do this and you let him take us anyway. You let him…"

Maya couldn't finish the thought. She covered her mouth with one hand then stumbled to the side, pulled her hair out of the way and threw up, retching well after she'd emptied what little had been in her stomach to begin with.

Bell tried to help her up but she slapped his hand away.

"He put Neve out there to lure Locke in, and he had the Ringmaster as his inside man," the Spider continued. "So now you know, Maya. This whole time you've blamed Neve, maybe because it was easier to hate her. But if you want to hate the one who did this to us, you shouldn't look any further than your boyfriend. He's the one who brought us into Arcanium, most of us against our wills or through deceit. He's the one who didn't protect us when he promised to. And he's the one who put an innocent woman on the slab as meat for the beast."

"Is that true?" Maya searched Bell's face, searched his eyes as though she could see into his mind the way he could see into hers. "Did you do this?"

"I didn't know what he would do," Bell said.

Maya punched him square in the mouth, much harder than before.

He spat blood. If they'd had to put their sacrifice on the altar, it only seemed right that he add his own.

Shrieking like a falcon, Maya punched him again and again. A crack signaled something in her hand breaking. She held it to her stomach and used her other arm and hand like a club instead, pummeling his face and the back of his head. When her arm grew tired, she started kicking him. If she'd still had parts of the carousel to grab, Neve had no doubt she would have made more of a dent in Bell's hide than Locke had.

Bell did nothing to stop her, and neither did anyone else, human or demon. Maya beat him down onto the concrete and he let her.

When he finally raised his arms to block the blows, she staggered backward. Then she stretched her broken hand away from her abdomen and flexed the fingers. He'd rendered it like new. She started to punch him again, but he rolled away and raised himself back to his feet.

Bell stood there with the wounds that Maya had inflicted — cracked teeth, swelling eyelids, broken nose, bruises, scratches over his chest. But it didn't seem to bother him more than the regret in his eyes, and that might have been why Maya didn't go after him again, although she kept her bruised fists clenched.

"I couldn't see him," he said through a swollen lip that slowly subsided. "He'd done something to hide himself from me. I knew after he breached the haunted funhouse and set my prisoners free without repercussion that I had to prepare for the worst — a demon who could disguise himself from my sight, who lived in my blind spots and who had the power to unravel the spells I'd woven through the circus. I couldn't see a future for Arcanium. I can't tell you how that terrified me, not knowing the fate of something so vital to me — and knowing that the fact it is vital was the reason I could not see."

"You sat there and you planned for a demon to come after Arcanium," Maya said. "You fucking roped the Ringmaster into it, so he knew it was coming, too. He knew he had to pretend to be on Locke's side when it happened."

Now the Ringmaster joined them, naked as Adam, with Kitty holding his hand but otherwise staying out of the argument, which didn't seem characteristic. Perhaps she'd already reached a similar conclusion as the Spider.

"I tried to protect her," the Ringmaster said to Bell. "I asked for her. But though he indulged my weakness for Kitty, I could not convince him that Maya's compliance for pain would justify my saving her."

"That's not the point!" Maya shouted. "What about the rest of them, Bell? It was okay for the rest of them to go to hell as long as Kitty and me were safe? What about Valorie? What about the Spider? And what about the ones you never had any kind of relationship with? They're just *supposed* to suffer?"

"There has never been anything, demon or jinn, capable of conquering Arcanium before," Bell said. By now, most of the damage Maya had done to him had faded, which did nothing for Maya's mood. "I caught and captured every one of them. Those I didn't destroy, I condemned to serve until they understood Arcanium was not for the taking." Bell raised his eyebrow to the Spider and gestured to Neve. "May I help her? Or would you rather she heal the natural way by principle? Wasn't it you who advocated against principle when it mattered?"

"Don't you dare use what I said to Neve against me. It's not the same thing at all." But the Spider withdrew her arms and went to Neve's other side, as though to ready herself to lash out.

Bell knelt next to Neve. "I'm going to have to make skin contact," he said softly, bringing his hands near her forehead and cheek, framing the gash. "I'm depleted. Contact makes it easier."

Neve nodded, and he closed the brief gap between them. The healing started immediately, more seamless and quicker than the work he'd done on her tongue.

"With the Ringmaster watching when I could not, I thought I would see my adversary coming sooner. I thought that when I put Neve out on a hook, I would notice when someone tried to bite and I could pull her from the dangerous waters before the damage was done. And I thought that if those two plans failed, I would always be able to find Arcanium again, that I would be able to find you, Maya. But much of my power is woven into the web of Arcanium, and he tied more of it in and stole the circus in such a way that I was left weak in its wake—jinn still, but damaged so badly that I could not heal myself. I couldn't find you again until I collected more power, and I couldn't collect more power without more wishes. It took far more time than I believed possible before I could spin another web. Even then, Locke ensured I couldn't find Arcanium myself. He blocked it from my mind the way he blocked himself. I had to find someone else who knew where it was and come in the back way."

When he was finished with the gash and she could see him from her regrown left eye—blurry, but getting

189

clearer every moment — he brushed his thumb over the smooth skin along her cheekbone. "There's that beautiful eye again, good as new."

Neve moved her face away from him, but he guided it back.

"I'm sorry. Let me finish with your mouth and I will leave you alone again."

He completed his work on her tongue and healed the damage she'd done to herself cutting through the skin muzzle. "It was never part of the plan that Locke would succeed. I didn't bring you into Arcanium to be taken, Neve. I didn't even bring you in as bait. That was a secondary, even tertiary consideration. I brought you in because I thought Arcanium could offer you something that your world did not. Your wish, though idle, was genuine. And I could give that experience to you here. I promise, Neve, no one was supposed to get hurt."

"Well, we did," Neve whispered.

He brought his fingers to her throat, healing her voice. When he made to stand, Neve closed her hand around his wrist and pulled him back down. She guided his hand to her breast, where the silver piercing was so tight it had nearly cut off circulation, but it rubbed and twisted and caressed her as well. Without the other pain to distract her, the simultaneous pain and pleasure from the piercings had risen to the fore, and without Locke to stop them, the silver continued to tighten.

"Please take them out."

Bell ripped away the flimsy cloth that barely covered her anyway. "Damn it. It's magically fused with you. This is going to hurt."

"It'll hurt if they cut off the oxygen to the flesh and they all fall off, too. Just get it over with."

The silver resisted. The Spider grabbed Neve's flailing hand to give her something to hold on to as Bell conjured the silver from one of her nipples. As soon as it was out, the silver writhed in his hand like a wasp. Blood dripped from her breast, but with the other two piercings twisting harder and the blood flow moving through the freed nipple, Neve gritted her teeth.

"Sweet Jesus, what the hell is that thing?" Maya snatched the stilling silver from Bell's hand and threw it as far away as she could.

"Keep going," Neve gasped. "Don't stop."

Bloody tears streamed down her face by the time Bell reached the piercing that was latched to her clit. It hurt so much more coming out than going in, but the worst part came after, when freeing her engorged clit sent the signals to her indifferent brain that she could orgasm, and she did—a hard, uninspired orgasm that was solely physical, sending nausea through her in cold and hot waves.

"No, Bell, don't you look away from that." Maya took him by the sides of his head and made him keep watching.

As her dry orgasm finished, it left behind what Neve could finally call relief, which she didn't think she'd had since Locke had put them in.

"You look at her," Maya said. "Look what you've done. If you're not going to look at a woman who still thinks you're better than the demon that did this to her, then maybe you should look around at the rest of them, because you're not anywhere near done fixing what you helped make happen."

"I know." As soon as Neve's piercings healed over and her pleasure-pain subsided, Bell finally pushed Maya's hands away and stood. Neve couldn't see Bell's face from this angle, but Maya took a step back. "There are no words for my grief. There is no apology that will assuage the pain. All I can do is heal the wounds that I can and give them time to heal the wounds I can't." He swept past her to tend to someone else.

"So that's it, then." Maya spread her arms then let her hands fall as though she didn't have the energy to maintain her own anger. "The demon is vanquished, the king is dead, long live the king all over again. We're no longer going to be tortured for a thousand demons' pleasures, but some of them are still going to be tortured to entertain the human guests who don't know what happens on the other side of the curtain?"

The Arcanium cast had gone quiet. Most of them wouldn't dare talk to Bell the way Maya was, the way Maya always did, as though he was just another man. No one else would have dared to strike him once, much less try to beat him bloody. But they were listening, and a few nodded.

"Sure, maybe I thought they deserved it," Maya said. "Maybe they even did. But they didn't deserve this. None of us deserved this. But *this* is what dungeons are actually for, aren't they? This is what Arcanium would have been under someone else. And this is what allows you to make Arcanium what it is, with your prisoners and your involuntaries and your golems. It's demonic rules that let you do all that. You know, Neve defended you in the ring. She called you a collector. She said you made Arcanium better than a dungeon. But I don't think that's true. I think your Arcanium *is* just another dungeon, just another hell on earth. And what you do is so much worse than what Locke had the demons and monsters and goblins and whatever do to us."

Bell lowered his eyes. "Maya…"

"Don't you tell me that it isn't. You didn't live this. *We* did. Don't tell us how *sad* you were to lose your playthings to a bigger bully in the schoolyard and how *hard* it was to get them back. Don't tell us how you care. It doesn't matter. You weren't here. You don't know what they did. You have no conception of what they did." Maya brought her hands to the side of her head as though to hold in her emotions, press down the memories still too fresh to forget.

"I know *exactly* what they did," Bell said. "If I could do to them what they did to you for all eternity, I would. As it is, they can't think where they are, much less torture. I'll handle them later, one by one. I'll make them suffer for every last thing."

"Oh, because you can see into our minds, right? Because you *know* what they did, you think you know how it feels. Because you know how we felt, you think you can understand what it was like for us in the moment—but you can't. That's where your limitations are, Bell, the ones you didn't choose. You think you understand us because you can read us, but you'll never be like us, and you can't understand what you can never be."

"What makes you think I don't understand," he snapped, "that I don't feel everything you felt as though I was their victim in every moment? I can feel every single one of you in my mind. You're all silent, but your minds still scream, crowded with the ghosts of dead days that haunt you as though they live."

"Where are we going, Bell?" Maya said, quiet now instead of shouting. "When you're through with us here, where are you taking us?"

"Back home. Back to Arcanium. He didn't take the tents or the caravan. He didn't need them. The infrastructure was left behind, and it was there I brought the new members as I used their wishes. It's ready for us to return as though he never stole you away."

"See? That's the problem right there. You think home is the old Arcanium. You're going to take all these people and put them back in the circus. Somehow, your jinn brain thinks that's better. And that's why your Arcanium is worse, because you made us think it was better, too. You made us think Arcanium was home. You made us think we needed it, that we needed you — after *you* took us from the world, after *you* remade us to *your* liking and made sure we had these sexual or romantic entanglements we'd never want to leave, even if we hated what we'd become. I thought I needed you. For the last I-don't-know-how-many days, I've suffered the worst of what any demon has to give to a woman like me. But I can't even look at you anymore."

"Arcanium was never meant to be a hell." Bell reached for Maya's hand, but she jerked it from his grip. "Never. Even the prisoners would be set free in time. You say it yourself all the time, Maya. Arcanium is no hell. It's a purgatory — a forge's fire instead of a demon's. I bring souls in to help. I care what happens to them. I harbor affection. Love. These things are not of hell."

"I'm sure you believe that." Maya backed away when he tried to touch her face. She wrapped her arms around her abdomen, looking anywhere but him. "All these people are tied to Arcanium. They're all going back to the hell you made. But I don't have to."

Bell shook his head, forehead furrowed from a complete lack of understanding. If anything marked Bell as inhuman more than all the things he'd ever done, it was that bewilderment.

"I'm out, Bell. I'm done." Heedless of her own state, Maya turned and picked her way gingerly through the crowd then slowly walked toward the path to the parking lot, toward the streets of the city around them.

Kitty took a few steps toward her, far more human grief written over her face. "Maya..." When she reached for Maya's hand, Maya let her have it. For a moment.

Then she pulled away. "I'm sorry. I'm happy that the Ringmaster got you out. But you can't understand either."

She was halfway to the path when Bell said, "Wait. Take these."

He tossed a pair of keys through the air. Maya whirled around just in time to catch them.

"Everything you need is in the front seat. An address. The bank account with your earnings and compensation. Clothes. Your belongings. Whatever you need."

Maya stared at the keys in her hand.

"You will always have a place in Arcanium, Maya."

"Screw you."

Bell watched her long after she'd disappeared behind the dense cluster of cars. There was the beep of an alarm for her to find the car then nothing. She didn't come back.

Chapter Seven

Neve slept in her own bed without anyone's limbs entwined with hers, without their dreams becoming hers, without waking up to a demon's mouth hot on her stinging breast.

The first night, she'd been too tired to dream. She'd crashed for fourteen hours. The second night, she'd been afraid to close her eyes. But no one entered her RV and her bed stayed otherwise empty, quiet.

Sometimes the quiet was deafening. She'd stare into the darkness beyond her room and wonder whether the door handle would turn, whether someone or something would slink into her bed and hold her wrists down and make her beg for them.

No one ever did. It was getting a little easier to close her eyes at night, but she still had a good two hours of insomnia before weariness did her in.

Neve ran her fingers through her hair, peering up at the blinds, where the strung lights outside poured through in golden lines — not like daylight but perhaps like sunrise. It illuminated the bedroom, made it better for her when she would open her eyes to check for the four hundredth time that she was alone.

She sighed, tried to relax every part of her body from her eyelids down to her toes, one part at a time. She seemed to sink into the mattress, the duvet heavy, warm and soft over her. Her thoughts untethered, making less and less linear sense, although she was still aware of the room around her, still awake enough.

Enough to open her eyes when the duvet at the end of the bed dipped down next to her foot.

The same thing happened on the other side.

Neve sat straight up.

Hands made of shadows moved like black spiders on the white duvet. Then a figure rose from the darkness at the foot of her bed and emerged into the dim golden light, his eyes a familiar blue glow.

She started to scream, but Locke climbed onto the bed with inhuman speed and clapped his hand over her mouth.

"Shhh, love. No one's going to hear you. No one will know I'm here. It's just you and me again, the way it will always be."

When he ran his tongue up the length of her neck, she couldn't help the moan, muffled by his palm. He pushed the covers down her body, purred at finding her naked. When he took his hand away and lowered his lips to hers, she scratched her nails down his back and spread her legs for him. His every touch, the caress of his tongue, the dent of his teeth, the slow, hot slide of his cock into her, satisfied every craving that had risen in her since Bell had brought her back to the old Arcanium.

Dark cravings—of silver, of pointed tongues, of a demon's indifference but shared pleasure, her ambivalence serving to make the thrill keener. He hurt her as he took her, shoving his cock in at the speed and force he chose, what made him feel good, but she closed her teeth over his shoulder in her own hunger, raised her hips up to meet him.

"I'll never let you go."

Neve's eyes flew open. She was alone in her bed, the duvet kicked to the floor, her skin slick and her panties wet. She crawled to the wardrobe for another pair, pulled on another tank top as well, a fresh one that hadn't been soaked through with cold and hot sweat.

The dreams were getting worse.

* * * *

For the first time in any cast member's memory, the Arcanium gates stayed shut. On the bars, Bell had fastened a sign that read, *Closed indefinitely due to illness. Visit arcaniumcircus.com to show your support and learn when we open again.*

Arcanium seemed more than just ill. It seemed on its deathbed, if not already in the grave.

The golems were given more direction, but they still lacked purpose without a working circus to take care of, and they sometimes just wandered aimlessly about or stood in groups like mannequins.

If the golems were zombies, Arcanium had a cast of ghosts.

The relationships that the circus had forged—either through demon-enhanced sexual chemistry or from the adversity they'd experienced in the old Arcanium— had been shaken or shattered entirely. Neve wasn't the only one who couldn't stand to be touched, although her sexuality had awakened again fresh and strong with the piercings removed and the sex demons' magic weaving through the circus.

Lovers who had depended on each other now couldn't look each other in the eye, knowing what they'd gone through, knowing what the other had suffered. Bell had healed every last wound and infection, internal and external damage, whatever Locke or his clients had inflicted, but he couldn't heal the mental and emotional wounds, not without removing memories, and he'd never done that to his people before.

In the midst of his cast's suffering, Bell walked the circus with the same deadness in his expression, dwelling on his own loss that, if not as physically painful, had dealt a blow that he might not have known would be so powerful.

The ones who recovered more quickly from Locke's Arcanium were the demons — which struck Neve as logical but also somewhat ironic. Ciarán and Moss were inseparable once more, although that might have been more out of necessity than choice. The clowns had resumed their strange hive threesome as though nothing had happened.

The Ringmaster and Kitty's relationship had only deepened, which raised more questions about what had happened after he'd saved her, but no one dared to ask.

Lord Mikhail and Lady Sasha, in particular, came out stronger together than before and were constantly in company, the chill in their relationship thawed. Neve would feel their gazes on her, together or apart, but they didn't approach her.

The demons in general gave the humans of Arcanium a wide berth, either because Bell had told them to or because they somehow sensed their humans' fragility.

The rest of the humans of Arcanium had to still feel the sex demons' effect, the same as Neve did, but what she saw on the few occasions she crossed paths with them was division, fractures. They mostly stayed in their RVs and trailers, alone, much as Neve did. Christina, who had been with Troy for so long, returned to the twins' trailer, where she'd apparently been before Seth and Lars had started visiting their vehicle more often. Seth and Lars didn't leave their RV at all. The golems had to bring food to them after they'd refused to come out for three days straight. And though Christina came out to talk with Troy, the twins also stayed in their trailer twenty-four-seven.

Carlo and Misha, Caroline and Riley and Colm, Valorie and John… They acknowledged each other, spoke in lowered voices when they were out in the circus proper, but they'd return to their individual homes in the caravan at the close of the day. Lennon still had to take care of Melanie, but he didn't stay in her part of the trailer nearly as often as he once had.

Aside from the Ringmaster and Kitty, the only other human who appeared to have emerged from Locke's Arcanium still able to endure intimacy with someone else was the Spider.

"I told you, Neve," she'd said dryly, "none of this was new to me. And what the Creature is helps. He's not human, not demon. He takes the fear away. He'll take yours if you let him."

Neve wasn't ready to let hers go. It seemed rational and irrational in turns. Locke couldn't hurt her anymore, not beyond the dreams that were becoming increasingly intense, increasingly realistic. But if Locke had shown them anything, it was that Arcanium was not safe. Had Bell rescued them all on the first day, he would still have betrayed the trust they'd placed in him. All his assurances that they were safe would always be lies, even if nothing ever got through again.

For the new faces in Arcanium, the veteran cast must not have been the warmest welcome. Kitty tried, but a one-woman welcome wagon in the midst of so much despair could only do so much. In dealing with their own problems that Bell had given them, they mostly stayed out of the old cast's way. At least Bell would have a batch of fresh talent to bring out when he decided to open Arcanium again, even if his old cast still hadn't recovered.

Neve was sure she wasn't the only one without the heart to learn any of their names.

* * * *

"I want to thank you for meeting me here tonight."

Bell stood in the middle of the ring, the center spotlight too bright over him. He'd sent out a compulsion to come to the big top that evening, and for the first time since Locke's Arcanium had fallen, every familiar face had been out in the circus proper all at once.

The new cast had not been invited. When they'd seen the rest of the cast heading for the big top, Kitty had told them not to follow. The invitation had been strictly for those stolen.

There were gaps between most of them on the bleachers—even when a pair or trio sat together, they didn't sit near anyone else. Everyone had their own space, enough room to stretch without reaching another body. Bell had to turn in a circle to address them all.

"During this interim period, I've been more than willing to give all of you time, and I will continue to do so until enough interest in continuing the circus justifies the opening. Even then, I will not force any of you to serve or perform until you're ready. Some of you speculated that what Locke did would lead to Arcanium closing for good, but in that you are mistaken. Arcanium is my child, the culmination of a long life's work. It sustains me and I sustain it. I'm a wish-fulfilling jinni with a need for wishes, and Arcanium offers and fulfills that need. If anything, what Locke did to pervert Arcanium reinforced that which I love. Everything I do, I do for this circus. Once you are a part of Arcanium, you are a part of that which I love. I protect it, tend it, make it grow, cull the elements that harm it. No, Lars, let me finish."

His jaw tight, Lars sat down again.

"When I wanted a larger cast, I gave more trespassers the chance to serve rather than pass them to the clowns or the incubus and succubus. When that larger cast went rogue because they were kept apart, I reintegrated them. I thought I could sustain a presence beyond the borders of Arcanium and keep you safe at the same time, but Locke used my complacency to make his move during the Funhouse, which I may choose to discontinue. The more I changed, the more variables I put into the spells around the circus, and that made me more vulnerable. Power has returned with the rest of Arcanium — more power than ever with the addition of the new cast. Now that I've been made aware of the spells' weaknesses, I have reinforced them so that a breach such as what Locke did will never happen again. But after some introspection, I believe the time has come for another change."

The spotlight followed him as he walked to the edge of the ring and sat on the edge of it. Not for the first time, Neve thought about how delicate he seemed and how much that illusion lied. But he also appeared resigned, sad, and those weren't lies. She could hear it in each deliberate, considered word.

"It is my wish, powerless though it is, for the circus to continue as before. The Funhouse events will be postponed at least until next year. Leaving Arcanium has been and always will be at my discretion. The men and women who have entered the circus in your absence will be held here by the same rules, serving Arcanium until I am satisfied. I am a collector, yes, but a collector with purpose.

"For those I brought in because of a voluntary or involuntary wish, I did whatever I could not to cause you harm. For those brought in through punishment, the rules against harm were far more flexible. But once your punishment had been served and I could discern an altered mind, an altered heart, you became one of mine, under the same protections. I punished you for hurting my people, but if anyone came in and tried to hurt you, even as my prisoner, I would do the same. By now, you should know that what I've done to you, no matter how you resent it, is nothing compared to a hell. I am as capable of hell as any demon, but I cannot abide it."

He looked to John, Misha, to the Sphynx, to the Man Doll, to the werewolf, to the diseased, to the human knot.

"When Locke stole Arcanium," Bell continued quietly, lowering his head, "it was my greatest fear come true — a fear that I believed could never happen. Everything I'd built, everything I cared for, was gone. But there's no joy in having you back. Maya may believe me incapable of empathy, but what happened to each of you replays in my head through every second of every day, knowing that I was the cause by failing to keep my promise. My betrayal allowed Locke's crime, and it caused irreparable harm — indelible scars that, with all my power and the blessings of every wish you have given, I cannot heal.

"I would very much like to keep you here, keep those who are mine closer than ever. But if I am to follow my own law, I cannot force you to stay any longer. For those to whom I gifted adversity, you have endured far more than you needed. For those to whom I assigned punishment, that punishment has been served ten times over. Arcanium still offers everything it ever did — a place to celebrate strange, wonderful things both natural and supernatural, a place where demons and humans may walk the same paths without blood or souls spilled. A place to thrill, inspire, terrify, imagine, to reach beyond the limits that the world outside so callously imposes. A place that illuminates the weird, odd, terrible things shoved into corners as though they have no value. It may sound silly to you, but it is an ideal I carry, the one star in my darkness.

"It would be my wish for everyone to stay, to let Arcanium be that pinpoint of light but also the safe place in a welcome darkness. But if you want to go, you will be set free, given everything you need to start out in the world, compensated for the service you gave me as well as for your suffering. And if you ask it of me, I will take your memory of what transpired in his Arcanium. It won't take away the scars, but it may dull the pain."

He turned toward the section of the bleachers where most of the prisoners had congregated.

"You'll notice I didn't offer to take away the memory of my Arcanium. For those who were my prisoners, I will not spare you what you suffered for what you did to my people, in case you dared to repeat it. With those memories carved into your skull and with the knowledge that memories were removed because they were too painful to bear, you will know better than to seek retribution. Next time, I would give you to Arcanium's guards without a second thought. Being my prisoner in service to the circus *was* your second chance, and no matter what Locke did, I won't give you another. Have I made myself clear?" He waited until enough of them nodded in response. "Good. I would also like to be clear that you are included in my invitation to stay. Should you remain, you will know me as a more generous host going forward."

He stood again and went back to the center of the ring. The spotlight dimmed, not quite so blinding in the middle of the dark tent.

"After tonight, the contracts forged between us, either through a wish or through a literal binding document" — he nodded in the direction of Caroline and David — "will continue as before. This is a one-night offer. If you stay, I will take it as an agreement to my terms, with your freedom at my discretion once again. But if you want to leave Arcanium, released from any alterations made, come to me now. There is no need to wish. If you ask, I will set you free. Many of you will not be able to go back to your old lives, but you will be given everything you need to start a new life, and I will not pursue you again. If Arcanium has become your hell, I desire nothing more than your freedom. Please…"

Bell held up his hands, palms up, in invitation.

At first, no one moved. Neve knew what they were thinking. Underneath the chaos and enigma, Bell was usually sincere, even when saying terrible things. But as a jinni who had sought to capitalize on their idlest wishes, he wasn't entirely trustworthy.

Some of them just sat there, eyes glazed over in thought. Others muttered among themselves. Neve tucked her hands into the sleeves of her oversized sweatshirt and continued to look around at the rest, wondering who was going to make the first move, if anyone was brave enough to try.

Troy stood to carry Christina down a few bleachers then set her into the ring. She took herself the rest of the way.

Bell crouched down to meet her. From anyone else, it would have been offensive, belittling. But Bell kept his back straight, his balance perfect, so that it wouldn't seem like he was leaning over for a child. The pain in his face mirrored hers.

"Christina, I'm so sorry."

"I know you are. But even in your Arcanium, someone always goes after me, and I can't fight back. Troy does what he can, but…I can't stay here anymore, even with him."

Bell tilted his head, scanning his gaze over her. "You don't have to justify yourself to me. Are you ready?"

She nodded.

He extended his hand. Hers emerged from the stump of her arm to meet it. As he raised her up, in the same motion, her legs grew out from the tops of her thighs. The whole process was simple, innocuous as a fern unfurling in the morning light. When it was done, there was just a Chinese-American woman in a singlet—nothing more, nothing less.

He kissed the back of her hand. "There's a suitcase in your RV with what you need. I wish you luck."

Christina kept looking at her arms and hands, silent tears pouring down. She turned away, dazed, and walked to Troy. He kissed her forehead as though he didn't want to let her go. But when she left, he didn't follow her. Nor did he go into the ring.

John came down next. The scars over his face, shoulders and hands receded, rendering him almost unrecognizable to those who hadn't known him before. John hesitated, then he solemnly held out his hand for Bell to shake, which Bell did.

He knew she was coming before she stepped into the ring. Resignation weighed through his limbs as he turned to meet her. "Valorie."

"We both knew it was temporary. Twenty years is a long time, Bell. He was the last thing keeping me here, and after—"

"I loved you."

"No, you didn't. But I know what you mean."

She was cautious touching him, her fingers trembling, but she took his face in her hands and kissed him. "I'll keep my flexibility, if you don't mind."

"I thought you might."

Joanne and Jane were next. They didn't say a word, barely reacted when Bell rested his hands on their heads and gently brought them together, which confused Neve. She'd expected him to push them apart.

For a moment, they resembled what Locke had done to them, which confused her even more.

Then they fused together, Jane melding into Joanne, until they were one person, and everything made a lot more sense. A few subdued exclamations of surprise suggested Neve wasn't the only one who hadn't known they weren't actually twins. Bell said something that only the single woman could hear. She nodded then left without a word or looking back.

Lars stood up. Seth put a hand on his shoulder and whispered something to him. They had what appeared to be a heated conversation that no one else could hear, except for the sharp sibilants that reached everywhere in the giant room. Finally, Seth bowed his head, but he nodded and reluctantly led them down. Bell swallowed hard as he touched their cheeks with an unexpected depth of tenderness no less powerful for the contact being so brief.

It was a small thing for Seth and Lars to part, just a release of their intertwined fingers. But it wasn't a small thing at all. Lars left first. Only Seth looked back.

Other cast members came forward, most of them prisoners in some form whose decision to leave was more predictable. Even the circus animals took advantage of the offer. The only prisoners who stayed were Melanie, who'd been rolled into the big top in a portable swim tank, and the Sphinx. Whatever their reason for staying, they kept it to themselves.

Caroline entering the ring made Tragedy whimper, but Comedy put his arm around her tightly and neither clown tried to stop her. Murphy, however, with one look back at Tragedy, took his own exit visa out. Tragedy and Comedy's distress increased, the chittering and clicking from their strange throats one of the more unsettling noises Neve had ever heard.

Riley and Colm came up next, but separately. Caroline waited for them at the edge of the ring.

Bell grabbed Colm's forearm in a bruising grip. They stared at each other. Whatever they had to say happened between their minds, but in the end, Colm nodded and Bell released him. Caroline, Riley and Colm left with space between them...but together.

The demons and monsters stayed. Lennon, Ciarán, Moss, Tragedy, Comedy, Lord Mikhail, Lady Sasha, the Gentleman, the Ringmaster... Kitty remained on the bench one row down from the him, leaning against his leg, the color gone from her face. She'd worn nothing but black since they'd all returned to Arcanium. She looked like a Victorian woman in mourning.

Neve thought the Spider would be a shoo-in to take advantage of Bell's offer, but she didn't move from where she sat with the Creature.

From all the surreptitious glances her way, Elizabeth expected Neve to ask for freedom, too. After everything, she almost felt like she should. Have him take away the memories. Take back the desire. Return to a life of science, experiments, equations, hypotheses and conclusions. Hire that divorce attorney. She'd only been gone for a little while, especially in comparison to Valorie. She could conceivably get her old life back with few repercussions.

But despite everything that had happened to her, she didn't want Bell to take the memories. It was irrational, her fear of losing parts of her mind. Having someone take them from her seemed worse, even if she'd take a cheese grater to her limbic system if she could. But those terrible memories were a part of her, a cause-and-

Haunted

effect chain that had brought her to the woman she was in this second, and in the next second, and the next, and she couldn't conceive of being anything other than that woman. If she was going to keep the memories, though, there was no returning to her old life. She didn't believe in taking things back. She didn't think that was possible, and if it was possible, it shouldn't be.

If she left Arcanium, it wouldn't be to go backward.

Maybe that made her less pragmatic than usual, but it had a dash of scientific principle, too. Broken glass couldn't remake itself after shattering. It was more foolish to expect it to than to leave the pieces on the floor.

Misha left. Carlo stayed. The Rotting Man left. The Serpent King stayed. The odd chef stayed. The Horned God stayed. Victor stayed. Based on the body language and expressions of those who didn't get up from their seats, it wasn't always the easiest choice.

"Anyone else?" Bell looked straight at those who remained, one by one, urging them to come forward while they still had the chance. What he felt about the ones who'd left was clear, but he kept close what he thought about those who stayed. "Very well. Though we have many new recruits waiting in the wings, our diminished numbers mean I must amend the performances and the funhouse exhibits. If you have changes you would like to make in what you've been doing, you are encouraged to bring them to me. In the meantime, I know many of you have experienced loss tonight. Please get some rest. We begin rebuilding Arcanium tomorrow. If you are still unsure whether you want to leave, you have until midnight to decide."

The spotlight dimmed. By the time Neve's eyes had adjusted, Bell had stepped over to speak with Kitty.

The Spider made her creepily elegant way down the bleachers, using all her limbs to support herself. "I noticed you didn't invite Hank or Dez to this little absolution exercise."

"Oh no, I wouldn't do that to you," Bell said. "I made a promise to you and to them. After what happened, their punishments have been amended, alleviated, yes. But given their proclivities and continued lack of remorse, they belong in the special hell I've made for them until such a point that rehabilitation is possible."

"I can live with that." The Spider fiddled with the robe tied around her waist. "I'm sorry for your loss. It can't have been easy for you to let them go — for you to be *willing* to let us go."

Bell's smile lacked conviction. Once again, he looked unusually tired. "What a coincidence. Kitty offered me similar condolences."

"Do you think any of them will come back?"

It was a strange question after everything everyone had gone through and essentially escaped now, after everything the Spider had endured — especially given that her history extended well before Arcanium.

Maybe not so odd. After all, the Spider was still here.

Bell nodded. "A few. But it's not my responsibility to tell them they will return."

The Spider raised her dark eyes to meet Bell's without blinking. "Maya?"

Kitty made every effort not to appear eager for his answer, as though she'd been afraid to ask the question — either fearing how Bell would react or fearing his response.

"I don't know. She's too important for me to see."

* * * *

Without enough prisoners to fill it, Bell had to renovate the haunted funhouse. He improvised with props and oddities he could spare from Oddity Row, but his work was complicated by his old cast's trauma — even simulations of torture were too much.

Bell kept a few tableaus open for new cast, but to fill the space, he also created more experiences with classic funhouse elements rather than focusing so much on haunted house vignettes. Moving floors. Disappearing doors. Dead ends. The funhouse became a real maze, its paths ever-shifting, its horrors unpredictable.

The hands from Neve's tableau had been reused. At first glance, one of the corridors seemed innocuous, but as guests walked through, hands emerged from the walls, grabbing at them in an effort to pull them in.

He also included a Hall of Mirrors. The usual funhouse mirrors reflected distorted Wonderland bodies back at the people who passed through — too fat, too thin, too short, too tall. Other sections of the corridor disoriented with perfect reflections mixed with clearest glass, and the sections would shift so that a person couldn't memorize the way through. Some of the mirrors showed inhuman handprints along the otherwise pristine surface. Others showed gibbering monsters behind the reflection, lolling tongues, lantern eyes. Others distorted reflections in ways that couldn't be explained by the design of the mirror — with disease, decay, infestation, death — or showed no reflection at all. In some instances, the mirrors shifted on their tracks, and it would seem like a ghost or a dark creature darted through the reflections.

On its surface, the effects could have seemed laughably cheap, but it was done better than any low-rent fair, with the same exacting standards Arcanium prided itself on. Nothing looked like an LED light or computed-generated effect.

Neve moved slowly through the Hall of Mirrors, unhurried by any monster or demon behind her creating anxiety or urgency that would lead to mistakes or a bruise on her forehead. She observed the harmless lies of the distortion mirrors with a kind of detached delusion that the reflection was — or should have been — truer than the object reflected. She took her time through the maze, reaching out to keep from running into any clear glass. Except for the deliberate ones, all fingerprints faded to spare the crew from constant polishing.

She stopped in the middle of the corridor, surrounded by mirrors and shadows and light, surrounded by herself. Narrowing her eyes, she peered into the reflections, ignoring the tricks. She still wasn't sure why she kept coming back, but she had all the time in the world to figure it out with Arcanium still closed — although now 'on the mend and under construction', according to the website.

The soundtrack to the Hall of Mirrors was a steady litany of whispers that, like the ghosts the reflections created, moved through the corridor, sometimes sounding like they were right next to her ear or right behind her. In comparison to the rest of the haunted funhouse, though, it was eerily quiet — like listening to true silence until heartbeats rushed through one's ears.

She stared at her reflection, expecting to see something. She listened to the whispers, expecting them to tell her something.

A hand slid down her arm to weave fingers through her own. His arm curled around hers. That was all she could feel, all that was visible in the reflections, as though he'd grown out of her rather than stood behind her.

"Have you ever seen anything more beautiful?" Locke's voice joined the whispers at her ear. "More beautiful than any of the others, because you're the only one who's still mine. I made sure of that, didn't I, love? Bell can keep you in his freakshow menagerie if he pleases. But he's glad you stayed, because he can't untangle me from you."

He curled his other arm around her, finding her breast and massaging it until the nipple showed through the fabric. "Do you ever miss this, Neve? Do you ever wake up in the middle of the night and wish he'd left them in? But your wishes no longer have power with him. You used up the last of them. Now you can't wish yourself out, nor can you wish me away."

He pressed his mouth against her spine between her shoulder blades. She saw him first over her shoulder as he emerged from behind her, nudging away her hair to kiss over her neck. Then he was in all the reflections — full, real, his form human, naked. Beautiful.

"You've been looking for me. And you've been looking in the right place." He reached their clasped hands in front of them to touch the reflection. "I never tire of seeing you through your own eyes."

He slowly brought her other hand to the glass, telling her without words to stay. Then, smiling at her through the mirror, he lowered himself to his knees.

She jerked awake in the golden darkness of her own bed again, on her stomach, her mouth open in a prolonged moan in her pillow, nipples and clit hard and aching as though they, too, remembered what Locke had done to them but had forgotten its agony.

The worst part was that he never came to her as the demon. She suspected that he knew better. He haunted her all the worse by luring her in with the honey he could pour down her body.

The pleasure he gave her in dreams served as a greater reminder of the desire she couldn't satisfy when she awakened, although Mikhail hovered — at a more respectable distance than before and without emanating quite as he had in the beginning. Bell's slowly dwindling crystal collection indicated where he and Sasha were getting their food while Arcanium was closed, which minimized trespassers.

Mikhail waited — cautious, concerned, grieved, pained. If she could tell that from his distance, she could imagine how much more intense he would be if she allowed herself to go to him. But she wasn't ready for either of the Mikhails she had known since being brought into Arcanium, and he'd either decided on his own to give her space, or Sasha or Bell had convinced him it would continue to be wise. He'd grown better at reading her moods, so she suspected he'd figured it out by himself.

She let him keep his distance rather than deny him even that.

Locke didn't give her the same courtesy. In her dreams, she had none of her hesitation, none of the avoidance or trepidation, none of the nausea or unpleasant crackles of electricity through her head at the very idea of another hand on her. The memories of what he had done with her during his reign surfaced with her arousal, was colored by it, and left her with nothing but unadulterated longing that culminated into orgasms that woke her without fulfillment.

It was the curse of staying in Arcanium—a curse she'd chosen to keep, although these were the hours she most regretted it. Outside Arcanium, she could have been content never dealing with anything other than platonic contact, which she could gracefully minimize.

But that was a bit of a lie to herself. Even if she never dated again, hands always found her. Not as obtrusive as the grasping hands from the haunted funhouse or the demon hands from the Funhouse events, but in the outside world, nothing had ever left her alone. When she hadn't felt her own sexuality, when she hadn't been so sensitive to touch, it hadn't occurred to her how many times fingers followed gazes and words, sometimes surreptitious, sometimes outrageous. On the outside, she could lose her sexual sensitivity, but she might not ever lose the awareness. She looked back at her life even before puberty, when strangers would stroke her hair or pale skin or ask if she needed a ride home. Strangers would call her a pretty thing, and men would look at her twelve-year-old body and somehow still think they needed some of that. She'd chosen solitude in her professional and personal lives as much for protection as temperament.

And when had a man ever taken denial of his touch with the grace they all expected her to show to them? She considered most of the men she'd worked with and felt only relief, but working with men who respected her and didn't try to grab her ass or comment on how pretty her hair was should have been expected, not a relief.

Her whole life. That was what the Spider had said.

Her whole life. Neve's whole life had been one groping hand after another. That hadn't changed in Arcanium. It wouldn't change if she left.

Locke's palms ghosted over her in admiration, the memory of him in her dream strong enough that she could practically feel it.

She punched her mattress, screamed into her pillow, aroused and nauseated in waves. Her hair caught in her mouth. Her tank top twisted uncomfortably.

Neve gathered her knees under her to raise herself up. She pulled her tank top off, replaced her underwear then shrugged into one of her oversized sweatshirts. She didn't bother with pants in the middle of the night.

She grabbed a root beer from the fridge and brought it outside. The brown grass crunched with frost under her slip-ons. She left the light of the caravan to immerse herself instead in the near-pitch darkness of Oddity Row. She didn't need to see much — the canvas of the tents made them look like stone monoliths under the crescent moon. The big top became a temple. But she had no interest in worship. She just wanted to breathe fresh air that didn't have the musty smell of her own arousal trapped in it.

With a complete lack of surprise, her feet brought her to the stairs that led up to the haunted funhouse. The door didn't have a lock. The caravan vehicles were the only things in Arcanium that locked, besides the gate. Everything else had the clowns and Mikhail and Sasha to take care of them, although she'd seen neither hide nor hair of a demon during her walk.

She'd grown used to the haunted funhouse these last few weeks, immersing herself among all the adjustments, even giving her opinion on the changes when Bell had asked her. He seemed to trust her judgment on matters of the genre, which she found weirdly endearing. The lighting did its work on her nerves, but when the Gentleman emerged from a corner in his shadowed room, she didn't jump. He looked at her without eyes, considered her without expression. Then he gestured with his long fingers for her to continue and withdrew back into his shadow. She hadn't known he lived there, but he'd always protected her before, and beyond the heebie-jeebies naturally induced by his appearance, he gave no other indication of threat. Neve had never asked him whether Locke's Arcanium had distressed him or not. He seemed too alien for her to do so.

Aside from the Gentleman, her only other company was the automated spell work that suffused the haunted funhouse like a fog. She'd become deft at avoiding the hands in their hallway, and she knew to wait for one of the disappearing doors to appear again before going through.

Brighter lights switched on when she reached the Hall of Mirrors. Once there, she carefully made her way to the middle of the maze. Then she sat down, cross-legged, and considered her reflections as she continued to drink her root beer.

The mirrors showed a tousled, faintly freckled woman — a soulful ginger, still with more curves than she knew how to handle, whether they were weakness or power. Strain showed on Neve's face like age, but aside from some white hairs, she'd been otherwise untouched by her own mortality. Serious, subdued green eyes were cautious under the engaging, deceptive invitation.

Neve set the finished root beer bottle on the ground then got to her feet. She pulled the sweatshirt over her head to stand only in her underwear, unable to escape herself.

Nothing from Locke's Arcanium had been left behind on her skin—no sign of the deep nipple piercings, not so much as a cloud in the eye he'd destroyed. Her tongue had hurt for a few days after Bell had repaired it, but she'd suspected that, along with her watering left eye, the pain had been psychosomatic rather than residual damage. She couldn't remember which tooth had cracked. There were no scars where she'd cut through her own lips to make her wish. The same was true with everyone else. Bell had eliminated every trace within his power. As far as her image was concerned, Locke might not have happened at all.

She ran her hands over her body. It wasn't sexual, although parts of her couldn't tell. She inspected how her skin gave under her fingers, the shadow of the dents, the way she looked in different angles of light. She lifted her breasts, turned around to feel her way under her buttocks, down her thighs—searching not for him but for something that wasn't his. Bell had taken all the scars, but it felt as though her whole body was a scar that she couldn't see. No one could. Her body, which everyone thought belonged to them first, was all she could see, all anyone could see. The more closely she looked, the less it felt like it was hers anymore. The less she felt it was *her*.

"*Hello, gorgeous.*" Neither Bell nor Locke, but her own mind conflating the two voices in her head into one.

She struck her hip. The pale skin flushed bright pink, which quickly subsided. Sometimes, Locke had struck her until her buttocks and thighs were black, blue and chartreuse. Nothing left from that either. For those who had been tortured, perhaps it was a relief to have lost the memory melted into each ghost of a wound. With few scars to her name for the same amount of time, she felt as though she'd somehow cheated with her one hell. And if she kept going back to that hell in her dreams, how much of a hell could it have really been?

She hit herself again. The physiological response was too fleeting.

Neve brought her fingernails to her face and raked them down the side that Locke had gashed open. Those marks lasted longer, but they, too, faded in the reflections.

She stepped back then kicked her heel against the mirror in front of her. If it had been a mirror in any other circus, she was sure it would have shattered, but Neve fell to the floor, holding her foot until the red alarms in her skull had quieted. She didn't think she'd broken anything, but she couldn't put her weight on the heel yet.

'You put me in that hell out there. It's no less than what I deserve. But I won't sell my soul for a softer bed.'

Even though Maya was gone, what she'd said had never completely dissipated. It haunted her as surely as Locke did, hovering around the edges like Mikhail, like Bell's persuasiveness in her ear.

You got off easy, nymphomaniac. Wasn't much of a change, was it? You were already a demon slut. You still are. Took till the last day for you to get anything worth healing.

You shouldn't have let him heal you.

She stroked gentler fingers over her cheekbone where the scar should be.

The sound of breaking glass rang through the quiet corridor. Neve stood up to shuffle closer to the unshattered mirror. Then she held the jagged edge of the root beer bottle to her cheek. The cloying smell of it misted over her face. She'd done this once. She could do this again.

She'd cut less than an inch over her cheekbone before Bell's hand covered hers to lower the bottle. He didn't show in the mirrors until after she'd closed her eyes.

"Damn it, Bell, why'd you have to stop me?"

He removed the bottle neck from her fingers, tossing it to the side without caring where it landed. A brush of his thumb over the dark red line on her cheekbone healed it over.

She turned around to shove him, tears hot and stinging in the corners of her eyes, but he grabbed her wrists before she could try.

"I understand the impulse, my dear. I really do. What Maya did not manage to teach me, I unfortunately had to learn for myself. But what you're doing is dangerous." He loosened his hold on her to touch the blood smear left behind on her face. "You know that better than most. One wrong move... If I hadn't read your intentions, my dear, you might have bled out before anyone could reach you."

"You shouldn't have healed it." She yanked her wrists from his hands then rubbed her knuckles over the healed cut. "And you shouldn't have healed what he did. No matter how I begged, you shouldn't have saved me. I deserved it for saving my own flesh over theirs, just because *he* liked it."

"Disfigurement isn't something to be earned. It merely *is*, whether natural or by design. It's not a punishment. Well...not usually," he conceded. "Do you need me to tell you that you suffered enough without having to wear wounds like sackcloth? Do you need me to tell you that Locke dug his claws into your mind, skullfucked you into this state of seeking penance, when the sins were committed *against* you? There should have been no shame in choosing what seemed like the lesser of two great evils. It would have served no one to join the rest. But by making a choice you never actually had, you were still able to surprise a telepath when you finally found a moment to fight back. Does it help for me to tell you that, if you have sinned, your balance has been more than met? Your credit has been paid for longer than a lifetime, love. You've been absolved."

"It doesn't help."

"I didn't think it would. It rarely does. Turn around."

Bell came up behind her, but neither his proximity nor his touch triggered the panic she expected. Instead, a kind of peace poured over her like warm water.

"So you want to become someone else. I can do that for you, but not with a broken bottle edge." He opened his loosely closed fist. A stiletto switchblade like the one she'd used to cut her mouth open rested in the palm. He pushed the button that made the blade emerge from the hilt. "This is sterile, and I know how to avoid the major arteries."

Her sigh came out nearly sexual. She heard it, but she couldn't take it back.

"I can do this all at once," he said. "Painlessly. Wasn't what he did enough?"

Neve shook her head.

"If you want the pain, I'm not going to take the pleasure." He ran the slender edge between her breasts, not yet pressing. "You know by now that they go hand in hand, and I cannot abide causing you pain."

She stroked lines over the tendons down the back of his hands when they flexed. "Just do it, Bell."

"Very well. Brace yourself, and don't try to hold back the screams. The haunted funhouse won't mind."

Her hand slammed against the mirror just as it flecked red.

When Bell was finished, the Hall of Mirrors looked like a murder scene. She looked like a horror movie. He looked like its villain.

"Please," she whispered through the trembling, "tell me I'm not pretty anymore."

He wiped the blade on the back of his trousers. The front had been nearly soaked through. He'd replenished whatever blood she lost as he went, so she'd remained awake and alert the entire time.

"I'm afraid that's not up to me. I couldn't make you ugly if I tried, not without rendering you completely unrecognizable, and it's your own reflection you wanted to alter, not someone else's. You are what you are." He disappeared the blade back into his palm as though he'd never held it. Then he wrapped his arm around her abdomen, inspecting his handiwork. "But they'll fear your beauty now, love, more than they did before."

She traced the thick, corded stitches on her skin above his arm. It would have to do.

Bell raised her bloody right hand. From the same palm he'd held the blade, he drew out her wedding ring. The larger diamond in the center had gone a deep, rich red, like rhodochrosite.

"I keep the other demons in my tent. But I thought I would give you yours."

He slid the ring onto the third finger of her right hand. He stroked her hair when she shuddered, but he didn't let her protest.

"You're safe from him, Neve. He's trapped in the diamond. Even if someone were to crack it open, he'd still be in the diamond's pieces. He can only be freed if I release him, and on the day you ask me to do so, he'll be weak, human, mortal. I stole everything but his spirit. He's not conscious. He only dreams. Some of the dreams you've had, he has shared. But that is only because his last words of power led to the haunting. He can't hurt you anymore, but every word you speak still causes him agonizing pain, and one day, you'll tell me to release him so you can kill him."

He met her gaze in the spattered reflection. "This is my promise to you. This is *my* word."

She turned the ring to watch the red diamond sparkle in the light.

Chapter Eight

A knock brought Neve to her RV door. She peered through the small window before opening it. It was the middle of the afternoon, so she didn't expect strangers, but one couldn't be too careful anymore and she didn't want to field questions from the new cast yet.

Lady Sasha waited on the other side of the door with Lord Mikhail behind her.

Sasha was actually wearing clothes, which was new. The little black wrap dress seemed a bit fancy for a bohemian caravan, especially when accessorized with a king cobra, but the fabric was jersey and she appeared comfortable with the low V-neckline and the high hem. Mikhail, too, looked odd wearing jeans and a long-sleeved ivory shirt. They could have been a beautiful normal couple at a shopping mall, which jarred Neve's immediate perception the way the oddities had on her initial walk through the Row.

When she opened the door, both of them showed the exact same shock as they got their first look at Bell's newest work of art.

For all that they'd seen worse, Mikhail appeared horrified. "What happened to you?"

Her mouth wasn't quite ready to smile, but inside, she laughed a little at his reaction.

"Unfinished business," she replied. "Hurt like a bitch, but Bell dampened it afterward and it's healing fine."

"In need of a change of scenery?" Lady Sasha asked.

Neve nodded, touching the leather that ran over her forehead. She was still getting used to the eyepatch, though she kept expecting it to slip off. It had been constructed to follow the line where her hair had been shaved off on the right side of her head. Bell had used a straight razor for that part, smearing her fresh blood like cream over the scalp to ease the way. He'd taken his meticulous time until the aesthetic satisfied him. She still didn't know what she thought about the change, too unused to baldness on the one side of her head and unused to the darker red hair on the other side. But it was the same color as the red diamond in her wedding ring, and it matched in hue to the large crystal glass rhinestones set into the eyepatch, among a collection of smaller rhinestones of purple, green, black and gold.

The eyepatch didn't cover the whole gash that Bell had recreated, but it wasn't supposed to. The line of stitches over the gash extended up her forehead and down over her cheekbone to counter the line of her widened smile stitched back together.

She wore comfortable, loose clothes over the rest of the stitches that patchworked her skin in stark black that would eventually meld with the new scarified skin, like sand irritated into black pearls. But she hoped the dramatic, jagged colors would never fade or else she'd have to get Bell to do it again, and she didn't think he wanted to.

"Why would you have him do this to you? Bell ensured you would be unscathed," Mikhail said.

"I needed to be scathed." She didn't want to sound cold, but for the same reason she had trouble smiling, the warmth she felt seeing Mikhail this close again didn't make it to her voice. "What do you want?"

"I brought a peace offering." Lady Sasha lifted the small, clear terrarium she held. A juvenile albino ball python had curled into the corner.

"I wasn't aware we were fighting," Neve said.

"Not an offering for peace. An offering of peace." Sasha lifted her shoulder in sheepish self-deprecation. "A little of it, anyway. What peace we are capable of. You admired my collection with great respect. I have literature on how to take care of her, but I would very much like to help you as well. I rescued her from someone who never would have appreciated her."

Sasha lifted the container higher and murmured to the snake, her whispers like hisses. "So many people who keep these creatures don't deserve the gleam of their scales or the jewels of their eyes. But I know you will appreciate her. And as she grows, she may offer contact that comforts you when you cannot stand a different kind of touch, the way my serpents soothe me. You offered your solution. I've come to offer mine."

Neve took the terrarium and brought it closer to her one good eye to peer over the white and yellow coloring that made up its dramatic morph. "She's beautiful. Does she have a name?"

"None that you can pronounce. She'll take whatever name you can," Lady Sasha said with a smile. "I'll bring in a heat lamp and help you establish a more comfortable environment for her later today."

Neve tucked the terrarium under her breasts, as though to offer her body heat until then. "Thank you. I've never taken care of a snake before, but I'm eager to try. You didn't come here just for a peace offering, though."

"No." Sasha stroked the strong body of the cobra wrapped around her shoulder and looked back at Mikhail.

"I confess, Neve, we are not skilled at knowing how to respond to what the demon's Arcanium has done to the humans under his control."

"There's no great human knowledge here that you're missing," Neve said. "If we were in a human world rather than Bell's Arcanium, the people who love us would be awkward, uncomfortable, grasping at straws, going about getting back to normal in all the wrong ways. We were never taught how to take care of people who go through trauma. Even in grief, which everyone goes through, people tend to fall short."

"When in the demon's circus, he wouldn't let us hear you, wouldn't let us sense you or any of the others we had touched," Mikhail said. "It was as though he'd taken an entire part of our perception from us. We couldn't even sense each other. But when he brought us to his quarters, we did what we could to ease the torment he caused. I don't know if that was the right thing to do, to intensify pleasure so that any pain he inflicted could be subsumed. We could not do that at all times, and the longer he withheld food from us, we lost much of our control over the magic we sent out. But when I could, I still tried to soften the sharper edges, still not knowing if it was right."

Neve couldn't answer him. The amalgamation of emotions and sensations of that first time and every time to follow made absolutes like right and wrong inane. She'd hated, needed, loved and feared what Locke had done, and whether she'd been served by the incubus and succubus sending her more pleasure couldn't be answered. There had been no better or worse to Locke's bed.

"And I don't know whether keeping my distance from you is what you need from me now," he continued. "I don't know if you ever want me near you again, if you'd flinch from the very suggestion of my skin against yours. In my ignorance and concern, I might have stayed away indefinitely unless you came to me first."

"Both of us might have. Of all the rifts Locke created, we would have been just another," Sasha said. "We don't understand, you see. We don't understand why so many of you are broken. We see that you are, and we mourn. But the torment we suffered, though it seemed similar, was quite different."

"I don't understand you either." Neve took a step back into her RV, but she didn't close the door. "I don't understand how you can touch anyone ever again. I don't understand how you can still want sex without remembering all the people who used you. Without feeling disgust."

"Sex isn't the same thing for us as it is to people. What he did to us was more like starvation than sexual sadism, although we understand it was intended as both. Even so, though we experienced some strain, stress—shame, I suppose—the worst part was how he filled a room with a magnificent feast every night, smeared the food over our faces, but tied us down and covered our mouths so we couldn't enjoy any of it. It's not as though we can stop having sex, Neve. We won't die, but to avoid sexual contact the way that all his remaining humans are doing would only create more discomfort."

"We are not here because we seek you to alleviate that discomfort," Mikhail said. "I would not do that to you, not again. We have the demons Bell trapped to feed upon when the pressure becomes too great without having to come begging to you before you can stand the sight of me."

Neve lowered her head to hide her eye, as though he would be able to see too deeply into it, but then she looked up again to meet his gaze without flinching. "I can stand the sight of you. I wouldn't have opened the door otherwise. I wouldn't have stayed in Arcanium." She didn't add that it was herself she hadn't been able to stand the sight of.

"We came," Sasha said gently, "because you've called to us — not in words, but in the night. Before we forged our connection, I could hear you, but now that the spell has been cast, I understand why Mikhail called it deafening. I don't know whether you realize how intensely you call."

"You respond to our magic when you're awake, Neve, but the screams you send to us when you're not? It's excruciating not to answer." Mikhail rested his hand on Sasha's shoulder, nudging the cobra's body. "And the longer I stay away, the more I cannot say if doing so helps or harms you more."

"From what we do know of human trauma, I warned that you might not want him to touch you," Sasha said.

"But if a woman's touch wouldn't offend like a man's, I thought I could offer myself to satisfy the hunger in his stead."

It was almost sweet that Sasha could be just as awkward as Mikhail when it came to taking care of their human. They looked so normal, which made it harder to comprehend that they weren't human and didn't respond to things like humans did, and no matter how much time they spent with humans, there would always be things they just wouldn't understand. It reminded her of Bell, although now she'd seen what was behind his unassuming façade.

If they'd come to her RV because they needed a human to suck dry without any regard to her circumstances, she'd have shut the door and probably never would have talked to them again, pheromones or not. However, despite their good intentions, Neve's stomach spun and blood drained from her head, leaving her dizzy. Whether or not she was capable of a sexless relationship with Mikhail, the fact was that he *was* sex. He was an incubus, and that wasn't something he could change or control. Just thinking about him made her imagine his hands on her when she didn't want anything but the blades Bell had brought against her skin.

Bell had been able to touch her, though. He should have terrified her. He wanted her, and she didn't think that had changed because of Locke. A man like him — a being who might as well have been a god in comparison to her — wanted her, and if he decided to take her in spite of his rules and laws, he could. He should have triggered her so hard that she'd have tried to slice him open from ear to ear with the broken bottle for getting near her, but she hadn't. He'd been able to touch her to cut her, had been able to bring himself close.

Because he'd had something *she* wanted, and he'd been willing to give it to her for nothing in return. In the cosmic balance between them, he still owed her and he knew it.

She didn't think she could take Mikhail coming near her, with his size, his shadow, the memories of the times he'd preyed upon her in his own way. If *anything* else ever tried to force itself between her legs, she thought she'd burn the circus to the ground, screaming to tear Locke apart in his diamond.

But just as Mikhail couldn't help what he was, and just as he couldn't stop having sex even if Locke's Arcanium had done its own damage upon him, Neve wondered whether she had a choice either.

The sex demons had come to her out of concern for the strength of a desire she hadn't known was so strong. Had she become so detached from her own uncommon sexuality that she couldn't tell what she needed? Or had some part of her blocked it out to protect her from herself? Either way, she doubted it could continue indefinitely, and when the pain from the cuts subsided, what would rise in its place? What would happen when Arcanium opened again and the sex demons sent out their magic on purpose? What would happen when the lust from her dreams bled into real life?

"I've been dreaming of him," she said finally. "I'm not sentimental. I don't miss his Arcanium. I never loved him. But in my dreams, he still screws with my head."

"You don't need to explain yourself," Mikhail said. "Pleasure and consent are not always the good, safe things they should be, little girl. We understand that better than most. If he gives you pleasure, it does not mean that you belong to him, nor is it a betrayal. Pleasure is a feeling. It is not always a choice. And just because you agreed to submit to him does not mean you did not suffer. Suffering is what a dungeon was made for. No one brought in as a prisoner is spared, no matter how gentle the touch. Are you ashamed that you let him brand you by choice?"

"Maya said I sold my soul for a softer bed."

Sasha actually smiled, shaking her head with amusement. "Maya saw too much of herself in you. It is easier to criticize a reflection."

"She could have been like the Spider and me. Locke offered her that choice. She chose to join the demon brothel, become one of his *Hellraiser* exhibits."

"Do you think she blames herself for the demons who used her because she chose not to submit to Locke?" Sasha asked.

Neve didn't know how to answer that. It had been difficult to understand what was going on inside Maya's head during the best of times, but she and Neve had gotten off on the wrong foot from the start.

"Maya had trouble reconciling her beliefs with her actions from the moment Bell brought her into Arcanium," Sasha said. "Becoming his consort did nothing to uncomplicate that conflict. She's far from a reliable moral arbiter. If she hated you for your choice, she likely hated herself five times more for her own." Sasha bit her lip, as though unsure whether to continue. "Leaving Arcanium might have been the best thing for her. Kitty has always belonged, even before she came to Arcanium to wish herself in. But Maya struggled with her love for Bell in a way Kitty has not struggled with hers for the Ringmaster."

Mikhail frowned. "Even if many of us think she should."

Sasha hovered her fingers over the eyepatch, her usually flawless forehead showing genuine concern, as though such extreme modification pained her to see. "If this is because Maya passed her own inner demons to you..."

Neve shook her head, bending back a little so that Sasha's skin couldn't brush hers. "No. These are mine, not hers."

At Neve's recoil, Sasha's face smoothed over again. Before Neve had approached her, she'd always been so aloof — a statuesque ice queen who'd had to hold herself apart for protection from her own effect on the people around her, the same as Mikhail. It couldn't have been easy to be among human beings all her life but to keep herself always away, to watch the demons of Arcanium become lovers with its humans while she and Mikhail always had to restrain themselves.

Until me. Sasha hadn't even known Neve could be an exception until just before Locke had stolen Arcanium. Now human frailty distanced the one woman they both could touch from exploring that development. And Neve had wanted to explore it.

"Have I miscalculated? Have I committed as great a sin as my dear Mikhail with my own misunderstanding?" Lady Sasha withdrew her hand and took a step back. "Are you afraid that I would be as aggressive as when we collided? I can be gentler, Neve. I am capable of much greater control than Mikhail. You caught me by surprise at the event, between the accident and the reaction it caused. You will not catch me by surprise again. Should we leave? Have we come to you too soon?"

"Or has what happened left wounds too deep for a demon to comprehend, with no hope that we might help heal?" Mikhail backed away as well in anticipation of being dismissed. His sad puppy eyes had returned, but he lowered his head to conceal them, as though aware how they affected her, a different kind of influence than the sexual magnetism he also withheld. "Would you say our experiment is at an end?"

Arcanium could be a special kind of hell for them, but Neve couldn't let their discomfort manipulate her choice. She'd been manipulated by jinn since the wish that had started everything. If she wasn't ready, she damn well wasn't ready.

But if she had to dream of Locke every night for the rest of her life, if she could never remove the brand he'd placed upon her, if she could only put her scars on the outside to justify the pain inside to herself, if she could let *Bell* touch her...

"Wait."

"Please, don't do something you don't want because we—" Sasha started.

"Stop," Neve said, extending her arm, "or I'm going to lose my nerve." She hesitated halfway to Sasha, taking a moment to remind herself to breathe. The oxygen spun her head.

"I'm holding back," Sasha said quietly, reaching up to give her less distance to cross. Her palm was just a few inches from Neve's, close enough that Neve could sense the heat of her skin. "I'm holding back as much as we're capable of. If you can't stand to have me touch you without my magic, I promise that I won't touch you with it."

"I'll hold mine back as well." Mikhail had stopped stepping away to watch the two women with intensity Neve couldn't define as mere intrigue, arousal or curiosity—the emotions there were too complex to distinguish. "So that you don't confuse what you feel with what we want you to feel."

Neve nodded in gratitude, unsure whether she'd be able form words with breath such a precious commodity. Research said encouragement worked best to change behavior. It had certainly worked with Mikhail. He wouldn't have so readily offered to tamp down his magic in the beginning, nor would he have comprehended why it was considerate.

The sex demons pulling back their magic created a vacuum that seemed to steal the rest of her air. In its wake, her head cleared, although there hadn't been as much sex-demon-induced fog as there had been in the past. She felt like she saw them more clearly, without the haze that softened edges and enhanced the attractive qualities. Even before Neve had stumbled into Sasha, she'd experienced a mild form of that effect, she realized now. It had just been so subtle in comparison to what she'd experienced with Mikhail when he emanated that she hadn't recognized the desire as anything but woman-to-woman admiration and a slight serpent-based crush. Perhaps at least part of that could be attributed to Sasha's control, but Neve thought the more pertinent reason was that she hadn't been *trying* to create an attraction with a woman the way Mikhail always was.

Neve's fingertips had gone cold, but she closed the gap, bringing her palm to Sasha's and aligning their fingers.

Despite Lady Sasha's effort to hold back her magic, she couldn't cut it off completely, and the effect was instantaneous.

As soon as the sun rose every day, the strength of Neve's arousal from her dreamstate hauntings faded, a companion to the rest of the numbness left behind after Locke's Arcanium. Sasha's sex magic forced Neve to connect to her desire again. And all at once, she understood why the demons had thought she was screaming.

Neve shakily lowered the ball python's terrarium to one of the stairs inside the RV then braced herself against the door frame, afraid she might fall. "Oh."

Sasha's face animated, a warm glow rising in her features that melted the ice she'd carefully constructed in anticipation of Neve's refusal. She already had good color, but her dark eyes deepened and the pink in her cheeks and in her lips flushed darker. "'Oh' is right."

The immediate electricity from their moment at the Funhouse event came back to Neve even stronger, as a memory rather than an experience. She could tell how much Sasha kept back, but there was no denying the succubus' effect on her now, as undeniable as Mikhail's and not dismissible as mere magic making her feel something that wasn't real.

This was real. Neither of them might have felt it before her first wish, but Sasha was a succubus drawn to opportunity and Neve was an equal-opportunity nymphomaniac. The way Mikhail had described it, Neve's attraction would feed Sasha's, even if Sasha didn't feel an instant attraction herself. But if the reaction was this intense with Sasha holding back....

The desire men had for her had never been in question. The idea of being desired by a woman, succubus or not, was something that had never occurred to Neve—right up there with desiring a woman herself.

"Is the cobra going to bite me again?" Neve asked.

Sasha curved her lips into a smile. "Amil apologizes. He was only doing his job to discourage contact. He can't tell the difference between accident or purpose. *I* can tell the difference." Her voice had taken on a huskier quality, her alto deep enough for Neve to feel through their palms. "When all that skin met mine by accident, it was like getting hit from all sides by a two-by-four. I don't think I've ever been struck so strongly by another woman. Bell broke the mold with you, Neve."

The cobra, who had been more or less still around Sasha's shoulders, lifted its head to stick out his tongue in her direction. But Mikhail came up behind Sasha to draw it from her and wrap it around him instead.

"Are all sex demons snake charmers?" Neve asked.

"I should think so." With a grin, Sasha mimed jerking off.

"The two are nothing alike," Neve said. "Difference between cold- and warm-blooded, for instance."

"Reptiles were once warm-blooded. Perhaps we're reptiles of the old kind," Mikhail replied.

"Not if you can breed with humans, you're not. It explains where some of the evil serpent myths might come from, though."

"Lilith didn't need the serpent." Sasha slowly interlocked their fingers into a coupled fist. "The serpent needed her." She raised an eyebrow in query as she brought her other hand to Neve's face, near her eyepatch.

Neve nodded.

"Sweet girl." Sasha traced around the eyepatch, unflinching over the still-healing skin and stitches.

Neve hadn't known a wound could ache with arousal, especially not one through an eye.

Mikhail stroked the cobra's body as he observed them, his own dark eyes going black, eyelids heavy with interest.

"Do you want to stop?" Sasha eased closer, the angle between their forearms narrowing. "Is it causing you distress?"

"Eustress, maybe." Neve untangled their fingers to caress down the length of Sasha's forearm and draw her closer. "You're right. I didn't know I needed this. Hell, I didn't even know I wanted this. If I have a panic attack, I'll warn you it's coming."

"It will help if I release my magic. It can distract you, at least for now."

"Wait." Neve acted before she could convince herself not to, leaning in and pressing her lips against Sasha's. Without the full brunt of succubus magic, Neve could evaluate whether she liked kissing Sasha on her own merits.

She liked it just fine.

"You know, I could murder my ex-husband for everything he's put me through," Neve murmured into the corner of Sasha's mouth.

"I'll do it for you, if you like." The succubus licked her cheek playfully.

"Don't you dare touch him after touching me."

Sasha laughed, crowding Neve back against the side of the RV. Kissing Sasha was nothing like kissing Locke, her body soft where a demon man's was hard. She was only a little taller than Neve, so she couldn't loom, couldn't control her with height. And when

Sasha rocked her hips, there wasn't a cock to threaten or promise.

"Does this hurt? These cuts go under your clothes, don't they?" Sasha followed the line of one to the neck of Neve's shirt. "He cut you all over then sewed you back up again like a torn doll."

"It hurts, but it's a different hurt than anything *he* did. Don't stop. Let go. Just… I just want it to be simple. I want pleasure to be pleasure and pain to be pain. Don't stop."

When Sasha kissed her again, she opened the dam. Her sex magic swept through Neve like heat bursting from an oven. They both moaned into the kiss, both clutched at each other's bodies as a handhold against the force of it that swept from Neve to Sasha to Neve and back, lust feeding on lust until Neve had to break the kiss, gasping, because she'd started to black out.

"It's been such a long time since I've been with a woman." Sasha combed Neve's hair back from her face, admiring the color. "They're not usually what I go searching for. Really, with all the ripe young men just begging to be picked off, there's no reason for a succubus to hunt women. They have quite enough to fear without worrying about things like me in the night."

Neve leaned her head back against the side of the RV and laughed a little. "I've never done this before at all. I have no idea what I'm doing."

"Much of it is the same," Sasha said. "Do unto others as you would have them do unto you."

"I'm pretty sure that's blasphemy."

"I'm a demon. I'm allowed to blaspheme." Sasha kissed up Neve's neck to her ear, caught the lobe between her teeth and licked along the shell. On that side, there was no hair in her way, and she stroked over the bare skin with interest. "What do you *want* to do to me? There's no wrong answer here. I respond to almost everything. It serves me well to be easily pleased."

Neve slid her hands up Sasha's sides to cup her breasts. She wasn't wearing anything underneath the wrap dress. Her nipples pressed against the cotton without obstruction. Neve had lived with a pair of large breasts since puberty, but it felt so different on someone else.

Sasha hummed as Neve parted the sides of the wrap dress to push the fabric under Sasha's breasts. It was the middle of the afternoon and anyone could come along, but right now, Neve couldn't care less, and given that Sasha walked around nearly to completely naked on an average day, she doubted the succubus cared either.

Really, another woman's body shouldn't have fascinated her as much as it did. But Sasha's skin was warm butter, like it had soaked in the sun despite the late, wet winter cold. Her heartbeat was rapid and strong underneath Neve's hand.

On a whim, Neve dipped down and pressed her ear to Sasha's chest to hear it, the way she sometimes listened to a cat purr.

Sasha's nails pleasantly scratched her scalp, and she drew Neve's hand up to her breast again, covering her fingers to guide them to her nipple. The areola flushed the same dark pink as her lips under their firm touch. It drew Neve to close her mouth around it, sucking at the hard bud and bending it with her tongue.

"There's my girl." Sasha pulled on the tie to her dress. The two sides pulled open between them until Sasha was completely naked against her.

Neve suddenly felt overdressed, her comfortable layers heavy, hot and cumbersome. But the more skin Sasha bared, the more effect she had, because more of Neve's bare skin could come into contact with hers.

Touching Sasha was almost as arousing as stroking her own clit, except she'd barely been touched so far. Whether the reason was to let Neve set the pace or because Sasha was still wary of the effect contact would have on her fragile human psyche, Neve still appreciated the patience, but she was pretty sure she couldn't turn back now if she tried. The connection had been forged, the decision made.

She could technically tell Sasha to stop, but Neve understood that her own altered physiology wouldn't allow it, not now that her body knew what it had been denying itself. In spite of the inherent dangers of sex demons, they weren't dangerous to *her*, so she was still safe.

Still safe, still horny as hell whether she liked it or not and Locke wasn't anywhere in her mind now, whispering, ghosting his fingers over her. In fact, the more she spoke, the more he would suffer instead of her.

"Would you like to see how far the stitches go?" Neve asked, dragging her lips up Sasha's chest to her neck then to her mouth for another kiss.

"If Bell hadn't already submitted himself to the Ringmaster's whip, would I call for him to submit himself now?" Sasha asked.

Neve pulled back, startled. "Bell had the Ringmaster whip him?"

"Oh yes. The demons acted as witness. He didn't call his humans to him because you were in pain, and he didn't want all of you to assume he was trying to perform for forgiveness, as though five hundred lashes over the course of five nights could ever repay what he'd allowed to happen. But he broke his promise of protection, and he is subject to his own law as much as the rest of us."

Neve ruminated on that for a moment, idly rolling Sasha's nipple under her thumb as she imagined Bell's back bloody from the lashes. A human being couldn't endure five hundred, not from the Ringmaster. In Bell's human guise, it must have cut through to the bone, though there hadn't been scars on him the last Neve had seen.

"He shouldn't be punished for something I asked for," Neve said. "I actually had a choice."

"I don't like that *this* was your choice, Neve, to do to yourself what Locke did to you." Sasha unbuckled the strap that kept the eyepatch steady on Neve's head. A rush of cold wind brushed against the warm wound, breaking her skin out in goosebumps.

"It's not your pain. It's not his. It's mine. Besides, Arcanium needs new freaks, and I couldn't go back into the funhouse being fondled all day again. Bell understood that."

"He didn't need to make it painful."

"I told Bell to let it hurt. It's nothing like what Locke did to me, okay? It's real, not manufactured, not tangled with emotional and physical and sexual torment until I can't tell what it is anymore. It's healing faster than it should, but I don't mind, because the pain is just...pain. I can live with that." Neve leaned back, sliding a hand underneath her shirt. The fabric lifted with her hand. Above the waist of her leggings, stitches segmented her abdomen like lines on a map. "This is what I am, for now. This is what I need to be. Do you still want it?"

She looked between Sasha and Mikhail, her eyebrow arched in query.

Sasha took the bottom of Neve's shirt with both hands and lifted. Neve raised her arms to make it easier to remove. Unlike the succubus, Neve wore a bra, but enough of the patchwork was visible over her abdomen, back, arms and chest. She'd been segmented then sewn back together in what looked like a desperate Frankenstein science experiment — a nod to one of the first pieces of sci-fi horror, written by a woman about male hubris and scientific folly and in which the real monster wasn't so clear. Neve appreciated the homage, as Bell had known she would.

Sasha didn't comment again, but she was overly gentle along the angry red flesh under the thick black stitches. In Locke's Arcanium, Neve would have had to endure infection, but Bell had assured her the wounds would stay clean. Controlled injury, pain without risk... It was nothing like Locke's Arcanium at all, no matter what it looked like to Sasha.

Neve covered Sasha's hand with her own, bringing it more firmly against her abdomen. "It's okay. The stitches are strong and the wounds are sterile." She turned her arm over with a slight grin. "He did let me keep one old scar."

They were just puncture marks, two little knots of pearly skin. But they made Sasha smile again.

"I think I can come up with an adequate apology for Amil to give." Sasha ran her hands down Neve's abdomen then around to lift her up by her thighs with preternatural strength as powerful as Mikhail's, though her appearance didn't give the same indication. Neve gave a shout of surprise, but she crossed her legs behind Sasha's back and wrapped her arms around her neck.

"This is not for prying eyes," Sasha whispered in Neve's ear.

Neve beckoned to Mikhail as Sasha carried her up the stairs into the RV. "Are you coming?"

He wasted no time following them in and shutting the door behind him. He picked up the ball python's terrarium and carried it up into the living room with them.

Sasha scoffed as she looked around. "As though he can't afford to give you more space. He certainly affords to give himself what he needs." But she maneuvered Neve through the slender aisle, and when they reached the bedroom, Sasha hummed reluctant approval, then tossed Neve onto the duvet in a sprawl of limbs.

Mikhail sat on the edge near one of the bookcases. He rested the peace-offering ball python on an empty space on the shelf then handed the cobra back to Sasha when she stretched out her arms for it.

"Remove the rest of your clothing, please. I want to slide my body against yours to feel its silk. If you must wear those cuts, I want their texture as well. One day, I hope to take you as you were, as I first desired you. But I am more than pleased to take you as you are, my lovely little patchwork doll."

Sasha tilted her head curiously when Neve bristled. "What sets your teeth on edge? Lovely, little, patchwork or doll?"

"I didn't do this to be pretty."

"It's not something we decide, darling." Sasha climbed onto the bed, her knees on either side of Neve's legs. "It's something we use. I watched you during the first Funhouse event. It may be a long time yet before you can do anything like that again, but despite your reluctance to embrace your new sexuality, I watched you find the power in it. There's power in sex, danger in beauty. Some of the most dangerous things in this world are very beautiful. Some of the creatures of this world that they call ugly have their own beauty. I hope you didn't think surgical scars would mar you or that one lovely eye would be too few for beauty."

Sasha leaned down and licked the riverbed of new scar tissue over her eye. "You could be flayed, burned, dissolved and somehow what was left would still be beautiful. Take it from a succubus, Neve. Beauty is in everything, and your adversaries will try to use it to destroy you. My secret is to use it to destroy them first."

She raised herself upright again so that Neve could push her leggings down her legs. Sasha helped her pull them off. Then Neve unhooked her bra and tossed it aside.

It had been quite a while since locker-room days. Even back then, Neve hadn't been comfortable being naked in front of other girls, especially since she'd developed curves so much earlier and they'd caught attention from boys and girls alike who didn't know how to handle the changes or their reactions to them.

But Sasha's ease with her own nudity, even under non-sexual circumstances, gave Neve the courage not to cover herself, although Mikhail's gaze heated her in entirely different ways than Sasha's.

His breathing quickened, deepened, not quite a groan. Though his cock pressed against the front of his jeans, he kept his clothes on. He adjusted himself but didn't keep his hand on the erection—presumably in case the sight of a cock triggered a negative reaction when things were going so well.

Neve couldn't tell him it was okay, because she still wasn't sure. Sasha was safer, her strange body still familiar, like something Neve would see in a mirror, and though her sexuality was aggressive, it wasn't quite like a man's.

She turned back to Sasha with a squeak at the first cold glide of scales over her thigh.

The unhooded cobra's tongue flicked over Neve's skin. He'd be able to taste her scent, sense the heat from her hot-blooded mammalian body. But he remained unthreatened, exploring her contours and sending shivers through her.

As he slithered between her breasts, Sasha slowly parted Neve's legs, climbed between them, then lowered herself to nuzzle against Amil's body and Neve's thigh. She blew cold air over the spread flesh, drawing attention to the tension of arousal that flowed unhindered through it. Then, raising her eyes to gauge Neve's willingness, Sasha brought her lips to Neve's folds.

A swirl of tongue against the hood, light licks, then all at once hot, wet suction.

Neve fell back against the duvet once more, closing her eyes at such sharp, exquisite pleasure — nothing but pleasure. She arched to bring herself closer, her movements strong and quick, despite the cobra so close to her neck, to her face. He couldn't envenom her, but he was fully capable of striking her multiple times with lightning fast reflexes. With Sasha there, though, the cobra remained docile, active and interested, its scales a cool counterpoint to Sasha's insistent heat.

The cobra bumped its forehead against her cheek then swept back down her body with surprising speed compared to the leisurely pace from before. It nudged her breast, her nipple, seemed to rub its chin against her belly. Distracted as she was, it took Neve a moment to realize what it was doing. She whimpered as she grabbed a fistful of Sasha's hair and lifted her head away.

"I think your cobra wants to mate with me." Neve couldn't help but laugh at the absurdity of the words, the situation.

Sasha's grin was wicked. "It's a little late for him, but does it surprise you that succubus magic gets them in the mood? He shouldn't actually try to mate with you. He's just trying to make you a receptive female, much like I am." She extended her tongue much farther than a human could reach to caress Neve's clit. Her black eyes glittered when Neve shivered.

"It's a little weird, and I'm ticklish." The cobra rubbed his chin just under her ribs, and Neve squirmed with a giggle.

Sasha dipped down to take Neve's clit in her mouth again, sucking with deliberate, powerful rhythm. Neve immediately stopped giggling, keeping one fist in Sasha's hair and grasping with her other hand for something solid, but the duvet was too soft and slipped over the sheets. She finally reached the bookshelf and gripped the railing that kept the books from falling out during travel.

At the first press of fingers at her entrance, though, Neve tensed.

Sasha immediately pulled away, squeezing her thigh in reassurance. She redoubled her efforts on Neve's clit.

Neve should have been as sensitive to contact there as she apparently was to penetration, given the deep piercing that Locke had given her, but it was somehow different. Neve could experience the pleasure under Sasha's mouth freely without association with the piercings, because there was no shooting pain, no silver cutting off the movement of her blood, nothing to keep her from coming as Sasha quickly brought her to the peak and sent her over.

The amount of relief the release gave her couldn't be expressed in anything but the cries that filled the small room—which she hoped made Locke hurt like hell—and the hot, unstinging tears that poured from her unmarred eye as the climax spread warm and sweet and wet from Sasha's mouth outward.

Sasha fed from her, too, draining energy that left Neve's limbs heavier, body lethargic and mind blissfully slow, but it didn't shut her down or short-circuit her like a full feed. If Neve recalled the explanation correctly, Sasha *could* feed from her completely, the way Mikhail had fed from her when she'd sucked him off, but it took more effort than when Mikhail's cock was inside her. The difference made her slow, sleepy mind curious.

Sasha licked her lips with relish then crawled up the bed to settle next to Neve as she recovered. Sasha alternated between stroking the cobra and the woman, staring at Neve as though she was some kind of precious treasure. Neve supposed she *was* precious. The succubus hadn't had sex with a woman she couldn't kill before. Sasha curled her leg over Neve, rubbing her foot gently over Mikhail's thigh as though to keep him a part of it while Neve was out of commission.

"Do you feel better now?"

Neve carefully lifted the serpent from her body, listening for any angry hissing and making sure it didn't hood. For all that her first introduction to Amil had been violent, he seemed otherwise equanimous to sudden movements and heat spikes and who knew how many disturbances to his environment.

Neve rested him on his mistress then on impulse rolled to kneel over her and kiss her. The weight of her breasts pulled against the stitches over her chest, abdomen and back, which hurt the way her muscles ached when she stretched farther than her natural flexibility. Amil moved between them, finding his way out, and Neve sank down over Sasha to bring their bodies together completely. Mikhail was a big man, but there was a marked difference between her breasts resting against firm, built pectoral muscles and resting against another pair of breasts. It was as foreign to her as a cobra trying to make her receptive.

Neve took the moment to explore, running her hands all over Sasha's body, feeling her, almost molding her skin to test size and pliancy by touch rather than by sight, because touch made a fantasy woman reality.

She was more tentative when she brought her hand between the succubus' legs. Sasha bit Neve's lip with a moan as Neve trailed her fingers along the folds. This was where she had no idea how to proceed. Touching herself had never been as effective before she'd come to Arcanium as using a vibrator had been, so she had a dearth of knowledge of how to touch herself, much less another woman. She had to draw instead on what men had done to her, caressing up to her clit, not quite touching it more than a glance.

As though sensing her ignorance, Sasha brought her hand down to cover Neve's again and direct her to give more pressure until she could pull her hand back and let Neve rub over her clit with more confidence.

She was sure she was still fumbling, but Sasha's breathing quickened and went shallow, her hips rising to the rhythm that Neve set, and when Neve kissed her again, Sasha's softness and gentleness had faded. Though she'd fed, her kiss became hungry, her body against Neve's more insistent, every move a caress, as though every inch of her yearned for completion and would do anything to Neve to get it. And the more passionate Sasha became, the more Neve was compelled to make her lose even more control.

Is this what I'm like to everyone else?

Sasha broke the kiss, throwing her head back, her neck an enticing column, as she brought her fingers back to join Neve's to bring herself to completion together. Even her moans were the most sexual sounds Neve had ever heard, giving her as visceral a reaction as Mikhail's growls, purrs and groans that seemed to take her over when he made them. The frequency of his pleasure reached deeper places inside her, but Sasha's pleasure went right to her head.

The succubus' orgasm pulled at Neve through her fingers with a fraction of the power of Sasha's mouth on her clit. It acted more as a magnet to keep her rubbing through the climax. Rather than draining her, it fueled Neve's desire for more. She rocked herself over Sasha's thigh, driving herself forward, although she wasn't sure to what end, what more Sasha could offer her without the penetration she wasn't capable of accepting yet, even with sex demon magic.

Neve broadened her strokes over Sasha's folds, easing off of her clit, but Sasha continued to push up against Neve's hand. Her eyes had darkened to their deepest black, and she ran her tongue over her teeth as though to keep herself from biting down. Between their two orgasms, Neve suspected she hadn't been any more satisfied, which meant that Sasha still had more to take, and Neve had infinitely more to give. She also suspected that what Sasha had done to her so far wouldn't have been fatal to another woman. Curiosity got the better of her.

"Mikhail said that a woman is a succubus' safest victim. So how does a succubus kill another woman, exactly?"

"I haven't killed you enough?" Sasha sat up to playfully kiss Neve's neck. Amil had abandoned them entirely at some point for the romance section of the bookshelf, where it was more peaceful. He'd settled there in a rich brown coil across the bed from the ball python.

"You haven't killed me yet."

"You're right. I haven't. So you can tell the difference, can you, between a little death and a proper kill?"

"I've been killed many times," Neve said. "Don't hold back on my account. It's not death you need to protect me from. Bell's taken care of that."

"Are you sure?" Sasha brushed the hair from Neve's face. Sasha's hair was naturally wild and tousled without too much tangling, but Neve was sure her own hair was a mess. She didn't know how to manage half a hairstyle yet.

"Isn't that why you're here?" Neve asked. "As long as you're not satisfied, I won't be either."

"I'll need to do more than just let go. It will require me to seduce you, to pull you in, to sink the tendrils of my magic inside and wrap around you so tightly you won't want me to ever release you. If you're feeling sensitive to manipulation at the moment..."

Neve pressed her forehead to Sasha's, her breathing stertorous, but still she inhaled Sasha's scent. Their limbs were tangled in a loose knot, their bodies connected at so many places of contact. Neve already felt pulled in, manipulated the way a fly was manipulated by a pitcher plant.

But she felt safe. That could have been another manipulation, but Neve didn't think it was. She felt safe with Mikhail there, in spite of the anxiety the bulge in his jeans created. And she felt safe here in Sasha's arms, with her reassurances and patience and care in the face of what Neve had gone through, even if the execution hadn't been perfect.

Any other sex demons outside Arcanium wouldn't have given a damn, but they cared. That mattered to her so much more than she could explain in words right now, with her naked body against Sasha's and clouding all higher thought.

"Call it a scientist's curiosity. I know how two women have sex, but how does a succubus feed?"

"You might wish you hadn't asked me once I show you."

"Now I'm even more curious."

Mirth glittered in Sasha's eyes, but she also showed clear signs of hesitation. "It's similar to tribbing."

"Okay, I'm not *that* well-versed in lesbian sex."

"More commonly known among straight men as scissoring." If anything, Sasha was starting to look a little embarrassed. "Some women get nothing at all from it and think it's male fantasy alone, but other women favor it. And it's one of only two ways I can feed. You see, from a purely biological standpoint, which you seem to like, we feed based on genital penetration. Men with men and men with women, that's fairly straightforward. With women, it seems impossible, doesn't it?"

"You're not going to tell me you grow a cock. That doesn't seem…right." Neve settled back on the duvet rather than on Sasha's leg, less a lover and more the student, but it was a position she'd always loved.

"It doesn't, does it? And no, I don't grow. It's just… Most hybrids—including our closest cousins, the vampire and even the Creature—feed using their mouth, even if what they feed upon isn't always physical. You already know we don't feed from our human mouths, or at least that's not how we're designed to. Have you ever wondered what we use to feed, Neve?"

"You've got to be kidding."

Sasha parted her legs farther, which separated her folds. They looked like normal human labia until Sasha brought two fingertips near her entrances. The inner folds undulated, tightening around her fingers. Like a mouth. Like a freaking mouth.

Neve covered her face, caught between shock and a mad grin. "Oh my God, short of a goblin shark, that's the weirdest thing I've ever seen." But she leaned in to get a closer look.

The tension in Sasha's shoulders relaxed at Neve's mostly positive reaction. "Just wait."

She used both hands to part the labia again and probed her entrance with her fingers to spread the soft, pink, wet flesh. Nestled along the walls of her cunt, less than an inch in, were little white nubs.

"Shut up. Not *vagina dentata*," Neve said.

All at once, the nubs shot out, revealing themselves as sharp, curved teeth like extended cat claws in a spoked-wheel shape.

"Holy shit, that is awesome. That is just too perfect." This was why Neve had always loved biology. Nature was never boring. She squealed with delight as a slender, pointed tongue emerged like a tentacle from between the teeth, curling familiarly around Sasha's fingers.

"More often than incubi, succubi have to contend with people trying to have sex with them against their will, and we're more often caught unawares. We have many of the same vulnerabilities and struggles as human women. But we have more ways to fight back. Locke muzzled our human mouths, but he also muzzled us here, both so we couldn't feed and so we couldn't defend ourselves."

"Wait." Neve straightened and twisted around toward Mikhail, who'd actually gone red. She guessed he'd never been part of this particular kind of biology lesson before. "I've had plenty of sex with you, and I've never seen a mouth or teeth or tongue or anything like that."

"Do you want to see?" he asked, covering part of his cock with his hand.

"Of course I want to see. I *have* to see this." This wasn't sex. This was science. Science she could deal with.

"Please don't be afraid." He carefully undid the front of his trousers and lifted his cock out as soon as he could, letting out a sigh at no longer being held down.

"Oh, I've been afraid for weeks now. No use trying to stop me. Now come on, big man, show me your teeth."

Mikhail stroked over the shaft, urging it to thicken even more now that he'd been released. It darkened and pulsed in his massive hand.

For a moment, Neve's chest tightened, and she saw Locke surging over her, into her, in his demon form.

But as soon as Mikhail had grown to his natural size, he stopped stroking and instead pulled back the foreskin to expose the ridge of the head and just below. Where foreskin met glans, he had his own white nubs like milk teeth. They snapped out rather than in, but they were nearly identical in appearance.

"Holy mother of Darwin." Neve crawled closer now. "How does that even work? Wouldn't you just tear through the foreskin?"

"Ours are less frequently used. The cock itself is more of a weapon than the teeth. They're the last line of defense, if defense is needed, but yes, our foreskins must be fully retracted, and we have to be fully erect. It's…more often a way to cause pain to prey, to lock us into their flesh if we do not use our magic to make a body welcome us."

"Okay, that's less inviting." She pushed herself upright again, but though Locke had sometimes taken her without magic to ease it, Mikhail never had. It had always felt like part of what he was, part of what it meant to be an incubus — to seduce a woman to death rather than make her last moments painful. But she had no way of knowing whether other incubi were the same. All she could know was Mikhail and Sasha, each demon at a time.

The teeth around his glans curled back in, and he released the foreskin so that they covered the circle.

"There is no tongue. Whatever creates us must have decided we didn't need one, with enough penetrative force provided by the rest of the phallus. Unlike Lennon, whose maker decided there are never enough tentacles."

Neve couldn't help the grin that spread across her face, stretching the scarified skin on either side.

"I've missed that." He ran a thumb along one of those scars. Her grin faded, but she leaned into his hand. This time, regret instead of panic pulled at her heartstrings.

She wove her fingers through his. She hadn't been this close to him since the last Funhouse event. His black hair fell around his shoulders and curtained one side of his face. His skin was darker than Sasha's and he was hotter than her, as though he'd soaked in even more sun. His black eyes were just as dark as hers, though, with quiet ferocity behind them.

But he was in control, so much more in control than he had been when she'd first met him. Maybe because he wasn't hungry for the first time, but she thought it was more than that. She thought that with all the practice holding his breath, he could do so with more ease.

She wanted to kiss him, and it wasn't just from skin contact. But she slowly withdrew, unable to look at his lips and not see Locke's. As men, they were so different, but somehow when Locke went demon, she saw their resemblance—even though they still didn't look anything alike.

There at the foot of the bed, she turned around and lay back to beckon Sasha over her. She wasn't so far from Mikhail now, and he gently stroked over her shorn scalp, tracing the clean edge of the burst of dark red hair. From her angle below on the bed, his cock seemed huge and improbably tight against his abdomen, but he didn't touch himself again, and when he noticed her looking, he adjusted his shirt to cover most of it.

Neve squeezed his thigh through his jeans. "It's okay. As long as it's not over me. You can take care of yourself. You can... Oh."

Sasha crawled between Neve's legs, lifting them up until her knees were almost at her breasts. She slid her body against Neve's like a serpent herself before licking a hot trail up her neck.

"I'd love to see you two together one day, riding him at a gallop. Fuck, just the thought of it is the sexiest thing I can imagine right now. Mmm..." Sasha undulated against Neve, her hips simulating far more masculine sex than Neve expected — nor did Neve expect how strongly she'd react to it. She raised her hips with a whine, desperate to meet something, but the angle didn't give her any of the contact she wanted.

"So you want to know how a succubus feeds on a woman?" Sasha murmured against her lips. "Don't worry. I can't bite this way — at least, not with my cunt."

Sasha climbed further up her body, throwing one leg over and keeping one of Neve's legs hooked in her arm for her to hold onto, tucked around her hip. She brought her folds flush to Neve's clit.

"Oh. My. God." They were *like* lips, but not. The labia were more dexterous, closing around the hood and the clit like something blind. The suction *like* a mouth...but not. The tongue swirled around her clit like a molten version of the silver Locke had wrapped around it, except it was hot, smooth, wet velvet instead of cold metal.

"Believe me, Neve, I haven't even started yet. Come here to me. Help her up, Mikhail. I want my girl."

Mikhail lifted her upright, their bent legs mirrored. Sasha clasped Neve against her with greater strength than Neve could find, her limbs like jelly as Sasha's folds adjusted to the new angle.

"Damn, that feels so strange." Neve dug her fingers into Sasha's shoulders, holding on as though on the edge of a cliff.

Her nipples caught on Sasha's skin, leaving them aching as intensely as her clit. Sasha's magic was weaving around her, inside her, getting under her skin like Bell's thick black stitches. It was less insidious than Mikhail's, less subtle in its efforts to get inside. Sasha pierced her way in and didn't let go.

Neve moved against her, incited into the rhythm by her suddenly unbearable lust. She pushed her clit against the odd, grasping, sucking mouth of Sasha's cunt. Sweat beaded down her temples and back, but Sasha didn't relent. The succubus took her over with a kiss, rocking her hips, riding Neve's clit. She moaned as though starving, and Neve felt her already drinking. Each suck of that lower mouth took something from her.

The angles were awkward. Without Sasha's strength, they might not have worked. But the succubus didn't stop, and Neve didn't want her to. The pleasure was purer, one hundred percent proof, unfettered by any attempt to hold it back or control it. It swept every last second thought from her mind, every last memory, every last fear. It was bliss, not remembering, not having Locke in her mind for a few minutes, though it couldn't last.

"You delicious little peach. I could drink you all day and night," Sasha groaned, throwing back her head. "No wonder you didn't tell me how tasty she was, Mikhail. No wonder you wanted to keep her all to yourself. I should hate you right now, but I can't, because she's so goddamn good."

Neve bit along her neck and closed her teeth over Sasha's shoulder. Sasha gave a cry, perhaps of pain, but she pushed Neve back down on the bed, nearly sobbing as she frantically worked her lower mouth over Neve's clit.

"Don't stop," Neve begged. "Don't ever stop."

She gripped Sasha's ass, pushing her harder against her. And when she turned her head, she caught sight of Mikhail stroking himself, his hand a blur, his cock flushed red and its veins purple. He ran his free hand over Sasha's back, sending a ribbon of his magic through her and — as though lust could be conducted — through Neve as well.

Neve reached to take his erection in her own hand, parting her lips as though she would twist around to take it in. Her cunt was hollow, her mouth hollow, her body hollow, with Sasha pulling everything out of it instead of filling it. But Mikhail covered her wrist and lowered her hand.

Sasha turned Neve back to her, taking her mouth to satisfy at least one of her desires. And with magic siphoned from two ends, Sasha came, her arousal flooding around Neve's clit, but the mouth closing even more tightly around it, its rhythm that of her orgasm.

For what felt like minutes, their orgasm was one and the same — the same heartbeat, the same spasms, the same back-and-forth waves of mind-numbing pleasure like a drug. Finally, Sasha broke the kiss, loosening her hold on Neve and raising herself up to grind the final pulses against her victim.

This. This was how it was when a sex demon's feed was supposed to kill her. Neve was boneless on her duvet, unable to move, her mind a terrible, wonderful blank as Sasha shifted her hips away, releasing her and allowing her release to reach completion.

Almost without pause, Sasha leaned over, and Mikhail pulled away his hand to let her take him in her mouth instead. Her throat rippled and cheeks hollowed from the intensity of the suction. Mikhail shouted, pulling up the duvet in a fist as he shoved his cock up into Sasha's mouth in an almost instantaneous climax like the one Neve had let him have the night of the first Funhouse—a climax for its own sake, none of the other trappings. Neve and Sasha together had been the trappings tonight.

Without Sasha muddying her head, Mikhail not letting her touch him even when she'd been mindless with sexual magic gained all the more significance. She couldn't—shouldn't—let him have sex with her right now, and sex meant so many more things than his cock inside her, she knew.

In that one moment of watching him come down from the orgasm Sasha had given him, Neve thought she might love him—fierce, powerful love that had nothing to do with the sex he could give. It was the kind of love she'd thought she had with her husband, the kind that didn't *need* sex to work.

The feeling lasted for only a moment, but it shook her more than any orgasm that the incubus or succubus had given her, because everything after Locke had seemed like an everlasting, apocalyptic end.

And this seemed like a beginning.

Mikhail retrieved her eyepatch and Sasha's dress. Neve pulled on what clothes she could reach, tossed the duvet to the floor at the foot of her bed for the golems to eventually clean then grabbed a blanket and wrapped it around herself. Though it was the middle of the day, Sasha tucked herself against Neve's side. Mikhail settled behind the succubus to keep a body between him and Neve. After a few minutes, the cobra came to join them, drawn to their collective, welcoming heat.

Sasha drifted off, but Mikhail stayed awake. He brushed Neve's gashed cheek as though he'd been afraid he would never touch her again.

And Neve kept her one good eye open, unable to tear her gaze away.

Just the beginning.

Arcanium: Skeletons
Aurelia T. Evans

Excerpt

Vivian had expected more from Arcanium.

When she'd arrived at the Renaissance faire that the freak-show circus had paired with, Arcanium was little more than a collection of small tents and booths attached to the far edge like barnacles. The way her friends had described it the previous year, it was supposed to be the kinky steampunk party everyone needed in their life. But she'd been in the hospital again back then and hadn't been released until after the circus had already moved on.

There were harnesses everywhere the eye could see, leather and lace, bustiers and kickass boots. The Spider Woman creature…thing…person was tied up in white rope, and to Vivian's untrained eye, it looked authentic. But kink was more than outfits, and steampunk was more than cogs and gears, although there was a good bit of that, too.

And to Vivian's disappointment, the big top that her friends had all talked about was nowhere to be found. Any tents set up along the perimeter were small, and any open-air performances were seemingly spontaneous and limited in scope. There was no sign of the hot, homoerotic trapeze artists Lupe had mentioned.

As Vivian slipped through the crowd in her flowy gypsy skirt and peasant blouse—the closest she had to appropriate for the venue, although if the circus had been actually kinky, she would have had a few other things to contribute, she noted the performance times were unpredictable and the offerings slim, but the freak show was fucking beautiful. The kink and steampunk nods in the circus were more perfunctory than devoted homages, but the parasitic circus' enthusiasm for natural and unnatural weirdness seemed unmatched by anything she'd ever been to or seen before. Sure, she'd seen circus movies and shit, but those cheated enough that these freaks—the ones that were definitely real, at least—were worth a look.

But a look only lasted about fifteen minutes, and what else was she supposed to do with her time?

She abandoned the circus to return to the faire, where at least they had turkey legs she could pick at while watching falconers, wondering whether anyone would catch the irony. No one did, but the birds of prey kept her attention and the falconers weren't too bad either. She supposed they'd seen plenty of pressed cleavage in their day, but she leaned forward with her elbows on her knees and she wasn't wearing a bra. After the act, that distracted the sandy blond with an overgrown but somehow sparse beard. She smiled, finished what she was going to finish with the turkey leg, which was a little dry and how the hell did a single person eat the whole thing without looking pregnant when they were done? Vivian had only chosen it for the irony, anyway, and if even the falconer couldn't spot it, she needed to move on.

She was that close to throwing in the towel and leaving to drink heavily elsewhere—someplace where the pissy beers didn't cost an arm and a turkey leg to buy—when she heard music. And not the usual Celtic crap that sounded like it belonged on one of those soundtracks found at souvenir gift shops.

Vivian abandoned the falconer without a thought to follow the siren song of rock and roll where it didn't belong.

There was no stage, no curtains, nothing but a bare-bones set-up of amps, speakers and instruments next to the circus' food court. On the bass drum, someone had painted 'Skellies' in spiky script. And on an easel, a sign with the same script read *Karaoke—Auditions for Lead Singer*.

"Seriously?" Vivian muttered.

"Seriously," a man said behind her.

She could have sworn no one had been there, and as he stepped around her, the continued impression that he didn't displace the air was the weirdest, most unsettling feeling. Even though he was pretty as sin, she leaned away.

Pretty, indeed. Gently toned muscles wrapped around his bones. He was shorter than her, but when he looked up, he didn't seem to take it personally. He walked with absolute confidence as far away from arrogance as Vivian had ever seen on an attractive man who looked like he hadn't met a weight machine he hadn't tried.

Actually, there was fluidity to his strength that suggested something other than the gym. He wasn't a bodybuilder, wasn't absolutely ripped like the strongman. He was lean but not slender, like someone who could do all the weird fitness moves—a trapeze artist or a dancer, maybe. Since he wasn't with anyone, she wasn't sure whether he was supposed to be one of the trapeze artists she'd been looking for, although she was pretty sure one was supposed to be blond and the other black, while this man's close, curly hair was on the brown side of auburn.

He wore nothing but a gold bracelet around his arm — which had to be fake, because this kind of circus couldn't support that amount of real gold — and a pair of cotton pants that practically invited her to look. She couldn't see detail, but with the light beige color of the pants, he certainly wasn't wearing anything under them.

She didn't hide that she was studying his body, and he appeared unfazed by the inspection. He didn't preen or flex, didn't glare, didn't inspect her back — just sat down on one of the picnic tables that had been set up in front of the band. In spite of decent guitar riffs and beats coming from the practicing instrumentalists, people hadn't congregated yet.

"I didn't know circuses were in the habit of gleaning talent from their audiences," Vivian said. "Seems kind of desperate, don't you think?"

His hazel eyes looked a little sad — something in the set of his eyebrows — but he curved his lips in a grin. "Oh, it *is* desperate, in its own way. I'm afraid a good number of my performers had to leave en masse due to an illness that swept through my circus, with many lingering side effects. Now I'm working with a skeleton crew. I'd ask you to pardon the pun, but it just seems all too appropriate."

Vivian raised her eyebrow. "*Your* performers?"

When he didn't seem to mind her sidling closer, she climbed onto the picnic table and sat on the edge next to him — close enough to telegraph a certain amount of interest, although she wasn't in heat or anything.

"My circus. My monkeys." He raised his chin in acknowledgment to the guitarist, a pale man in a see-through shirt screened to look like the bones of a torso. He'd pulled back his long black hair, and when he glimpsed her talking to the shirtless man, he gave a too-wide smile. Despite his white teeth, he reeked of cigarettes from all the way where she sat. Yet she still couldn't get anything but a visual off the man next to her, who crossed his legs like some kind of bohemian model.

"So you're the one who's desperate, then," she said.

"I'm always on the lookout for talent, love. There's no shame in soliciting, and our audience has some fun in the process."

"You ever found anyone this way?"

The man nodded toward the acrylic drum sheet. "Shane, our drummer. Bringing her on allowed Lennon to take a permanent place as guitarist, which he much prefers."

Shane transitioned into a new beat, shaking her bald head and clenching her teeth—at least the ones in her mouth. The place on the left side of her scalp, which Vivian had initially thought was a tattoo, was dimensional in the right profile. Vivian blinked, squinted to find where poreless latex smoothed into pored skin—because if Vivian didn't know any better, a fang-filled mouth formed a crevice along Shane's scalp, like some kind of science fiction brain surgery gone horribly wrong.

As Shane moved, twisting on her chair and closing her eyes to the music, she revealed other places where the eerily realistic mouths opened in wet, red gashes wherever the skintight, bloody, white latex dress cut away from her body—along her shoulder, slashed diagonally over her belly, in place of a navel. Her entire body seemed to have been prepared for a glimpse of horror from every angle. She was skinny, her jutting collarbone, hipbones, knees, elbows and shoulder blades accentuated by the light layer of makeup that made a suggestion of a skull on her face and bones over her exposed ribs and spine.

Vivian dwelled on the beautiful angles of her thin fingers around the drumsticks with more than a little envy.

"Like oddities, talent is everywhere if you're willing to do what it takes to find it," the man said. "Or create it for yourself. Arcanium is undergoing a much-needed transformation, and if we are to survive, it needs to be fast. Bell Madoc, fortune teller and illusionist, at your humble service, my lady. I don't believe I caught your name." He held out a hand for her to shake.

At least when she took his hand, his flesh was solid and warm, almost hot.

"Vivian. I've never heard Bell as a first name before."

"It's short for a number of names I have taken. I am the Bell, book and candle behind the magic of Arcanium, and it does as well as anything."

Vivian turned back to the practicing band. A woman had stepped behind the keyboard and was fiddling with the volume. She wore a long black lace skirt and bralette that appeared to cover only what was absolutely necessary for legal reasons, all the better to show off the incredibly detailed body paint that created the illusion that the woman was only a skeleton.

Vivian was beginning to sense a theme.

Unlike Lennon, the guitarist, who only briefly nodded to the band's name, and Shane, whose skeleton makeup was soft, like a faint overlay of a skeleton illustration, the keyboardist had gone all out, filling in her body with black where the bones hadn't been painted on in minute anatomical detail. The woman wasn't as slender as Shane, didn't have the same skeletal structure already exposed. Instead, she seemed downright soft—which seemed to be coming back into fashion, but Vivian preferred angles to curves and bones to flesh. When she turned an envious eye, it was to women like Shane every time.

The keyboardist clearly had a background in belly-dancing, because she swayed sinuously to Shane's beat as she joined the warm-up, her hips seeming independent of her spine.

A pair of similarly skeletonized women gradually took their places behind Lennon, one of them picking up a steampunked electric violin. They were even thinner than Shane—emaciated, with their skin tight on their bones. In comparison to them, Vivian felt bloated, the flesh over her stomach like gelatin, her hips too broad, her breasts heavy, her thighs pressed too tightly against each other.

She could starve herself for months and die less skinny than they were. With her arm pressed to her belly, which felt like rolls of fat to her, she fought against the grumbling in her abdomen telling her how hungry she still was. Her eyes burned, as though the hatred she felt for their skeletal bodies could literally shoot out through her sockets. No such luck. The two girls muttered to each other—the instrumentalist smiling, the backup singer not—and none of them spontaneously combusted.

"More stray talent?" Vivian asked.

"The violinist, Lily, answered a classified. It wasn't what she'd thought she'd be using her classical training for, I'm sure, but she seems to enjoy the circus' particular challenges. The other two were mined from auditions like this. Oh, they aren't strictly auditions,

Vivian. If you simply want to sing with my Skeletons, you're more than welcome to take the mic."

Vivian tore her gaze from the women of the band. "Okay, mind telling me why you're buttering me up?"

If he'd been giving out any kind of signal for sex, she'd get it—maybe even be down for something somewhere private, since he was a lot more attractive to her than the falconer—and not just in the looks department. But he wasn't signaling. In fact, despite the bare chest, suggestive pants and the way he sat too close for an acquaintance, he seemed to deliberately not send fuckboy vibes in her direction. But the performer-owner of a circus just deciding to cozy up to a random stranger in the middle of his barebones circus? It seemed like more than coincidence, even suspicious.

"Because you didn't seem happy," Bell said. "Happiness is certainly not guaranteed here, but boredom simply won't do."

"I followed the music, didn't I? It sounds better than your average midlife-crisis garage band. What were the odds I'd find a good, hard sound at a freak show?"

"I thought I'd try something new." Bell rested his chin on his fist and narrowed his eyes in the classic Thinker pose that somehow looked deliberate and unpretentious at the same time. "It's definitely new. But test audiences like you seem to like it and so does my cast. The whole circus stops whenever they do their set."

"No offense, but this isn't a circus," Vivian said.

"Oh?" Vivian expected him to get defensive, but his expression remained neutral, and she couldn't tell whether he was hiding anything behind it.

She was used to understanding men. Men, like dogs, were easy. They wanted money, power, sex and a maternal figure. Period. All a person needed to do was figure out which one they needed to be at any given time. But Bell wasn't giving away his position. Vivian twisted her skirt between her fingers and tried not to clench her teeth.

"This is a freak show with circus elements. If it can't stand on its own, it's not a circus. It's circus kitsch."

"Before my cast got sick, it was a circus."

"Talk to me again when it doesn't need a geeky craft fair pretending to be Renaissance to prop it up." Vivian shrugged. "Don't get me wrong. I'm here at the geeky craft fair, aren't I? I didn't come here to mock it. But just because I like pewter dragons on necklaces doesn't mean everything's okay. I *came* here for the Two Thousand Twenty-Second Cumming of Mick Jagger, but this is kind of just…Steven Tyler in his grandma's wardrobe. It's not that he can't pull it off, but it's not what I came here for."

"I understand." He rested a hand on her shoulder, his thumb brushing the edge of her collarbone. Warmth deepened his eyes, his hold the first stirring of something sexual. Not blatant, like a hand to the thigh or the ass, but his skin was on her bare skin, a caress light but deliberate. "While Arcanium is in transition, why not help make it the circus you wanted it to be?"

Vivian scoffed. "I still can't figure out what *this* is."

"This?"

"*This*." She gestured to the length of him then finished off at the hand at her shoulder. "Talking honey. Humoring me when I'm clearly not humoring you. Trying to get me to go up there."

He withdrew but not abruptly. He trailed his fingertips down her shoulder, suggesting again that he wasn't ashamed of what he was doing—whatever he was doing.

"I just want you to enjoy yourself. I'm allowed to narrow my focus to a single guest, Vivian. It's difficult to thrill a crowd of people every day the circus opens. I find it much easier to please one person at a time."

"Is that why you play fortune teller instead of Ringmaster?" She inclined her head toward the tall, dark drink of water who glowered a head taller than the tallest normal man. That, along with the breadth of his shoulders and the downright evil glare, kept everyone an arm's length away. Vivian didn't know him, but she already liked him, and not just because his bare chest was more ruggedly masculine than Bell's.

"I'm an entertainer. I like to see the sparkle in a guest's eyes when they experience the magic we offer. Faces blend together, but a single face in front of me? I'll remember that with an elephant's memory. For instance, I'm accustomed to boredom by those who come to an interactive buffet like this but still can't remove themselves from the constant stimulation of their phones. They're bored in lines, bored at exhibits, glowingly bored in my big top tent. But you haven't picked up your phone once. A pretty young woman such as yourself, yet you came here alone, not a single person to accompany you. Yours is a different kind of boredom."

Vivian stopped watching the dancing, playing and singing Skeletons in front of her and straightened. "Looks like they're not the only ones picking up their phones. What have you been reading up on?"

"Where exactly would I put a phone in this outfit?" Bell replied mildly.

"Same place they put 'em in prison."

"I'm afraid it's never become that dire. I own a computer, but I've never been able to abide phones. They've only become more annoying as time goes on.

And they all have this buzzing sound most people can't hear, like electrical wires." He gestured to his ears. "It's distracting."

"And your floodlights, Christmas lights and sound equipment don't use electricity?" Vivian said.

"It's not electricity. It's whatever whispers across space when people speak idle words into the universe."

"You're so melodramatic." She shook her head and looked away from him again.

"Thank you. Will you consider gracing us with a song? My cast likes to bet, and so do I."

"Bet on what?" Vivian asked.

"Talent."

"You haven't known me five minutes, man." She ran her hands through her hair and shook her head. "No. I think I'll just watch. This isn't really my scene. And to stand up in front of everyone looking like this when those women out there are... Talent doesn't mean shit. I wish I looked like them instead."

Bell sighed. "I don't suppose it makes much difference if I say you already look like them."

"It doesn't matter what you *think* I look like. It only matters what I see in the mirror, because I'm the one who has to live with it, not you." She slid off of the table and slung her purse over her head to hang crossways down her body. "Besides, didn't you say you were a fortune teller? Don't you already know whether I can sing or not?"

"I like to be surprised." Bell climbed down, too, but though he faced her, he didn't pursue. He gestured toward the band with an ironic little flourish. "Surprise me, Vivian, if you can."

"Is that a challenge?"

"Let's just say you remind me of the worst traits of people I have lost."

The insult came so fast from so far left field that she didn't expect it to hurt as it did. She wound the purse strap around her hand to keep from hitting him in front of witnesses.

"To be fair," he said, "it makes me homesick for what Arcanium was. But I'd like to think you have more to offer than that. I'll tell you what I do know, love. I know you're competitive as hell. Don't disappoint me. I have a substantial sum riding on you."

"Why should I go up there and help you win, asshole? Why shouldn't I just leave and make you pay out?"

Bell shrugged. The smile of a gracious host returned. "I only pay out if you try but can't. Do think about it. And if you want a real taste of the truth afterward, come to my fortune teller's tent. I think we'd both be much more satisfied discussing such things in private, don't you think?"

The smug son of a bitch bowed then wove through the thickening crowd to speak with the Bearded Lady. Vivian didn't know whether to sneak up behind him and kick him in the balls or whether she should just stalk away and not spare the circus any more of her time, money or energy.

She did neither, though she had the sneaking suspicion that Bell had switched tactics on purpose after buttering her up hadn't worked, that it had all been part of some grander manipulation.

But he was right about at least one thing. She *was* competitive as hell.

And it didn't help that people were starting to sing.

Apparently, the band's repertoire included not just rock, metal and punk but a number of pop and dance standards as well—with an edgier spin, of course, although the keyboard could bring it down to something gentler. Vivian almost laughed when they did, because it was really something to see a seven-foot-tall mountain of a man. She thought he was literally called the Mountain, because he was shaped like a barrel, almost as wide as he was tall but more solid than fat—with a tiny, disproportionate head in the crowd, bobbing to a nineties Celine Dion power ballad.

A nineties Celine Dion power ballad that was being slaughtered by someone who should never have been given a device that amplified sound. The woman appeared unwinded by the laughter, singing *It's All Coming Back to Me Now* on what had to have been her third or fourth tankard of ale.

Vivian didn't understand how people could drink like that without saying things they really shouldn't and doing things that made people give them more than a side-eye. Maybe they did say and do things they shouldn't, but most people didn't do or say the kinds of things she did when tipsy. She wasn't a nice drunk, and she'd learned early on not to drink when she was in danger of being in other people's company. When she was alone and didn't have to wake up in the morning, she could drink as much as she damn well wanted.

Control. She'd learned that after her first round at the hospital. If losing control had put her there, maintaining it kept her out, even though nothing had changed. There had been a few lapses since, but she had enough control that nobody had to know why. Nobody ever had to know *her*. And as long as no one knew her, she could do as she pleased—anything within her complete control.

For instance, leaving before the ear-splitting caterwauling could strip the paint off her toes. She didn't have to stay for this. There was nothing keeping her here — no gates, no fences, no walls, no chains.

Vivian stood from the table and pushed her way through the crowd. In a matter of seconds, someone else took her prime seat — just one more reason to move on. The press of flesh around her, the scent of sweat, of meat, of sugar and cream and beer knotted her hollow stomach, twisted it into a clenching cramp. And the noise didn't help. If someone would just hit that woman over the head with a two-by-four, nothing would ever come back to her again, no matter how someone touched her.

That particular agony finally ended just as Vivian reached the far edge of the not-insignificant crowd. Really, she hadn't realized how big it had grown, with circus folk, circus fans — she could tell by the costumes, which had more glitter than the ones there for the Ren faire — Ren faire fans and regular Joes and Joannas with their kids and friends and family. On the outside of that, a girl could breathe again.

By the time she caught her breath, a deep voice yelled to the crowd, "Good afternoon, everyone! *Now* who's ready to rock?"

She considered turning around just to make sure it wasn't the guitarist, because she hadn't expected that rich voice to come out of his white, reedy, nicotine-stained body. Vivian supposed some people went for that, but pale British rock wannabes had never been her thing. The accent was sometimes lovely, but grease was for fish and chips, not complexion, and she didn't actually want to fuck Mick Jagger. Billy Idol, maybe. And Bell kind of looked like him, if he ever decided to go platinum…

Shit, there her mind went again, to that infuriating rodent playing some kind of game with her. And with the return of Bell to her mind, she couldn't help but turn back, furious at the helplessness of her own reactions—as though someone had read up that free will was an illusion and decided to have a little fun with her.

Instead of the guitarist, though, a tall, thick, three-breasted, busty drag queen belted out a surprisingly good rendition of *I Would Do Anything For Love* in a rich baritone that shouldn't have worked—like something out of a campy Jim Steinman horror musical, which was somehow the charm of it. The drag queen strutted across the uneven ground in six-inch heels—not stilettos, but nothing a person wanted to be walking on grass in—bellowing into the microphone with every indication that she'd been classically trained and could probably dominate a concert hall even without a mic.

Vivian crossed her arms over her chest and stayed through the whole song. She even clapped at the end with the rest. The drag queen gave the Human Spider a high five as she left the makeshift stage, all three boobs jiggling like they were real in the blue-sequined black leather and lace dress.

But when another drunken crooner who thought he could sing ambled up to the mic, Vivian turned on her heel once more, pressing her hands to her ears as she headed back into the Ren faire for the exit.

Before leaving, she stopped at the fairground bathrooms, which were an exercise in degradation all on their own—just one step up from portable toilets, gross from the cinderblocks to the seat covers. But she didn't want to use a gas station or fast food restaurant bathroom either, and she had to pee.

Inside the stall, she could still hear the muffled butchering of *Radioactive*.

'Why not help make it the circus you wanted it to be?'

All she wanted to do was leave. That goddamn effete little elf. She'd talked to him for only a few minutes and he'd infiltrated her mind as though he'd been there for years. She was supposed to be the puppeteer, not the puppet. *Never* any man's puppet.

Vivian slammed her hand against the stall door, uncaring that there were other people in the bathroom. Then she stuffed her sleeve in her mouth, covered herself with her light cardigan and screamed, digging her nails into her cheek.

"Are you okay?" someone asked from a few stalls down.

Vivian spat out her sleeve then forced a smile onto her face to change the quality of her voice. "I'm fine. Thank you."

She closed her eyes and took deep, long breaths until the urge to throw herself against the wall had passed. Then she adjusted her cardigan to hide the wet spot on her sleeve where she'd stifled her scream, straightened her shirt and stepped out of the stall. In front of the mirror, she pulled lipstick out from her purse to touch up with dark red and checked her hair, ignoring the curious stares from other people going in and coming out of stalls.

Vivian stepped out of the bathrooms. But she stopped in her tracks right before the ticket booths, wincing, when another guest started butchering *Living on a Prayer*.

"Oh, for fuck's sake."

She turned on her heel and strode back toward the circus, where the band had transitioned into a much-needed instrumental break. Thank God she didn't need to hear someone ruin *Don't Stop Believin'*. The electric guitar and electric violin played the melody as a duet, and the audience sang along together. In concert, the tone-deaf singers were overwhelmed by the swell of the sound. Audience singing was always a little flat to the ears and slightly creepy, like praying or saying the Pledge. But *Don't Stop Believin'* was *Don't Stop Believin'*. People didn't just listen to a song like that.

Vivian edged the crowd toward the front, where most of the circus folk congregated away from the good angles but close enough to support their own. Here, she got a better look at freaks that hadn't been wandering in her direction during her earlier time in Arcanium. The drag queen was taller than Vivian had been able to tell from a distance. In her heels, she was half a head taller than the Ringmaster, who looked thoroughly unhappy to be there.

Up close, Vivian was almost certain the drag queen's boobs weren't some kind of stuffed latex prosthetic but actual implants, and those implants were quality. Girl showed some serious devotion to her craft. Her hair was a wig but a good one, and she was talking with another woman next to her—at least Vivian thought they were a woman until they turned their head to reveal a nicely trimmed sandy mustache and goatee, a shade redder than their feathery, ambiguous hair. They were dressed in a slim, natty suit and held a black and silver cane—more Marlene Dietrich than Cary Grant, especially with the second button of their shirt undone to expose the lacy edge of a bra that provided decent and undeniable cleavage. But their hips were slim, buttocks more masculine, and with facial hair, their face appeared male. If Vivian wasn't mistaken, there was quite a bulge in the front of the tailored, pressed trousers, enhanced by the cut, but they could have been packing.

Vivian thought Arcanium might get a lot of angry letters from both sides of the aisle because of those two, but it was no significant concern for her. She mostly just wished she could pull off a suit like that, plus the drag queen's heels.

Next to the suited individual, a man had coiled – yes, coiled – his long, glimmering tan body into a seat to watch the show, his scaled head nodding with the beat and a smile on his heavily made-up face. How long did it take these people to do themselves up every day? Vivian allotted thirty minutes to her routine, but she hated every minute of it, especially when it was still dark outside in the morning. Some of these transformations had to take hours.

The Mountain was indeed mountainous, and the Bearded Lady was a different creature entirely from the suited individual, furred all over like a dark ginger cat, with a pirate queen's cleavage and a long beard any lumberjack would envy.

Next to her, Bell hooked his arm through hers. If Vivian weren't looking closely, Bell would seem like the gay best friend – intense, intimate, ultimately nonthreatening. But when he kissed the Bearded Lady's neck, there was nothing playful about it.

This damn circus. No, like she'd said, not yet a circus. *This damn freak show.* She couldn't pin a piece of it down. If they'd just had men on stilts, a couple of tumbling, rainbow-colored clowns and an elephant, she'd know what she was getting into. But a skinless woman had nails, pins and letter openers all over her like a pincushion, an armless black man moved like a backup dancer to the music and the Patchwork Pirate was almost scarier to Vivian than the creepy-ass clowns Arcanium *did* have, because she literally looked like someone had taken apart a sweet-faced hooker and put her back together again. On top of that, Vivian had no idea what the little girl's body with the big-ass man's head on it was supposed to be.

Twisted or missing limbs, face paint, gymnastic skills — these were all things she would have understood. But in the harsh light of day, the freaks looked real, more real than anything computer- or makeup-generated, and they were different from any other freaks she'd ever set eyes on.

If Bell had asked her what she thought of the circus now, she might have been more generous. The freaks were all the stranger close together and against a backdrop of so many normal people. When walking behind the oddities, she was the one who felt freakish. She often felt that way in a crowd, but this was different — as though she'd stepped into the *Twilight Zone* world where pig-faced normals pointed and laughed at her deformities, where she was the trespasser to lock away and they the holders of the keys. It was an unpleasant, upside-down emotion.

But when the Bearded Lady turned around at the sound of grass crunching behind her, there was a brief flash of fear in the formidable woman's expression. Perhaps the Bearded Lady saw a brief reflection of her own fear, because she calmed and gestured Vivian forward, indicating the stage in an unspoken query.

A forty-year-old bar singer got there first, calling for *Piano Man*. The keyboardist and guitarist rolled their eyes, but they dutifully played the intro as unironically as possible.

Enough was enough.

"Would you be so good as to hold my purse and jacket for a moment?" Vivian's mother had raised a girl who knew how to say polite things in passive-aggressive ways.

The first line of the song made Vivian want to rip the man's throat out. Instead, she strode forward, stepped right in front of him, angled herself toward the band members rather than the audience and pulled the neckline of her shirt to the side to expose one breast.

The man's mouth stayed open, but nothing came out of it anymore.

"Great, now that we've stopped this train wreck…" Vivian covered her breast again and made a cutting motion over her throat to convince the instrumentalists to stop, which they did with a certain amount of gratitude. "Don't let the door hit you on the way out, bitch."

"Whore," the man muttered, but after being briefly stunned by the flash of bare boob, he staggered off.

That was more like it — more how men were supposed to act whenever she did anything.

Vivian assumed the place at center mic. She glanced over her shoulder at the band. "Do you do *Paint It Black*?"

"Thank the devil and all his minions," the guitarist said, changing the setting on his amp and checking back with the keyboardist. "But if you can't sing, I may have to kill you."

"Stuff it, ciggie. Just play the damn song."

The man smiled as he gave her the British two-finger salute. Then the keyboardist started on her first notes, a higher-register minor-key harpsichord setting that tickled the hairs on the back of Vivian's neck. She turned back to the microphone and waited for her musical cue.

With the abrupt shift from harpsichord to the electric guitar's power chord and the drummer joining in with a crash, Vivian closed her eyes. There wasn't a lot in the world she liked. Pizza was at the top of her list. Music that shuddered through her sternum was another.

After the keyboardist did a lead-in string of notes and the drums withdrew, Vivian grasped the microphone. With butterflies in her stomach but hornets in her head, she took on the first verse, favoring it with her warmer lower register, just a hint of a rasp within the sweetness. It wasn't perfect. They hadn't rehearsed, and it took a minute for Vivian's vocal chords to finds their muscle memory. But Vivian knew how to improvise, and once the guitar whined a third above her voice, something clicked.

The instrumentalists started following her, with dramatic pauses when they weren't sure what she was going to do. They were professionals, and she'd sung in bands before back in high school and college. She had no formal training, unlike the keyboardist, the violinist or the drag queen, and she didn't always play well with others, but she'd learned what her voice could do in the silences. And when she brought the melody up an octave, relishing in the demon rock goddess growl she could conjure on command, she soaked in the sound of cheers from the crowd and circus freaks alike.

In spite of the lyrics, she couldn't hold back a smile. It had been years since she'd performed, since she'd even sung along with the radio.

She'd missed this—the power chords, the electric violin soaring up to ugly-beautiful heights, the toothsome woman going Animal on the drums, words growling out of her chest like a demon. And at the end, she pulled the demon back, with clearer, sweeter notes floating up into her head, the entire crowd quiet to hear.

God, how I've missed this.

The applause didn't suck either, especially when the drummer did her own version through a descending drum solo.

"You got a standing O, rude woman." The guitarist grinned as he changed his amp setting again.

"I guess a standing O is better than no O at all."

"You're weird, and I like you."

Vivian bit back the impulse to ask if he wanted sex later. She couldn't stand even the slightest bit of cigarette smoke, but he did have a good smile.

"I think they want one more." The keyboardist had a pleasantly gentle alto, the kind that would do much better in the singer-songwriter genre. "What are you up for?"

"I was on my way out. I just wanted to stop the bad." Vivian put the microphone back on its stand and raised her hands as she backed away. "What you do now is up to you."

The keyboardist grinned then started on the first few notes of *My Immortal*.

Vivian tilted her head, saying '*Seriously?*' again without even opening her mouth.

"People love it even when they hate it," the keyboardist said. "Come on."

Vivian shook her head, but the crowd clapped to encourage her and the violinist added her plaintive strings to the repeating intro.

Vivian backed away again. "I don't remember the lyrics."

"Don't worry about that."

Vivian jumped then whipped around. Someone needed to put a fucking bell on Bell, because he just didn't *feel* like a person, the way all the little cells on skin could sense anyone else close by. She hated that he'd made her jump in front of hundreds of people.

"An audition is all about showing range," Bell said, "and never saying no."

"This isn't an audition," Vivian replied. "It's a rescue mission, and I've done my part. I'm out of here."

Bell nodded to the sign — *Karaoke — Auditions for Lead Singer*.

"Yeah, well, I did the karaoke part of it."

Bell caught her hand before she could walk past him. "You don't get to choose whether this is an audition, Vivian. You've been in dead-end office jobs for years because that's all you can manage while keeping your secrets. Don't you want something a little more exciting? Something a little stranger?"

Vivian hesitated, swallowing back another nauseating wave of fear, a different quality this time than when she'd been behind the freaks. She wasn't sure if Bell's hand would squeeze, grinding her bones within his grip.

"This isn't my audition." And when she pulled her hand away, he did release her. "I'll do one more song if it'll get you out of my face, but then I'm going home."

"I know how this day will end, Vivian, and it's not how you expect." He touched her chin, lifting her face, then brushed her cheek. She swore he was going to kiss her, and to her utter humiliation, she was weighing whether she'd let him or not. But Bell sank back into his freakshow crowd, clapping with the rest of them to encourage her to take center stage.

The crowd cheered harder and higher as she returned to the microphone. She waited for the keyboardist and violinist to cycle through the introduction again and cue her in.

She kept her voice soft, clear, reining in the vibrato and only bringing in the barest harshness during the bridge. And in spite of being in a fairground, with all sorts of ambient sounds and people doing other things—even though it seemed like the whole world had congregated in front of the band—everything else seemed to go silent. She'd rarely sung for people who weren't friends or friends of friends before, and never for a crowd this big.

The keyboardist was right. Even when someone said they hated this song, they secretly loved it, because a good minor key got through all the cracks and crevices, and for a few minutes, it made her feel something other than angry. Maybe that showed, because everyone—young and old, boomer and hipster, normal and freak—applauded again. And her smile might have been shy, without a trace of coyness.

"Thank you," she muttered into the mic. Then she determinedly walked back the direction she came, rounding the crowd away from Bell. The Bearded Lady handed her the jacket and purse with a smile. Vivian didn't bother checking her wallet. She was even agreeable when the drag queen raised a hand for her to fist bump.

She was almost out of the sparse Arcanium midway when Bell grabbed her by the back of the neck and covered her mouth to keep anyone from hearing her scream.

"You're not going to sneak away from me that easily, love. We have some unfinished business."

Sign up for our newsletter and find out about all our romance book releases, eBook sales and promotions, sneak peeks and FREE romance books!

About the Author

Aurelia T. Evans is an up-and-coming erotica author with a penchant for horror and the supernatural.

She's the twisted mind behind the werewolf/shifter Sanctuary trilogy, demonic circus series Arcanium, and vampire serial Bloodbound. She's also had short stories featured in various erotic anthologies.

Aurelia presently lives in Dallas, Texas (although she doesn't ride horses or wear hats). She loves cats and enjoys baking as much as she dislikes cooking. She's a walker, not a runner, and she writes outside as often as possible.

Aurelia loves to hear from readers. You can find her contact information, website details and author profile page at https://www.totallybound.com